SKYSPIRIT

Volume 3: Zen and the Art of Investigation

ANTHONY WOLFF

AuthorHouse™
1663 Liberty Drive
Bloomington, IN 47403
www.authorhouse.com
Phone: 1-800-839-8640

Published by AuthorHouse 03/11/2014

ISBN: 978-1-4918-6662-7 (sc)
ISBN: 978-1-4918-6663-4 (e)

PREFACE

WHO ARE THESE DETECTIVES ANYWAY?

"The eye cannot see itself" an old Zen adage informs us. The Private I's in these case files count on the truth of that statement. People may be self-concerned, but they are rarely self-aware.

In courts of law, guilt or innocence often depends upon its presentation. Juries do not - indeed, they may not - investigate any evidence in order to test its veracity. No, they are obliged to evaluate only what they are shown. Private Investigators, on the other hand, are obliged to look beneath surfaces and to prove to their satisfaction - not the court's - whether or not what appears to be true is actually true. The Private I must have a penetrating eye.

Intuition is a spiritual gift and this, no doubt, is why *Wagner & Tilson, Private Investigators* does its work so well.

At first glance the little group of P.I.s who solve these often baffling cases seem different from what we (having become familiar with video Dicks) consider "sleuths." They have no oddball sidekicks. They are not alcoholics. They get along well with cops.

George Wagner is the only one who was trained for the job. He obtained a degree in criminology from Temple University in Philadelphia and did exemplary work as an investigator with the Philadelphia Police. These were his golden years. He skied; he danced; he played tennis; he had a Porsche, a Labrador retriever, and a small sailboat. He got married and had a wife, two toddlers, and a house. He was handsome and well built, and he had great hair.

And then one night, in 1999, he and his partner walked into an ambush. His partner was killed and George was shot in the left knee and in his right shoulder's brachial plexus. The pain resulting from his injuries and the twenty-two surgeries he endured throughout the year that followed, left him addicted to a nearly constant morphine drip. By the time he was admitted to a rehab center in Southern California for treatment of his morphine addiction and for physical therapy, he had lost everything previously mentioned except his house, his handsome face, and his great hair.

His wife, tired of visiting a semi-conscious man, divorced him and married a man who had more than enough money to make child support payments unnecessary and, since he was the jealous type, undesirable. They moved far away, and despite the calls George placed and the money and gifts he sent, they soon tended to regard him as non-existent. His wife did have an orchid collection which she boarded with a plant nursery, paying for the plants' care until he was able to accept them. He gave his brother his car, his tennis racquets, his skis, and his sailboat.

At the age of thirty-four he was officially disabled, his right arm and hand had begun to wither slightly from limited use, a frequent result of a severe injury to that nerve center. His knee, too, was troublesome. He could not hold it in a bent position for an extended period of time; and when the weather was bad or he had been standing for too long, he limped a little.

George gave considerable thought to the "disease" of romantic love and decided that he had acquired an immunity to it. He would never again be vulnerable to its delirium. He did not realize that the gods of love regard such pronouncements as hubris of the worst kind and, as such, never allow it to go unpunished. George learned this lesson while working on the case, *The Monja Blanca*. A sweet girl, half his age and nearly half his weight, would fell him, as he put it, "as young David slew the big dumb Goliath." He understood that while he had no future with her, his future would be filled with her for as long as he had a mind that could think. She had been the victim of the most vicious swindlers he had ever encountered. They had successfully fled the country, but not the range of George's determination to apprehend them. These were master criminals, four of them, and he secretly vowed that he would make them fall, one by one. This was a serious quest. There was nothing quixotic about George Roberts Wagner.

While he was in the hospital receiving treatment for those fateful gunshot wounds, he met Beryl Tilson.

Beryl, a widow whose son Jack was then eleven years old, was working her way through college as a nurse's aid when she tended George. She had met him previously when he delivered a lecture on the curious differences between aggravated assault and attempted murder, a not uninteresting topic. During the year she tended him, they became friendly enough for him to communicate with her during the year he was in rehab. When he returned to Philadelphia, she picked him up at the airport, drove him home - to a house he had not been inside for two years - and helped him to get settled into a routine with the house and the botanical spoils of his divorce.

After receiving her degree in the Liberal Arts, Beryl tried to find a job with hours that would permit her to be home when her son came home from school each day. Her quest was daunting. Not only was a degree in Liberal Arts regarded as a 'negative' when considering an applicant's qualifications, (the choice of study having demonstrated a lack of foresight for eventual entry into the commercial job market) but by stipulating that she needed to be home no later than 3:30 p.m. each day, she further discouraged personnel managers from putting out their company's welcome mat. The supply of available jobs was somewhat limited.

Beryl, a Zen Buddhist and karate practitioner, was still doing part-time work when George proposed that they open a private investigation agency. Originally he had thought she would function as a "girl friday" office manager; but when he witnessed her abilities in the martial arts, which, at that time, far exceeded his, he agreed that she should function as a 50-50 partner in the agency, and he helped her through the licensing procedure. She quickly became an excellent marksman on the gun range. As a Christmas gift he gave her a Beretta to use alternately with her Colt semi-automatic.

The Zen temple she attended was located on Germantown Avenue in a two storey, store-front row of small businesses. Wagner & Tilson, Private Investigators needed a home. Beryl noticed that a building in the same row was advertised for sale. She told George who liked it, bought it, and let Beryl and her son move into the second floor as their residence. Problem solved.

While George considered himself a man's man, Beryl did not see herself as a woman's woman. She had no female friends her own age. None. Acquaintances, yes. She enjoyed warm relationships with a few older women. But Beryl, it surprised her to realize, was a man's woman. She liked men, their freedom to move, to create, to discover, and that inexplicable wildness that came with their physical presence and strength. All of her senses found them agreeable; but she had no desire to domesticate one. Going to sleep with one was nice. But waking up with one of them in her bed? No. No. No. Dawn had an alchemical effect on her sensibilities. "Colors seen by candlelight do not look the same by day," said Elizabeth Barrett Browning, to which Beryl replied, "Amen."

She would find no occasion to alter her orisons until, in the course of solving a missing person's case that involved sexual slavery in a South American rainforest, a case called *Skyspirit,* she met the Surinamese Southern District's chief criminal investigator. Dawn became conducive to romance. But, as we all know, the odds are always against the success of long distance love affairs. To be stuck in one continent and love a man who is stuck in another holds as much promise for high romance as falling in love with Dorian Gray. In her professional life, she was tough but fair. In matters of lethality, she preferred *dim mak* points to bullets, the latter being awfully messy.

Perhaps the most unusual of the three detectives is Sensei Percy Wong. The reader may find it useful to know a bit more about his background.

Sensei, Beryl's karate master, left his dojo to go to Taiwan to become a fully ordained Zen Buddhist priest in the Ummon or Yun Men lineage in which he was given the Dharma name Shi Yao Feng. After studying advanced martial arts in both Taiwan and China, he returned to the U.S.

to teach karate again and to open a small Zen Buddhist temple - the temple that was down the street from the office *Wagner & Tilson* would eventually open.

Sensei was quickly considered a great martial arts' master not because, as he explains, "I am good at karate, but because I am better at advertising it." He was of Chinese descent and had been ordained in China, and since China's Chan Buddhism and Gung Fu stand in polite rivalry to Japan's Zen Buddhism and Karate, it was most peculiar to find a priest in China's Yun Men lineage who followed the Japanese Zen liturgy and the martial arts discipline of Karate.

It was only natural that Sensei Percy Wong's Japanese associates proclaimed that his preferences were based on merit, and in fairness to them, he did not care to disabuse them of this notion. In truth, it was Sensei's childhood rebellion against his tyrannical faux-Confucian father that caused him to gravitate to the Japanese forms. Though both of his parents had emigrated from China, his father decried western civilization even as he grew rich exploiting its freedoms and commercial opportunities. With draconian finesse he imposed upon his family the cultural values of the country from which he had fled for his life. He seriously believed that while the rest of the world's population might have come out of Africa, Chinese men came out of heaven. He did not know or care where Chinese women originated so long as they kept their proper place as slaves.

His mother, however, marveled at American diversity and refused to speak Chinese to her children, believing, as she did, in the old fashioned idea that it is wise to speak the language of the country in which one claims citizenship.

At every turn the dear lady outsmarted her obsessively sinophilic husband. Forced to serve rice at every meal along with other mysterious creatures obtained in Cantonese Chinatown, she purchased two Shar Peis that, being from Macau, were given free rein of the dining room. These dogs, despite their pre-Qin dynasty lineage, lacked a discerning palate and proved to be gluttons for bowls of fluffy white stuff. When her husband retreated to his rooms, she served omelettes and Cheerios, milk instead of tea, and at dinner, when he was not there at all, spaghetti instead of chow mein. The family home was crammed with gaudy enameled furniture and torturously carved teak; but on top of the lion-head-ball-claw-legged coffee table, she always placed a book which illustrated the elegant simplicity of such furniture designers as Marcel Breuer; Eileen Gray; Charles Eames; and American Shakers. Sensei adored her; and loved to hear her relate how, when his father ordered her to give their firstborn son a Chinese name; she secretly asked the clerk to record indelibly the name "Percy" which she mistakenly thought was a very American name. To Sensei, if she had named him Abraham Lincoln Wong, she could not have given him a more Yankee handle.

Preferring the cuisines of Italy and Mexico, Sensei avoided Chinese food and prided himself on not knowing a word of Chinese. He balanced this ignorance by an inability to understand Japanese and, because of its inaccessibility, he did not eat Japanese food.

The Man of Zen who practices Karate obviously is the adventurous type; and Sensei, staying true to type, enjoyed participating in Beryl's and George's investigations. It required little time for him to become a one-third partner of the team. He called himself, "the ampersand in *Wagner & Tilson.*"

Sensei Wong may have been better at advertising karate than at performing it, but this merely says that he was a superb huckster for the discipline. In college he had studied civil engineering; but he also was on the fencing team and he regularly practiced gymnastics. He had learned yoga and ancient forms of meditation from his mother. He attained Zen's vaunted transcendental states; which he could access 'on the mat.' It was not surprising that when he began to learn karate he was already half-accomplished. After he won a few minor championships he attracted the attention of several martial arts publications that found his "unprecedented" switchings newsworthy. They imparted to him a "great master" cachet, and perpetuated it to the delight of dojo owners and martial arts shopkeepers. He did win many championships and, through unpaid endorsements and political propaganda, inspired the sale of Japanese weapons, including nunchaku and shuriken which he did not actually use.

Although his Order was strongly given to celibacy, enough wiggle room remained for the priest who found it expedient to marry or dally. Yet, having reached his mid-forties unattached, he regarded it as 'unlikely' that he would ever be romantically welded to a female, and as 'impossible' that he would be bonded to a citizen and custom's agent of the People's Republic of China - whose Gung Fu abilities challenged him and who would strike terror in his heart especially when she wore Manolo Blahnik red spike heels. Such combat, he insisted, was patently unfair, but he prayed that Providence would not level the playing field. He met his femme fatale while working on *A Case of Virga*.

Later in their association Sensei would take under his spiritual wing a young Thai monk who had a degree in computer science and a flair for acting. Akara Chatree, to whom Sensei's master in Taiwan would give the name Shi Yao Xin, loved Shakespeare; but his father - who came from one of Thailand's many noble families - regarded his son's desire to become an actor as we would regard our son's desire to become a hit man. Akara's brothers were all businessmen and professionals; and as the old patriarch lay dying, he exacted a promise from his tall 'matinee-idol' son that he would never tread upon the flooring of a stage. The old man had asked for nothing else, and since he bequeathed a rather large sum of money to his young son, Akara had to content himself with critiquing the performances of actors who were less filially constrained than he. As far as romance is concerned, he had not thought too much about it until he worked on *A Case of Industrial Espionage*. That case took him to Bermuda, and what can a young hero do when he is captivated by a pretty girl who can recite Portia's lines with crystalline insight while lying beside him on a white beach near a blue ocean?

But his story will keep...

THURSDAY, MARCH 17, 2011

The Zen Buddhist priest, Shi Yao Feng, still in his full-sleeved black ceremonial robe, hurried down Philadelphia's Germantown Avenue to the storefront office of *Wagner & Tilson, Private Investigators.* He wanted to reach his friends before they went to lunch.

The March wind blew his silk robe open, letting it flap behind him like a luffing sail, and his wooden sandals clopped on the pavement, causing a few pedestrians to stare at his tabi socks and tunic and wonder why he was dressed in such a bizarre way. "I know. I know," he muttered. "If I shaved my head they would figure it out."

He pushed open the office door. "You guys got time for me? I need help."

Beryl Tilson, sitting at her desk in the front office, was a member of his Zen sangha and knew that ceremonial robes are never worn on the street. If Sensei was wearing his full black robe, whatever it was that he wanted, it had to be important. "Sure," she said. "What's the problem?"

He sat down and spoke in an unaccustomed staccato beat. "You know how indebted I am to Tracy Baldwin. She's got a problem and she's asked me to help her. But in order for me to help her I need you to help me. Her sister has gone missing."

Beryl clicked onto a new folder and began to type. "Tracy Baldwin... like the piano?"

"Yes. The Reverend Tracy Baldwin... like the piano. Her sister is Olivia Mallard... like the duck. She's from Albuquerque, New Mexico."

"Have the Albuquerque police been notified?"

"No. It's complicated. The last time Tracy talked to Olivia was the morning of Valentine's Day, last February 14th. It was a Monday."

"That was a month ago. Where did she see her?"

"Here in Philadelphia. Olivia came unexpectedly to Tracy's house on the 13th. She must have been up here to see a man because Tracy saw a Valentine gift box from a men's store in the back seat of her car. Olivia had been crying. Tracy figured that the gift and a man were connected, but her sister refused to talk about it."

"Any clues?"

"Olivia had parked at the curb; but the Homeowner's Association rules forbid overnight-street parking, so Tracy put her car in the garage. That's when she found a gas receipt from a Shell station in Ephrata."

"Ephrata in Lancaster County?"

"Yes. She didn't know what Olivia was doing in Lancaster County. As a minister, she's trained to induce people to discuss their emotional issues, but she couldn't get Olivia to say a word. I don't want to mess up the story. I told her I'd ask you guys if you were interested, and if you were, I'd set up a meeting. What should I tell her?"

"It's Saint Patrick's Day. If she's a Methodist she's not likely to be wearing green and celebrating. How about if we meet in the temple kitchen after services tonight? Tell her to bring the gas receipt and any recent photos she has of Olivia."

Sensei made the call.

Before Sensei Percy Wong became a Zen Buddhist priest, he taught karate in his small but well-regarded dojo in Philadelphia. Tracy Baldwin had come to him, begging him to help her son who was being bullied everywhere he went - at school, in their neighborhood, and even when he visited his father, Tracy's ex-husband who had married a woman with four aggressive sons. The boy lived in fear. He couldn't sleep, eat, concentrate, and he never smiled. She had tried all the usual nostrums: psychotherapy and changing schools. As he grew weaker, he became even more vulnerable.

Since the boy was too shy to join a class, Sensei went to her home to give him private lessons. He was a good student and within a year he gained weight, self-confidence, and became an honor student. Soon he took classes in the dojo three times a week and competed at his grade level in tournaments.

When Sensei lost his lease on the dojo, rather than move elsewhere, he went to Taiwan to be ordained in a Zen Buddhist monastery and to take advanced martial arts' training there and in China. When he returned he was a priest without a temple and a teacher without a classroom.

Tracy opened a wing of her Church's recreation center to him. In exchange for giving free instruction to church members, Sensei could conduct his own classes at any time during the week. She personally paid the additional insurance premiums. She also owned a storefront row-house building which she sold to him for a dollar. He converted the downstairs into a small temple and the upstairs into his private residence. There was a room built over the garage which he used as a dojo for teaching a select group of private students, Beryl Tilson among them.

The boy was now a college man; but Sensei's dojo arrangement continued even after he came into his own money and could easily afford an independent facility.

Out of uniform, Tracy Baldwin looked more like a librarian than a cleric. Aside from the unfortunate choice of clashing plaids, she and Beryl were dressed similarly and appeared to be the same fortyish age.

"Can you give me Olivia's back story?" Beryl asked.

"By character, she's naive... an enabler... religious and the kind of optimist who believes in everyone's inherent goodness. She's a better Christian than I am. I'd study Latin and Greek. She'd volunteer to clean house for the sick and teach delinquent kids how to work with clay."

Tracy sighed. "In high school she fell in love with a football jock named Dan Mallard, a football jock who could turn on the charm. She planned to marry him after graduation. Dan was a lazy, narcissistic, arrogant drunk. Before he was eighteen he lost his driver's license after two DUI convictions. When my parents heard how he was bragging about the gold mine he was marrying into, they responded by putting the bulk of their property in trust for Olivia and me - with a very conservative bank trustee. Dan lied and said he was offered an athletic scholarship and they set a wedding date. Before that could happen, our folks died of carbon monoxide poisoning while they were staying at a mountain resort. Our lawyer sued and we, who were still minors, received a large settlement which went into the trust. None of these assets was community property.

"I moved into a seminary boarding school and Olivia and Dan married and moved into Mom and Dad's house. He had no college prospects and couldn't even pass an entrance exam. She had twins and he had friends. He rented out the pool house to them. If they paid any rent, he kept it. He ran up huge debts buying cars and boats. Our trustee hired an *au pair* to help Olivia, and Dan got her pregnant. There was a row in a public park, Dan took a shot at Olivia and at the police who answered the 9-1-1 call. He spent ten years in prison. Olivia got a divorce. By then I was married. My husband owned a shopping center and since her boys were old enough to go to school, we gave her one of the shops to use for her ceramics' business. She got a few contracts to make personalized mugs and commemorative plates and her business grew. She did beautiful work.

"Her life was the boys, the shop, and the church. The boys went to college and got navy commissions. She was lonely and now her life was just the shop and the church. She visited the sick. She wrote pen-pal letters to the lonely. She helped people."

Beryl asked, "Why are you referring to her in the past tense?"

"God help me," Tracy said, "I'm so worried that I'm assuming the worst. Since Valentine's Day, it's as if I wake up every morning and read her obituary."

"Did you bring the gas receipt and also some recent photos?"

"Yes." She placed the receipt on the table. "It's dated February 13th. I called her on the 25th. Her phones were disconnected. A woman had bought her business and took it over just as it was. Her house had a new owner. I had no idea she was planning such changes to her life. I called everyone I could think of. Nobody knew where she was. A few said they were under the impression she was leaving the country. I called our lawyer, but he invoked attorney-client confidentiality.

"Here are some recent pictures - one of us together and two of her alone. Her eyes are still a little swollen, but the likeness is good." She gave Beryl the photos. "Don't we have to sign a contract?" She got out her checkbook. "What will your retainer be?"

"A dollar." Beryl winked at Sensei as she placed the agency contract on her desk.

Tracy balked. "No. What Percy did for me, I can never repay. You should see my son today. He's gorgeous. I intend to pay."

"If you want our help," Sensei said, "just sign the contract. The expenses are on me. Period. Do not argue." She signed the contract.

"What kind of car was she driving?" Beryl asked.

"A new Cadillac coupe, white."

"Tomorrow morning I'll drive up to Ephrata and talk to the gas station people," Beryl said, hesitating, "There's just one thing. We're investigating your sister - a woman who did not care to tell you about her private life. It may be that she's in trouble; but it may also be that she's happy and might not appreciate our poking around in her affairs. If we locate her and she's not in any trouble, we'll just report to you and let you contact her."

"That's fine. I'd prefer it that way."

FRIDAY, MARCH 18, 2011

The sun was alone in a clear sky and the traffic was light as Beryl drove northwest on the Schuylkill Expressway. The road dipped and curved in the Appalachian foothills, changing her perspective of the barren farmlands and windbreaker trees. Scarlet farmhouses and barns glowed in the morning light, and here and there a burst of pastel pink or cream revealed the early blooming of a fruit tree.

She exited at Ephrata and saw the familiar sign of a Shell station.

After filling the gas tank, she went into the convenience store. "Do you happen to remember this lady who was here a month ago?" she asked the cashier, showing her the photo. "She was driving a white Cadillac, New Mexico plates."

The young woman gasped. "I remember this lady! She was wearing that same sweater. She was crying her eyes out! I gave her a soft pretzel and a Coke. I didn't want her to drive while she was crying."

"That was thoughtful. She's missing, and her sister's hired me to locate her. She found a receipt from here, so this is where I'm starting my search."

"She was on her way to Philadelphia."

"Yes... but Philadelphia couldn't have been her original destination. She must have driven north to Ephrata and then went southeast to Philadelphia. She bought only a quarter tank of gas, so there had to be another reason for her to be in the area. Whatever made her cry was something that happened here. Have you any idea what that could be?"

"Maybe she knew somebody who lives around here. But my guess is that she had gone to visit someone at the prison."

"I didn't know you had a prison up here. A state prison?"

"Yes, it's a Commonwealth prison. A small place - less than 300 inmates. Aardenaar Dehemel Reformatory it's called. It's in a Dutch community about fifteen miles or so from here. It's a really old building. It was founded by Dutch priests."

"Priests? Like... Catholic priests?"

"The Order was originally Catholic but hundreds of years ago they became Protestant, but they still do a lot of the old Catholic stuff. They're called 'Father' and not 'Mister' like Protestant ministers, and usually they're not married."

"That's a new one on me. A religious-run prison here in Pennsylvania."

"It's not run by the priests. The warden and the guards are regular state employees. But the Dutch folks over there have taken care of the prison for generations. They bake bread and pies and the ladies knit wool socks and hats for the winter, and the men teach the guys trades like bicycle repair and upholstery. The priests do counseling, but they don't try to convert the inmates, so the state's ok with it. Besides, they don't keep murderers in there and they take the overflow or the 'protective custody' guys from other prisons."

"And you think she might have gotten some bad news at the prison?"

"Well, she was here on a Sunday, and that's visiting day, so it's possible. And the next day was Valentine's Day. Emotional for some people."

"I'd like to visit it. Is it far from here?"

"No, but if you want to interview someone, you'll need an appointment. Sometimes they verify who you are before they'll talk to you."

"I guess the sooner I make the appointment, the better. Do you have the number?"

"Sure. Call now. They've been real busy. There's been a lot of trouble in the last month at the prison and the church, so it's best not to wait."

The clerk called the prison and handed Beryl the phone, whispering, "The warden's name is Conner."

Beryl spoke to the warden's secretary who gave her an appointment for 1 p.m. on Tuesday, March 22nd. She returned the phone to the clerk. "What did you mean by 'trouble' at the prison?" She looked around. "Do you have any of those pretzels left?"

As the two women talked, they drank Cokes and ate pretzels slathered with mustard in the old Pennsylvania style. "A few years ago they got a new priest," the cashier explained. "He was originally from around here but he went to Holland when he was twelve. Lord, he was so cute. And nice, too. Everybody loved him. He came back here as a community priest and he also worked at the prison. But then they said they'd caught him stealing from the church. He supposedly got away with thousands in just a few years. We didn't believe it. But they had to let him go. He wasn't arrested or anything like that."

"And this happened just in the last month?"

"Right around Valentine's Day."

"The sudden loss of a good looking priest and a woman's tears. Somehow that seems to go together. What was his name?"

"DeVries. Father Willem deVries."

"I'll look into it. Can you give me directions to the prison? I don't want to get lost when I come up again next week."

"Just stay on this road and follow the signs. It'll take you into Harderwijk - that's the Dutch town. Go another mile past it."

Beryl gave the cashier her card. "If you happen to think or hear of anything else, I'd really appreciate a call."

"When you go through Harderwijk you'll see a white church with a steeple, the First Holland Christian Church. There's a rectory there, too. They're the order of priests I just told you about."

"Well, thank you. I don't know your name!"

"It's Alison. And you're welcome. I hope you find her."

George Wagner decided to check into Olivia Mallard's sudden sale of her home and business. If the rumor that she had left the country was true, then it was likely that she put her business records and other personal property in storage. She probably had valuable art objects, and also, having moved into her deceased parents' home, she must have had sentimental pieces that she wouldn't sell or give away. Since the new owners took over the business "as is," they probably retained her old employees. He searched through "ceramics, Albuquerque, New Mexico" and found her former shop immediately. He called and was able to speak to Olivia's former truck driver who said that he had, in fact, helped her to put her possessions into a storage facility.

"Did she give you any clue as to where she might be going - to which country or part of the world?"

"The only thing she said was at some future time some items might have to be sent to Suriname."

Paramaribo was the largest city and the capital of Suriname. George searched "hotels" in the area and began to call them. The Hotel Tropical Haven brought results. His call was forwarded to her room. He planned to hang up when she answered, but the phone rang until the operator cut in to say that evidently Miss Mallard was not in her room and asked if he wanted to leave a message. He said he'd call again.

"Suriname? That's the old 'Dutch Guiana!'" Beryl said. "This is beginning to make sense. The gas receipt is from a station that's near a Dutch community in which an old Commonwealth prison is located. It just so happens that a handsome priest named Father Willem deVries, who ministered to the prisoners, was discharged in mid-February for embezzlement. Nobody knows where he is now. We need to locate him. The church is the First Holland Christian Church of Harderwijk."

"Did they remember Olivia at the gas station?" Sensei asked.

"Yes, she was crying. I have an appointment Tuesday at one o'clock with the warden at the prison."

"Do you want me to get on the Willem deVries location problem?" Sensei asked. "I'll call the church. By law, they have to know where he is."

"Why by law?" Beryl asked.

"Because the church has to carry ministerial insurance for as long as the statute of limitations is in effect for the type of serious crimes that could involve a cleric. It's like a doctor's malpractice insurance. He can leave an area but by law he must maintain malpractice insurance for several years after. The insurance company has to know where to reach deVries in case somebody files a suit against the Church for something he's alleged to have done while he was employed there. Every state is different. But trust me. The Order will have ministerial insurance on him. They'll know where he is."

Sensei called the First Holland Christian Church and asked for the pastor.

"Ah," the receptionist said in a voice that rasped with age, "you want Father Anton Haas, but he isn't here now."

"Who is next in authority?" Sensei asked.

"That would be Deacon Faber. I'll transfer your call." Deacon Samuel Faber took the call.

"I'm trying to locate Father Willem deVries," Sensei said. "I understand--"

"Who are you?"

"I'm a Buddhist priest, but ordinarily I use my secular name, Percy Wong. I understand that Father deVries is no longer with your Order; but it's important that I speak to him. Do you--"

"What about? What did you want to talk to Willem deVries about?"

The aggressive tone irritated Sensei. "I'm afraid that is a confidential matter."

"Then, confidentially speaking, you're not going to take me on a fishing expedition." Deacon Samuel Faber hung up the phone, angering the usually placid Zen priest.

Beryl frowned as Sensei related his encounter with Deacon Faber. "The problem with people who rely solely upon the martial arts for defense and offense," she teased, "is that they can't handle action at a distance. Everything is calculated to be done while in physical contact with an opponent. Women know how to fight when they're miles away. Allow me to call the First Holland Christian Church."

"Go ahead and try it. Let's see what you get out of that smart-assed clergyman!"

"I thought you said he was a deacon. A deacon is not a clergyman. I'll put the phone on speaker. Listen and learn." She called the rectory. The same elderly voice answered. "I hope I have the right lady," Beryl said. "I'm

Beryl Tilson, an investigator down here in Philadelphia. An associate of mine called a few minutes ago and spoke to a very charming lady and a rather rude man. Are you the charming lady?"

"I hope so, Miss Tilson. My name is Violet Miniver. I talked to your associate."

"And who, Ms. Miniver," Beryl said in a conspiratorial tone, "was that man who presumed to speak for Father Haas?"

"Deacon Samuel Faber."

"That man needs to learn good manners. Somebody should teach him."

"Somebody would be wasting somebody's time," she whispered.

"I know what you mean. Is Father Haas available? We're trying to locate Father Willem deVries, and Deacon Faber will not tell us where we can find him."

"Your associate should have asked me. I would have told him that Father Willem is the chaplain at a hospice in Camden, New Jersey. *Christ The Savior Hospice.*"

"Thank you so much. You're very kind. But tell me... Is Father Willem a nice man?"

"Yes. Will you be speaking to him?"

"I hope so."

"Please tell him that Violet Miniver says hello and that his memory is safe in her keeping and his name is always in her prayers. The only thing that man ever stole was my heart." She took a deep breath and spoke confidentially to Beryl. "What with Lent we've been very busy. If you still want to speak to Father Haas, you can come up Monday or Tuesday morning. I'll set aside time around ten o'clock for you."

"Tuesday morning is perfect. Thank you, Miss Miniver. I'll see you then."

Sensei shook his head. "*Touché,*" he said.

Ananda Moyer had gone through Suriname's citizen's entry port without any official delays. He presented his passport to the customs agent who read the deportation notice stamped on it and checked his name off a list. Overstaying his visa in the U.S. might have incurred American displeasure, but aside from sartorial considerations, it could hardly be offensive to the Surinamese authorities. Moyer was still wearing the denim shirt of prison garb as he deplaned in Paramaribo. He had in his pocket the hundred-dollar bill that the warden in Harderwijk gave him as release money when he was transferred into federal custody.

While he was in prison in Harderwijk, he had written to his old friends in Suriname, telling them of a wonderful scam he and a church deacon were running. He had communicated with several rich religious women who each sent him money for an attorney, which the deacon put into his own bank account. The scheme was that he'd induce one of the women to open a mission church and school in some jungle outpost. They'd sell her "the Brooklyn Bridge" as the deacon put it, and split the proceeds of the con. Faber would leave the church; and with the money he and Ananda gained they'd open a small resort in the Caribbean that catered to 'men of distinction who enjoyed pleasure and pain." Ananda's friends in Suriname had another idea about spending the rich woman's money, and it did not include Deacon Samuel Faber.

If this were not troublesome enough, Ananda Moyer had begun to like the woman chosen for this scam. Olivia Mallard was just about the nicest person he had ever known, and he seriously considered marrying her and really opening a mission in the rainforest. Ananda could read and write but hardly well enough to entice "a woman of quality." It was necessary for Deacon Samuel Faber to write all those poignant love letters for him, and, as expected, Olivia had fallen in love with him because of those letters. He was her "Bright Star" and she was his "Bright Spirit." Now she was waiting for him in Paramaribo. And so were his friends.

Before he committed himself to Olivia he wanted to see what she looked like. If she was as pretty and dignified as she appeared in her photographs, he would take her down to his village near the Gran Rio in Sipaliwini to meet his family. His mother would be ecstatic. She always feared that he'd bring a whorehouse floozy into their village. Even his village Captain had warned him about bringing diseased women into the area. Olivia would raise his status. She was intelligent. Deacon Faber had said so. And she could supply money for start-up industries that would give people financial independence.

Ananda had taken the Skyspirit English course which Deacon Faber administered, but he had not had the time to complete it. He had all the lesson handouts, but he needed to study and practice them. With the exception of one "scripted" phone call, all of his communication with Olivia had been by mail. He did not want to disillusion her by revealing the immense gap of knowledge that existed between the way he spoke English and the way he wrote it.

Of course, if she turned out to be ugly or nasty in person, he'd happily work the con on her that his friends had planned. He had not contacted them during the entire time he was in federal detention awaiting deportation, and they did not even know that he was in town. He'd go and meet her at the Hotel Tropical Haven. And then he'd decide whether he would live with her or just scam her with his friends. He was hungry, and he looked forward to the hotel's food. But he couldn't enter the hotel in prison garb.

In a discount store near the airport's shopping mall he found a traditional white Filipino shirt, slacks, and loafers that he could buy for just under three hundred Suriname dollars. He studied himself in the fitting room's mirror and decided that while he usually detested such conservative garb, it looked good on him. He pulled off the rubber band that had bound his hair at the back of his neck and shook his head. He had washed his hair that morning and the soft golden-brown mass of curls framed his face and neck like a nimbus's indication of sanctity. He brushed his hair and put the rubber band in his pocket. All of the jewelry he possessed when he was arrested had been contained in a sealed manila envelope. He opened the envelope and removed his gold loop earrings, chain necklace, and wrist watch and put them on. Having determined that nothing additional could possibly enhance his appearance, he stepped out of the fitting room, smiled at the clerk, asked for a shopping bag, and handed her a hundred dollar bill, which, at an approximate ratio of three Surinamese dollars to one American, more than covered the cost of his new garments. He put the contents of his overnight bag and his prison clothes in the shopping bag and threw the old worn overnight bag into a trashcan.

As he accepted his change, he asked the clerk, "Would it be possible for me to use your phone to call the Tropical Haven Hotel?" She nodded and he called, asking for his friend Anton "Tony" de Jong. The response he received was hostile. Mr. de Jong was no longer employed by the hotel. Moyer thanked the clerk and left to return to the shuttle station at the airport.

The airport mini-bus let him out at the front door of the hotel. He went inside and asked the desk clerk to connect him to Olivia Mallard's room on the house phone.

Olivia had been in Suriname for nearly three weeks. She did not know when Ananda Moyer would arrive. She had, in fact, no absolute knowledge that he would arrive at all, but she did have faith. She believed in him and intended to build a life with him and to do God's work there in his beautiful country. They would build a church... small but with real stained glass... with maybe a generator to run an air conditioning unit for the congregation's comfort. Maybe they would even get a small organ. She knew from his letters that he would deliver beautiful sermons. She would teach people how to make potter's wheels and fine, salable pottery.

The bedside telephone rang. She prayed that it would be Ananda at last. She answered slowly.

A man's voice answered, "This is the Suriname Astronomy Society callin', Ma'am. We're tryin' to locate the proper place to put a Bright Star."

Olivia squealed with delight. "Ananda! Finally! Where are you?"

"I'm down here at the desk, Ma'am. But I'm busy right now waitin' for a Bright Spirit to come down and have a cuppa' tea wit' me. Do you happen to know a Bright Spirit who is floatin' aroun'?"

"Give me five minutes and a very Bright Spirit will meet you at the desk!"

"Hurry, woman! Hurry!"

Olivia had been prepared for this day for weeks. She brushed her hair and put makeup on. She selected a prim blue pique dress and jacket and, since she wasn't sure of Ananda's height, she put on sandals.

Looking her best, she stepped out of the elevator and gasped with delight to see how tall and handsome he was. She smiled and her whole face registered happiness.

Ananda opened his arms wide and Olivia rushed into them. They held each other tightly, and when he released her, it was only to kiss the palms of her hands. Olivia had never before felt such joy.

They went into the dining room, arm in arm.

Before the waiter approached the table, Ananda began a speech that in consultation with his Skyspirit grammar notes, he had written and memorized. "A confession needs to be made, and it is I who must make it. I have no money. I owe you five thousand dollars already; and between you and me, I do not have even the prospect of repaying it. If you wish to order dinner, you should know that it is you who must pay the cheque. I have enough money in my pocket to order tea and cake for us both. But that is all." He bowed his head. "You cannot imagine how bad I feel. I am so ashamed."

"My dear," Olivia's eyes brimmed with tears. "Money means nothing to me. You are what matters to me. All that I have is not mine, it is ours."

"I do not deserve a woman like you." Ananda kissed her hand as he warned himself not to do anything that would make the statement an obvious truth.

The waiter placed menus before them. It seemed magical to Ananda that the table could be so quickly filled with so much delicious food and wine. He consumed them as a black hole consumed matter that slid over its event horizon.

With dinner, Ananda ordered a bottle of sparkling burgundy wine. He had never tasted it before that night; but he had heard people praise the wine and he wanted to know what was so wonderful about it. It was, he thought, as good as they said it was. Olivia drank iced tea, leaving the entire bottle for him to guzzle alone. He ordered another bottle.

At first, the more he drank, the more animated he became. His eyes would widen and narrow, and he'd punctuate his sentences with an exclamation's burst of laughter that allowed him to show his perfect teeth as he tossed back the spiral strands of hair that seemed determined to cover his face. Olivia found his gestures and laughter adorable. She wondered how she had ever lived without him. For decades, her eyes and ears had been functioning at a fraction of their capacity; but now they were fully engaged and the richness of what she saw and heard were the sights and sounds of heaven.

As he drank the second bottle of wine, his speech became so slurred that his words were incomprehensible. He lapsed into a patois of Dutch, English, and his mother's native language. After a few hours of rapt confusion, Olivia felt tired, and, with good-natured sweetness she told him that she needed to sleep. It was after midnight. She signed the check and asked Ananda to walk her to the elevator.

When the elevator doors opened, she turned to say good night to him, but he gently pushed her inside and managed to indicate that she should tell him which floor. She said, "Five," and he pushed the appropriate button. She then realized that he had no money or place to stay. He could not stay in her room, of that she was certain. She turned away from him and took five one hundred dollar bills from her wallet. "Here," she said firmly, "take this money and get yourself a room in a nice hotel. And sleep! You're home now and free. Call me in the morning, early if you want to come for breakfast. Or we can meet again for lunch."

He stood inside the elevator, staring at the money she had pressed into his hand.

She said, "Good night, Darling. Good night, Bright Star." The doors closed and she hurried to her room.

Ananda Moyer felt as if he were a starving man who had taken a mouthful of delicious food. He was between pleasure and pain and feeling both. He had not had a woman in months. He wanted pure, unadulterated sex. Olivia had rejected him. On the other hand, he had five hundred dollars in his hand. There were other places he could go to feel welcome and satisfied. Even gambling was legal in Suriname.

SATURDAY, MARCH 19, 2011

Ananda Moyer put the five hundred dollars in his pocket and pushed the ground floor button. When the doors opened he walked past the desk clerks who seemed to be relieved that he had descended so quickly.

Outside the hotel he marveled at the clarity of the night. March marked the end of Suriname's three-month "short" dry season in a weather-cycle that repeated itself endlessly. His watch told him that it was still only a little after midnight; but at the moment, time ceased to be linear. What was more significant was that he knew a place where he could get a drink, a woman, and a pair of hot dice. He felt lucky.

He walked along the Waterkant until, at Henck Aaronstadt, he found a taxi idling at the curb. He approached the driver's side. "You know how to get to Ellington's Jazz Club?" The driver, a Hindustani immigrant, said that he did and asked, "You got the fare?" Ananda Moyer waved an American hundred-dollar bill and asked if that looked like money. "You're the boss," said the driver as Moyer climbed in the back seat.

Fifteen minutes later the cab stopped in front of Ellington's, a seedy club that managed to be inconspicuous in a warehouse area. Aside from the patrons, only an occasional night watchman could hear the loud jazz music that blared from open windows on the second floor of the building. The ground floor, open except for support columns, served as a parking place for campers that functioned as temporary motels for the 'working girls' who congregated on the sidewalk.

A woman, wearing a skirt that was as short as a bathing suit and an elastic tube-top, watched as the cab driver counted out Moyer's change in Surinamese currency. She recognized him and called him by name as he tipped the driver and jammed the money into his pocket. "Nandy, Man... Nandy the Candy Man. Come ove' heah, Man! Gimme some sugah!"

Ananda Moyer's soul flew heavenward at the sound of the familiar lilt of his own native speech. He was home. He thought of the man whose name had been given to a long highway in his clean and beautiful country. "'Free at last!'" Moyer shouted, "'Thank God Almighty! I am free at last!'" He picked up the woman and swung her around.

She was filled with praise for him. She took his hand and led him back to her camper. "I got candy for ya' nose. Oh, Man. We gonna have a good time!"

After lunch, at 1 p.m. Beryl, lurching forward and then backwards half a dozen times, squeezed her Bronco halfway into the only parking place available. "How far out am I?" she asked, frustration edging her voice.

Sensei gauged the distance. "What's that old line? 'It's not far... we can take a cab from here to the curb."

"At least," Beryl said, "I did not hit anyone."

"I begin to understand the merits of 'action at a distance,'" Sensei said.

They stood on the sidewalk and looked at *Christ The Savior Hospice*.

It was a dilapidated building that had been created by cobbling together three brick row houses. All the windows on the ground floor had been covered by a chain-link grill. A fake stone facade had once been glued to the middle house. Near the roof, hunks of the stonework remained stuck to the crumbling bricks. Three separate sandstone 'stoops' led up to the three doorways. The first had "Enter" painted on the glass pane at the top of the door; the middle was nameless; the last had "Exit" painted on its glass. There was an alleyway beside the row house marked Exit.

Sensei noted, "This being a hospice, I guess they use the alley for the hearses."

"Let's get this over with," Beryl said as she walked to the entrance door and opened it.

Inside, they winced at the stench of pine disinfectant mixed with vomit, excrement, blood, urine, and the stink of cabbage and whatever else that had been cooked for lunch.

An emaciated man in pajamas and slippers pushed an oxygen dolly across the hall. "Can you tell me," Beryl asked, "where we can find Father Willem deVries?" The man weakly pointed to a door towards the end of the hallway. Beryl thanked him, proceeded directly to the door and pushed it open.

DeVries, younger, with blonde hair that fell in waves down to his collar, and far more handsome than she expected him to be, was bending over a patient, comforting him. The priest wore a lab coat over a black turtleneck sweater. A cross was pinned to the coat's breast pocket. "Let us pray," he began, closing his eyes as he knelt on the floor beside the bed.

The two visitors stood in the doorway and waited for the young chaplain, who seemed not to notice them, to finish. "Oh, Lord, be Thou the goal of my pilgrimage and my rest along the way. Welcome my soul. Let me find peace and refuge in thee."

With great effort the patient raised his hand and placed it on the chaplain's shoulder. "Amen," he whispered. "Thank you, Father."

The chaplain bent over and told him to get a good night's sleep and said he'd see him in the morning. He turned immediately to Beryl and smiled as he finger-combed his hair back. "Can I help you?"

"I certainly hope so. I'm Beryl Tilson, an investigator with Wagner and Tilson, and this is my associate, Sensei Percy Wong. Sensei is also a Buddhist cleric. Shi Yao Feng." They shook hands. Beryl continued, "We're trying to locate a lady named Olivia Mallard and we're wondering if you can help us."

DeVries led them out of the ward. In the hall, he said, "I never met Olivia Mallard, but I did write to her once. A month ago I answered a letter she wrote me about an inmate at the prison I worked in. She had written from New Mexico, I believe - and that's all I can tell you." He smiled again. "I'm curious. Why have you sought me out for information about her?"

"Her sister is our client. She last saw Olivia a month ago, on Valentine's Day, right after Olivia was at the prison which was..." she read from her notepad, "Aardenaar Dehemel Reformatory in Lancaster County. I hope I pronounced that correctly."

The priest smiled. "Close enough. It's actually Van de aarde naar de hemel - that's Dutch for 'From Earth to Heaven.'"

"I take it that she wrote to you in your function as a pastoral guide at the prison. Something happened the day before Valentine's Day. She drove to her sister in Philadelphia that day, crying and too upset to talk about it. She drove home to New Mexico and dropped out of sight. Olivia sold her home and business and went to Suriname. Our client doesn't want to call the police or do anything that might introduce a sensational element into what might be a private and reasonable act. So, I'm asking if you can give us a clue about what it was that troubled her around Valentine's Day?"

Willem deVries shrugged. "There's nothing confidential about what she wanted. She wrote to me about an inmate who was being deported. She had driven a great distance to see him and then was refused entry into the visitor's room. Somehow she got the idea that I was responsible for her being turned away. The tone of her letter was hostile. I assured her that I knew nothing about anyone's refusal to see any visitor. She also thought that I was remiss in not pressuring his attorney to act efficiently in his interest. I knew nothing about any attorney for him or anyone else. I suggested that she contact Father Haas or the warden. And you want to know the inmate's name. Ok. I see no harm in it. She wrote to me about a fellow from Suriname, a man named Moyer, Ananda Moyer."

The reply was unexpected. Beryl had suspected that the priest was the "love interest." She revised her suspicion. "Yes. Ananda Moyer. It's an unusual name. She apparently intended to start a new life in Suriname."

"Ah," deVries smiled, "he was an unusual man." He grew serious and his expression changed to one of concern. Incredulously, he asked, "And she was going to start a new life with *him*?" Then as if to say, "It's none of my business," he added, "Well, I cannot judge. In Christ all things are possible. Water into wine. Rough into refined." He turned to Beryl, "But I should tell you that though the name 'Moyer' is more German than Dutch, it's fairly common both in Pennsylvania and in Suriname. 'Ananda' seems to indicate that perhaps his mother or someone important to his parents was Indian or had Buddhist leanings. 'Ananda' might be unusual up here, but Suriname has a large Indian population."

Sensei nodded. "Yes, the Buddha's cousin was named Ananda. Many Mahayana Scriptures are attributed to him. Did Ananda Moyer have some connection to Lancaster County?"

"He apparently did have a relative there. He wasn't one of my prison church-members so I don't think I ever knew who that was. When he got into trouble, it was learned that he was in the country illegally. He had been staying with a woman he was supposed to marry."

A man with a clipboard approached deVries who excused himself while he signed a paper. When the man left, deVries turned to Sensei. "Do you have a temple in Philadelphia?"

"Yes," Sensei said. "And I also teach karate. I'm out of uniform, as you can see. My head is supposed to be shaved."

"My hair is also not what anyone would consider 'regulation length,'" said deVries, but since I'm in the ex-category of the ministry, I might as well take advantage of it. I wish I could be of more help. My dealings with Ananda Moyer were limited. He never attended my services or sought me out for private counseling. And he was there for only a few months. Actually, I left a few days after he was transferred to federal authorities. In fact, one of the last things I did was to answer Ms. Mallard's letter."

"And she never wrote back after that?"

"Not to me. She may have written to others. The locals apparently liked him - until he got into trouble with the law. That ended his sojourn, so to speak."

"What kind of trouble?" Sensei asked.

DeVries held up a hand and shook it, palm out. "I'm not comfortable discussing Ananda Moyer's troubles. He was in jail, so it's all a matter of public record. Suffice it to say that the charges were dropped, and that while he was being held, his visa expired. He was processed for deportation. An attorney would not have done him any good especially since no U.S. citizen was willing to support his residency here."

"Would the woman he was going to marry know his address in Suriname?" Beryl asked.

"She probably would. Her name's Saskia Deken. Her name should be in the newspaper accounts. Check the area paper, *The Telegraph,* for November of last year."

Sensei returned to the priest's previous statement. "You said 'ex' but once you're ordained, with or without membership in an order, aren't you still a priest? I noticed that you're still called 'Father.'"

"Yes, in a religious order they can cast you out, but they can't take away your divinity Ph.D. It's like being a medical doctor. You can lose your license but not that M.D. after your name. In case you're wondering, I was banished... accused of misappropriating Church funds. I don't suppose it matters that I was innocent."

"It matters," Beryl said. "It's terrible to be accused when you're innocent. Embezzlement's a felony. Shouldn't you have had your day in court?"

"Ecclesiastical courts have to practice what they preach. Better than any human judge, God knows a person's guilt or innocence. If a man has been unjustly convicted, if he keeps his faith, yet he will prosper. And if he is found to be innocent when he is guilty, his conscience will punish him far more than any human court or council can punish him."

"Ah," Sensei smiled. "That happens to be the subject of my next Dharma talk. *Honi soit qui mal y pense*. Specifically, The *Lex Talionis.*"

"I'd like to hear it," deVries said.

Sensei removed a card from his wallet and gave it to the priest. "Tuesday night. Seven thirty. I'll hold the curtain for you."

"A command performance? Then I'd better not be late."

"Oh," Beryl teased, "be late and make a grand entrance."

"Don't dress for the occasion," Sensei laughed. "My church is humble."

"As humble as this?" deVries looked around.

A light of recognition passed between the two men, and they laughed. "You got me beat," Sensei said.

"By the way," deVries asked, "how did you manage to find me here?"

Beryl answered. "It wasn't easy. When Sensei first called he spoke to Deacon Faber who was rude and hung up without telling him anything. If the good priest here could have reached through the phone line and poked him on one of his *dim mak* points, he would have left him dead in Harderwijk. I called again and spoke to one of your most ardent admirers. Miss Violet Miniver says that you are safe in her heart and your name is always in her prayers."

DeVries smiled. "Please tell Ms. Miniver that I never see violets but I think of her. And I hope you locate Ms. Mallard. And Sensei, your reaction to Deacon Faber is the normal one. He can be nice; but usually he comes off as being too busy with important things to be disturbed by insignificant things... such as the person he's talking to."

Sensei laughed. "Two minutes talking to him - and I needed someone's prayers. I didn't have enough of my own to do the job."

"I'll pray for you," deVries laughed.

"You could start," Sensei said, "by praying that this most excellent detective can pry her car out of the parking spot she wedged it into."

SUNDAY, MARCH 20, 2011

Ananda Moyer remembered getting into the camper. There was a red floral bedspread on the bed. He remembered that. On a table near the bed was a single-edged razor blade and a piece of glass. He remembered white lines being furrowed on the glass and pressing a nostril and inhaling. The flowers in the bedspread were roses. He thought he remembered that just a moment before he realized that he was lying on a table in a hospital emergency room. A doctor was sewing his ear lobe. Ananda said nothing.

As the doctor finished bandaging the wound, he said, "Keep it clean and dry. If it itches, don't scratch it." He rummaged through a desk drawer. "Here's a rubber band to hold your hair back. It's matted with blood and sand. Keep it away from the wound. I know you don't have any money," the doctor said compassionately, "but you need to get some rest and drink plenty of water. You were dehydrated when you were brought in." He opened a refrigerator door and removed a small carton of orange juice. "Drink this," he said, opening it.

Ananda's swollen and bruised hands shook as he tried to get the V-shaped spout into his mouth. His bottom lip, split and swollen, added pain to the task. The doctor took the carton and held it steady, telling him to take his time. "Oh, tha's good. Tha's good," Ananda muttered.

"I'll get you another one. And you can have this leftover donut. Wait until you're outside before you eat it. Your shirt's bloody and torn... and what happened to your shoes?"

Ananda was still groggy. "I don't know where they are. They were new. Where's my watch and my shoppin' bag?"

"You weren't wearing a watch. No jewelry at all. No shoes, socks, money, or shopping bag. Somebody tore your earrings out of your ears.

The closure snapped on your right side, but on your left it held and your flesh was ripped open. You were found on the waterfront. Wait a minute... I may have an old pair of flip-flops that fit you." The doctor went to a room marked "Private" and returned with an old pair of sandals. He put them on the floor near Ananda's feet.

"Thanks, Doc. Did I have my passport?"

"No passport. *Niets. Nada.* Nothing. They left you with your life. You're lucky to have it."

Ananda Moyer did not feel particularly lucky or particularly alive. "Where should I go?" he asked the doctor who had his back to him, washing his hands.

"I can only suggest that you not go back to where you were. You're finished here. Come back in four or five days and I'll remove the sutures." He left the room.

Ananda stumbled into the hall. He pushed open the door to the men's room and once inside, he ate the donut and, spilling as little of it as possible, drank the second carton of orange juice. Then, using liquid hand soap from the dispenser, he tried to wash the blood out of his shirt. The band-aids on his hands fell off. He ran cold water over his hair and rubbed soap into it until all the clumps of hair were reasonably free of blood and sand. The bandage on his ear fell off. He filled the basin with water and dunked his head in it repeatedly. After changing the water several times, he considered his hair to be clean enough, and he returned to the problems of his shirt.

The breast pocket had been torn three quarters of the way off the shirt. With a toothpick he found on the floor, he picked at the remaining stitches until he was able to remove the pocket, which he then put in his pants' pocket. It could serve as a handkerchief if worse came to worst - as it apparently had.

With his shirt and hair dripping wet, he exited the building. The morning sunlight struck his eyes like javelins. He squinted and tried to shield his eyes with hands that were swollen and scraped. The local anesthesia in his ear had begun to wear off. His head and arms and feet and hands... everything hurt. He wanted to sit down and cry, but he kept walking in the direction of Olivia's hotel.

Standing across the street from the hotel, he watched the people who passed by until he found one who looked like the sort who would help him, a young man in his twenties who had just put his cellphone in his pocket.

He approached the man and stood in his path. "Brother," he said, "I'm not askin' for money. But I could use a little help. I got mugged. Could you make a phone call to my lady? She's at the Tropical Haven but I can't go in there lookin' like this. Just tell her Ananda is out here waitin' for her, and could she come out and meet me."

With some suspicion the man used his phone to look up the number of the Hotel Tropical Haven. "What's her name?"

"Olivia Mallard. She's on the fifth floor. I can't remember the number."

A moment later the man said, "Olivia Mallard's room, please." As Moyer watched apprehensively, the man said, "I'm outside the hotel across the street with Ananda. He's been injured... mugged I think. He wants you to meet him out here. Yes, right across the street from the hotel. I'll tell him. You're welcome." He turned to Moyer. "She'll be here in fifteen minutes."

Moyer had tears in his eyes when he thanked the man. He shed even more tears when he saw Olivia walking towards him, carrying his shopping bag, He had left it there in the hotel. So he hadn't lost his passport and old shoes! A surge of joy crested in his smile, and he stepped forward and waved. She saw him and returned the wave. Immediately Moyer burst into serious tears.

Walking together, they went to the rear of the hotel gardens and sat on a bench.

"What did you do when you left last night?" she asked.

Ananda Moyer felt more in control of himself. "I went ta' look for a clean but inexpensive hotel. I wanted ta keep as much of the money ya' gave me that I could. I was about two blocks from here when three thugs grabbed me. I tried to fight 'em off. You can see my hands from hittin' 'em. Look!" He showed her the scrapes. "They stole my money, my watch, my necklace and earrings and even my shoes." He showed her his stitched ear lobe. "Then they hit me with somethin' and the next thing I knew I was in the hospital."

"Why didn't you call me?"

"I was in and out of consciousness. They had ta' x-ray my head ta' make sure it wasn't broke... so I couldn't get up and make a phone call. And then I'd lose consciousness again. And finally when they was sure I was ok, they sewed up my ear and let me go." He sighed and shuddered. "I tried to wash the blood from my shirt. The doctor gave me these beach sandals." He looked through the shopping bag and with great relief found his passport and his old shoes, socks, and shirt.

"Are you strong enough to travel?"

Ananda Moyer wanted nothing more than he wanted to get out of Paramaribo, but he still was uncertain about what he intended to do with Olivia.

As he sat there, feeling victimized and resenting having to be rescued from people he had trusted, an old tint of self-loathing became a vivid primary color. "Either you do it, or it does you," he told himself. If he went with Olivia, she'd see right through him and he'd wind up losing everything. At least with his friends, Henny and Tony - guys he had known all his life - he wouldn't have to pretend to be what he was not. And he'd be able to get a big chunk of that money.

Again she asked, "Are you strong enough to travel?"

"Yes," he said. "But I'm supposed to contact some people about where we can build the church. I don't want ya' to be upset if I don't come right back. I may have to go look at the property. Will you behave yourself till your Bright Star can shine on ya' again?"

"I'll try to be a good girl," she said playfully. "I may go shopping again. When you didn't come by for breakfast, I went out and found the most beautiful mauve silk... a whole bolt of it. And the shop had an old treadle sewing machine for sale. I couldn't resist. I kept thinking about redecorating that old plantation house you told me about, so I went ahead and bought it. They took the sewing machine apart and packaged it. It's in the hotel now along with the silk. Was I being too extravagant?" She pouted.

"No, no. Why... you might have some left over to make a nice altar cloth for the church! What's to be sad about? What is mauve?"

Olivia smiled and touched the tip of his nose. "It's sort of pinkish lavender. But you leave the curtains to me."

Ananda was absorbed with another problem. He had changed into his old denim shirt; but the words, "I.C.E. Federal Detention Center" were printed on the top of the pocket. He took the pocket he had removed from the Filipino shirt and put it inside the denim pocket leaving enough outside to fold down and cover the printing. He suddenly felt better. "I have ta' go find the real estate people."

"Do you want me to come with you?"

"No, my lady. I want ya' ta' go back into the hotel and have a good lunch and wait for my call."

"Well, at least let me give you some money." She opened her purse and extracted two hundred dollars. "Is this enough?"

"Ah, it is too much." It did not, however, seem sufficiently excessive to warrant returning any of it. He put the bills in his pocket. "Can I ask ya' to hold on ta' my shopping bag?"

Olivia was happy to do so. Ananda's passport was inside the bag, acting like a compliant hostage.

Ananda walked to a cheap discount clothing store and bought a shirt and shoes, and asked the clerk if he could call the airport. He called Hendrik Holman of Holman's Air Service.

"I'm back," he said. "And I'm hungry. I'm comin' now ta' your office."

"Finally! We've all been waitin' for ya. Meet us at the cafeteria instead," Hendrik replied.

Ananda said, "Ok," but he was puzzled by *'we've all'*. Who was *we all?*

Hendrik stood up in the booth and whistled as Ananda entered the cafeteria. "Jesus... you haven't been back in town long enough for the engines to cool down and already you've been in a fight. Get rolled, or what?"

"I don't need ta' give my personal history. I had trouble. It's over. Now what's goin' on here?"

Tony deJong, his blonde hair pulled back into a ponytail and a short stubbly beard on his face, extended his hand. "Nandy, my man. I've got all the paperwork here. You're gonna love the scam we worked out. As you can see, we've had to let another guy in with us."

"Who's this guy? I think I've seen him around Cajana."

"You do know him," Hendrik said. "Jackel Mazumi."

"I've seen ya' around *Springer's* or the *Pink Dolphin.*" Warily, he shook hands with Jackel.

Tony grinned, "You're gonna love the scam we've got planned."

"Jackel's a citizen of Guyana," Hendrik explained. "He's got an address in Georgetown so we don't have to get involved with phony passport shit. Everything is legit. Tony will lay it all out for you."

Ananda did not like the sudden increase in personnel. And he didn't like the way plans had been made without consulting him. He had brought the "prize" to the party, and suddenly guys who had brought nothing were telling him what they had decided he had to do with it. More bosses. He reconsidered his options. Everything was on hold until he alone chose between going with them or with Olivia. He looked at Jackel Mazumi. How, he wondered, could a pureblooded native possibly fit into a swindle. Jackel's heavy black hair came down in bangs that covered his eyebrows and stuck out over his ears and the top of his torn and dirty collar. Traces of red ocher tribal markings were still on his cheeks. Yes, he supposed that Jackel was a good man - if by "good" was meant loyal and honest. But a confidence man required a degree of sophistication, and in that department, Ananda thought, Jackel was a big minus.

Tony wanted to clarify his own position. "I lost my job at the Tropical Haven; but I'm still tight with a waiter there - so I know that the mark is registered."

"Don't call her 'a mark!'" Ananda snarled.

Hendrik responded to the awkward rebuke. "The good Mr. deJong is very sensitive about hotel guests and employees. He was fired a couple of weeks ago for having aroused more than a little suspicion that he was light-fingered and morally loose." He paused for effect. "Actually, he was accused of having stolen money and jewelry from a wealthy gentleman guest in whose room and rectum he had spent a few private hours. Can you believe that of our Tony?" Hendrik led the group in laughter. "What could they have done together that made the kindly tight-assed old gentleman decline to press charges? Do you like Tony's new watch?"

As everyone laughed, Tony flashed his newly acquired Longine. "I got his diamond pinky ring and some cuff links, too. Imagine an old guy wearing a pinky ring. Ridiculous. I did him a favor."

"Yeah, Tony, you're the man," Hendrik laughed and turned to Ananda. "Are you certain she brought the million with her?"

Ananda was pacified. They had spoken respectfully to him. He studied the menu. "Yeah. Nearly a million. She thinks we're goin' ta' buy that beat-up house the old loggin' company used for the manager's residence. I called it a 'plantation house.'" He grinned. "I told her the wreck needed a little repair."

"Guess what? It's not a wreck anymore," Hendrik said. "While you were gone it was renovated. The place was bought by a company that mines gold. The chief engineer lives in it."

"Oh?" Ananda looked up. "Now what'll we do?"

DeJong rolled his eyes. "Listen, this will work even better. After we found out it was already renovated, we put an ad in the paper to sell it - to lessen the coincidence for when you got back. The prospective buyers have to write for an appointment. Nobody's written yet. You should bait her with the ad as soon as possible. But remember, we have to time it perfectly. Everybody has a role to play."

As soon as the waitress took the order and left, Tony opened the satchel and handed Hendrik the documents.

Hendrik spoke confidentially to Ananda. "Read fast before the food gets here." He explained the significance of the documents. The first one purported to be an officially stamped Grant Deed which transferred title of the house and 100 hectares of land in the Cajana Township area of Sipaliwini District from the previous owner to the Wollenback Mining LTD of Georgetown, Guyana, for two million six hundred thousand SRD Surinamese dollars in January of 2011. "You can tell your American lady friend that these two hundred hectares equals five hundred acres, and that two million six hundred thousand Surinamese dollars equals eight hundred thousand American dollars.

"Monday morning Jackel and Tony are going to Georgetown to register our new company, Wollenback Mining. Then they'll open a bank account."

Hendrik placed a second document over the first. "This is a letter we wrote saying that the Wollenback Mining company has changed its mind about continuing its Cajana operation in Suriname. It says that a claim to extract minerals from a potentially richer source has finally been granted to them by another government and that they plan to transfer the personnel and equipment from the Cajana operation to this new resource. It tells the chief mining engineer that it will absorb the cost of those improvements made to the Cajana property and that he has accordingly been empowered to negotiate the sale. It says that all necessary documents have already been filed with the appropriate authorities in Paramaribo and in Georgetown." Hendrik looked at Ananda Moyer with a stern expression. "Pay attention to what I am telling you. Your lunch will soon be here and if I know you, you won't be able to think about anything but eating."

"What are you now? My mother or my wife? Finish your goddamned story!" Ananda intended to be respected. He had the Queen Bee... they were just workers.

Hendrik took a deep breath and softened his tone. "Tony, here, is going to pretend to be the chief mining engineer of the Wollenback Mining Company. The real company is Granger Mining and the real engineer is alone in the house now. Jackel sells him fresh fish every weekday.

"Now, the real engineer flies up here every Saturday morning with a competitor of mine, Kenyon Air. He's got a girl friend he sees. While he's up here he buys supplies - food, tobacco, booze, and other shit for the week. So it's important for him to go every weekend. Kenyon flies him back at noon on Sunday.

"This is the plan: Monday Jackel and Tony register Wollenback as a Guyanese company and open a bank account and order checks to be printed. Jackel can use his father's house in Georgetown as his address, so he can be the corporation's resident agent as well as its treasurer. Tony's going with him so don't worry. Today he's going to get Jackel properly cleaned up - a hair cut and manicure and some business clothes. Tony has also been his language coach. They'll fly back here with the bank account's information. It should take no more than three days to do this. Then they'll go back down to Cajana.

"Then next Saturday morning, that's March 26th, Jackel and Tony will go to the 'plantation house.' Jackel knows how to get into it through one of the windows. The real engineer will be up here with his girlfriend. You and Miss Mallard book a flight with me for Saturday at 10 a.m. round trip to Cajana. You mention that plantation house you're interested in buying near Cajana, and I say I heard people were looking at it, that it's a nice place, if you're lucky enough to get it.

"I fly you down and I wait on the veranda of the Vandermeer Lodge while you two walk back. Tony's gonna put a Wollenback sign up over the Granger sign. You'll see it as you walk back. You knock on the door and Tony answers. He'll say that there's another party interested in the house so if you want to buy it, it has to be immediately since he wants to go to Paramaribo that afternoon to complete the sale.

"You want to give it a good look. The house is in good condition. There's a big room they use for conferences. She'll see it as a good 'start-up' church room. Since the house isn't open to the elements - it has real windows and doors, she can see it as the perfect place for that little air conditioning unit she wanted. Tell her that. Get her excited about the possibilities.

"If all goes well, she'll say that she wants the place. And Tony will say, 'Great!' He'll say that he might as well go back to Paramaribo with you that afternoon since he also wants to meet me. You and he need a proper witness for when the title is transferred on Monday.

"Jackel will show up at the airfield and ask me for a lift up to Paramaribo. I say, "Sure," and say that sometimes two witnesses are necessary. So we introduce everyone to each other. I fly all five of us back here in the Cessna and we agree to meet in the cafeteria on Monday morning to complete the transaction.

"Miss Mallard, you, and Tony go to her bank, Trader's, as soon as it opens on Monday, the 28th, morning. Tony will give her Wollenback's Georgetown bank account number. She wires $800K to the account. He hands her the deed and some other papers. The money won't have trouble clearing the bank. The bank in Georgetown will know the money's good. She's had it in a bank here for a month."

"Wait a minute," Ananda objected. "You think that Jackel and Tony are gonna' open an account one week and then, after $800K is put in it a few days later, they'll go up to the teller and clean out the account? Just like that? And nobody's gonna get suspicious? They'll be questioned on the spot."

"It will be done by checks," Hendrik assured him, "by properly signed Wollenback Mining Company checks."

"And what happens," Ananda smirked, "if she goes down and finds out the place isn't hers at all. She'll bitch to the Sipaliwini section of the NBI, and there'll be somebody waitin' in the bank for Jackel and Tony to show up."

"That's why it's up to you to keep her away from Cajana until those checks have time to clear the bank here. We'll tell her she can't have access to the property until all the heavy equipment is removed... around two weeks. By that time everything will be a done deal.

"We'll each get a check for $200K through a Georgetown branch of an international transfer agency. You can open a bank account here today and they can put it right into your account. It's legitimate money. If you're ever asked you can say that you owned stock in Holman Air and Wollenback bought you out. If that time ever comes, we'll make up some phony papers."

Hendrick sat back into the booth. He put his hands behind his head, waiting for a reaction.

"What happens ta' her... Olivia... when she finds out the house ain't hers?" Ananda asked.

Hendrik shrugged. "Take her down to your mother's house. Be grief stricken when you find out she was swindled."

"I'm not too happy about takin' her for a ride. She really loves me."

Tony saw the waitress coming with the hamburgers. He gathered the papers together and returned them to the satchel. "All the better! Hey, that's why it will work. She'll believe it when you act as if you've lost as much as she has. She'll want to comfort you. She can't take you back to the U.S. with her since you've been deported. She's got to stay here with you or go home without you. If you're so hung up on her... well, you've got $200K to build your church down in Sipaliwini. You can tell her a kind Christian donated the money to help make up for her loss."

Hendrik Holman and Anton deJong sat in irritated silence while Ananda Moyer consumed his two hamburgers and fries. After he wiped his hands and face on a napkin and sucked on his straw until the ice at the bottom of the big cup slurped and rasped, he said, "Lemme' see if I got this straight." Much to their amazement, he repeated the plan correctly. Then he asked, "How you expectin' Jackel ta' register a corporation and do all that bankin' stuff?"

Hendrik sat up straight. "Good question, Moyer. First, we've already started on that. Today Tony is going to get Jackel groomed for the part. Barbershop, clothing store, and then tonight he'll make him go to the reception desk of one of the lesser hotels and request a room, and register, and do a kind of 'dry run' on conducting himself in a businesslike way. Tony will keep working on his diction and demeanor all day tomorrow and then they fly to Guyana Monday morning."

Ananda shook his head and looked at Jackel. "It's gonna take more than a shave and a haircut ta' get him lookin' like a businessman. And ya' better make him deaf and dumb."

Hendrik looked at Jackel. "Say a few words that a businessman might say."

Jackel smiled and slowly enunciated, "Thank you. That is excellent advice. Good morning. I would like to open an account. We plan to develop new mineral claims, here in Guyana and in Suriname. Big oak trees from little acorns grow. Here are the necessary documents, all signed and sealed and recorded. I would like to deposit one hundred U.S. dollars just to open the account. Like any other enterprise, it will take men and equipment and the will to succeed. A large deposit will follow."

"I told you," said Hendrik, trying to let the irony leech out of his voice before he spoke, "this guy is on board. And remember, Tony will be there, too."

Ananda spoke to Jackel as a fellow student of English. "Damn!" he said. "You sounded refined!"

Tony deJong invited them both to come along for the transformation. Hendrik looked at Jackel and declined, saying that his heart couldn't tolerate such a "high-anxiety" experience. Ananda said he'd stay with Hendrik and be pleasantly surprised all at once instead of at stages.

Hendrik issued a warning. "All of you... listen. I have to do a lot of flying, and I've spent a lot to get those documents created, plus I have to stake Jackel to clothes, airfare, and all those business filing fees. That's a big investment in money and time. See to it you deliver *your* end on time."

"All right, everybody, let's roll," deJong said, standing up.

"Hendrik..." Ananda said as he stood up with the others, "Is there any chance I could spend a few nights on your office couch. I'll eat elsewhere but I need a place ta' wash up and sleep. I'll go to the bank and open an account now. I've got a hundred dollars American on me."

Hendrik gave him one of his 'left hand' compliments. "Ananda, I'll also consider it a pleasure to have you safely in my digs at night. Knowing where the hell you were would do my nerves a lot of good. There's a key taped under the mailbox beside the door and clean sheets in the closet."

"Thanks," Ananda said. "I told Olivia that I'm searching out a mission site." He grinned. "I don't wanna' give her too much of me at once."

Everyone laughed.

At the hotel barbershop that deJong patronized, the manicurist looked at Jackel's hands and said, "I'm goin'ta need a jackhamma' to push these cuticles back." She smeared a softening agent over his hands and led him to the shampooing station. After two shampoos and a facial using deep-cleansing cream, he was ready for the barber's chair.

With scissors and comb and styling foam that had the properties of epoxy, the barber worked a minor miracle. "Voila!" he said, turning

Jackel around in the barber's chair. "He looks like he just got off the plane from Paris!"

Neither deJong nor the manicurist would have gone that far in their approval, but it was, both had to admit, a startling improvement.

The manicurist set to work with her orange stick and scissors. Finally, she applied colorless nail polish and then when the polish was dry, lathered his hands in a heavy-duty lotion.

Jackel was ready now to shop for clothes. On the way out of the shop, he lingered at the mirror to admire himself.

MONDAY, MARCH 21, 2011.

Wearing a pastel striped shirt, khaki pants, and loafers, and carrying an attaché case, Jackel Mazumi boarded the Georgetown flight with Tony deJong. Jackel, sitting in a window seat, said nothing until they had been airborne for fifteen minutes. Then he turned to Tony and said, "So this is what it is to fly high in plane. Henny fly low. I wonder many times. The people look like ticks."

The remarks had a sobering effect on Tony. He smiled in spite of the sudden fear he felt. He wondered what kind of trouble he could get into attempting to perpetrate a fraud of this sort. The vision of a Guyanese prison took form in his mind.

The flight required less than an hour and they gained an hour by flying westward into another time zone. Jackel did not quite understand how it was possible to land the same time that they took off. DeJong assured him that after everything was recorded and the bank business was finished, he'd get a globe of the world and teach him all about a place called Greenwich and what they did there.

Everything went smoothly at the Recorder's office and at the bank, although they were asked to return on Wednesday, March 23rd, to finalize opening a business account and to order cheques. They went to Jackel's insect ridden house and, at deJong's insistence, left it quickly to check into a hotel.

Beryl gave herself a couple of hours to drive the seventy-five miles to the area that was once known as the home of *The Mystic Order of Solitude*, a German group of pious "Dunker" Baptists, a religious group now nominally extinct. She arrived at Harderwijk, southwest of Ephrata, just before 11 a.m.

She had taken her time driving through the prosperous Borough of Ephrata. There was an old landmark Synagogue, several German Protestant churches, well-kept lawns and trees, and a freshly painted look to every building. Occasionally an Amish horse and buggy pulled to the side of the road to let her pass. It seemed to be an unlikely place to research criminal matters. Ah, well, she thought, what can you tell from the appearance of anything.

In Harderwijk, she saw the white-steepled church and a mile or so past it, a small brick building that sat back from the road. A simple sign erected at the private drive's turnoff read *De Telegraaf*. "This must be the place," she said aloud and turned onto the drive.

The publisher, editor, reporter, and ad salesman of *De Telegraaf* were merged into the person of one white-haired old gentleman who pecked away at a computer keyboard and shouted, "Hold that thought!" to Beryl as she entered. She watched him as he focused on the screen and mumbled to himself the lines he was converting to print. Not until he finished the page and wrote the traditional "30" at the end of the article, did he turn and look at her.

He stood up and smiled. "How can I help you? Command me."

Beryl handed him her card. "All right. You're commanded. I'm investigating a missing person who had a connection to a man named Ananda Moyer, and I need your help."

He looked at her card. "Ms. Tilson... I'm Willem van Kempen, the labor and management of this old rag. My morgue files haven't been kept up to date. You'll have to trust my memory or else check at the Ephrata public library."

"I will happily trust your memory."

"Then let me think. Ananda Moyer was a rather handsome fellow... in his thirties... mulatto... a mass of curly yellow-brown hair that he tied back with a rubber band. He was from Suriname.

"You'll want to know how he got here. That's easy. Last summer, Ananda Moyer happened to be in Aruba when a cruise ship docked and our own Saskia Deken came ashore. She's a rather well-to-do widow with a couple of kids... pretty, around thirty-five. They got to talking and discovered that his great aunt, Karel Hiemstra, lived between here and Ephrata. It's not such a 'small world' when you consider that Aruba's Dutch, Suriname's Dutch, Harderwijk's Dutch, and so are Moyer and Deken.

"In the short time that her ship was in Aruban waters, Saskia became infatuated with Moyer. Since his great aunt was well regarded hereabouts, Saskia didn't hesitate to invite him here. She even sent him the money for his ticket. By late September he was here and everybody liked him. He lacked polish, of course. He wasn't very well educated - but we chalked up his language deficiencies to the fact that English was not his native language. For that matter, Dutch wasn't either. He was born and raised in an isolated area in the rainforest. He was pleasant enough and since it was harvest time he helped, for free, some elderly farmers who were a little strapped for cash. How am I doin'?"

"Fine... but let me write down some of these names. Saskia Deken—"

"D-e-k-e-n. Her place is at the northwest corner of Millpond and Brooklyn. Eighty acres, but she let the trees grow back. She harvests pine nuts. Lots of deer. She keeps a salt lick for them. She doesn't need the income from farming. If you want to find her place, just go back down to the road and turn right. It's maybe five miles down."

"And Aunt Karel?"

"H-i-e-m-s-t-r-a. She lives on the west side of the road that takes you up to I-76. About a mile after you leave Ephrata and before you get to the Expressway. You'll see a sign, *Hiemstra Farm*. Follow that road back. You can't miss it.

"Moyer seemed to be a good match for Saskia and they planned to get married over the Thanksgiving Day holidays. One day Saskia went out to do some shopping with her seven year-old daughter and asked Ananda to mind her four year-old son. When she got back she went to change her boy's clothes and noticed that his underpants were on backwards. She said she was going to let it go, thinking she had made the mistake; but then she noticed that his privates seemed red. She asked the boy why his underpants were backwards and he said that Uncle Nandy put them on that way when he was in a hurry because he saw her car coming up the driveway. She asked him why the pants were off in the first place and he said he had promised to keep that a secret. She didn't do anything at that moment because she was in a state of shock and wanted to be sure before she made any accusation." Van Kempen shrugged his shoulders in a way that suggested he didn't quite believe the story.

"What happened next?"

"Next morning she told Moyer that she and her daughter would be going to look at quilts in Ephrata and asked if he'd watch the boy for a few hours. She drove to the road and waited half an hour and then walked back to the house. She found Moyer and her boy in the shower. Moyer was on his knees with his arms around the boy and his mouth at the boy's plumbing. Well, all hell broke loose. She called the police and Moyer was taken into custody; but instead of being taken to jail he was taken to the old prison. The jail holds many drunks when harvest's over; and nobody wanted to mix a child molester in with good honest drunks. He had no way to raise bail and while he was in custody his visa expired.

"Saskia saw no reason to subject her son to the trauma of a trial since Moyer was going to be deported anyway. She told the police that she could have been mistaken about what she saw and the charge was dropped. Moyer was taken into federal custody last month and transferred to Baltimore for a deportation hearing. I'm told he was supposed to be flown back to Suriname this month. And that, as we say in the trade, is all the news that's fit to print, brought to you by *De Telegraaf*."

"What was Moyer's response to the charge?"

"He denied it. He said that on the first occasion he changed the boy's clothes because the kid peed his pants while he was out playing with some of the older five and six year olds. He didn't want them to know he had peed himself. It was cold outside and when his wet pants almost froze he came in crying because it hurt and also because he feared his mother would punish him. Moyer said that nobody had to know, and he changed his underpants and blue jeans and socks. He hurried when he saw Saskia driving up and that's why the underpants were on backwards."

"And the shower incident?"

"He vehemently denied that, too. This time the boy pooped in his pants while he was playing outside. Saskia gave both her children prune juice regularly. She had that old fashioned belief that a full bowel was a germ-filled bowel that caused disease."

"I think that was called autointoxication," Beryl said. "People used to give enemas regularly for it."

Van Kempen agreed. "Yes. That was the technical name for it. At any rate, Moyer said the kid was covered in shit from the belly down. He stripped the kid and threw the clothes in the washing machine which, he insisted, was still running when Saskia came back. Moyer said he wiped the kid off with toilet paper as much as he could, and since he hadn't showered yet himself, he took the kid in the shower to wash him properly. The boy didn't want his mother to find out and made Ananda swear he wouldn't tell people that he pooped his pants. That was the big secret."

Beryl frowned. "I hate to say it, but of the two versions..."

"I know. My personal feeling is that Moyer's account made more sense. I even investigated as much as I could which is to say I asked my wife to get her hair done at the beauty parlor and see what the ladies had to say. My wife learned that Saskia, who was very social-conscious, had evidently been criticized by her former in-laws. They had ridiculed Moyer, and he suddenly became a great embarrassment to her. She had no intention of marrying him. Before Christmas she married her former brother-in-law, so her name stayed the same.

"Ultimately, we don't know what went on in that house. Moyer wasn't the sharpest arrow in the quiver. He was likable but he did lack social grace. Or maybe he was just lousy in bed. Who knows?"

Beryl laughed. "Even widows have standards." She closed and then reopened her notebook. "I think you covered all the bases. I have only a few more questions. Do you know Willem deVries?"

"Father Bill? Yes, he seemed to be a good man. I didn't know him well. He was accused of embezzling funds from our church. I can't imagine him doing it. He used to work at the prison, but the accusation ended that. You should talk to the folks at the Church."

"I'll be back tomorrow to interview Father Haas. Do you know where I might be able to get Moyer's address in Suriname?"

"Saskia would know."

"Would she mind if I called on her?"

"I'll call and find out." He went to his desk and consulted his Rolodex file. A moment later he was talking to Saskia.

Van Kempen began to write. He also began speaking Dutch which Beryl could only slightly understand. He thanked Saskia and hung up. "Moyer got his mail at one of those all-purpose jungle outposts... down in the south near one of the tributaries of the Suriname River. The place is named *Springer's Road House,* in care of the Cajana post office in Sipaliwini District. She doesn't know any more than that but she did say that after he was transferred to the Federal detention center, some mail came to him and the warden let his Great Aunt have the mail and a few personal things of his that he had left behind. Do you want me to call his Aunt and see if she still has the things?" He gave the note to Beryl.

"This is such an imposition! Of course, I'd appreciate it."

Again van Kempen consulted his Rolodex and dialed Karel Hiemstra. Beryl listened intently as he spoke Dutch. "She says she still has the things all of which you are welcome to and if you come right away you can have lunch with her."

"This is too easy," Beryl said. "Thank you so much. If there is ever anything that I can do for you, just let me know."

"I'll consider myself well paid if there's a story connected to your inquiry - a story that the folks around here might be interested in... and you give me the scoop."

"I will indeed," she said.

Karel Hiemstra opened the front door and said, "I am so sorry that I didn't ask you if you were a vegetarian. I had cook make roast beef sandwiches." She held the door open for Beryl to enter. "You never can tell who's a vegetarian - not by sight, anyway."

Beryl laughed. "Roast beef is fine. I'm what is called 'a vegetarian of convenience.' Some people call it a 'semi-vegetarian' but I rather like the 'convenience' term."

Aunt Karel knew nothing about Moyer or even his father's life. "My brother was his grandfather. After the war, he took a job running a shipping company in Dutch Guiana - that's what Suriname used to be called. He got married and had a daughter, Gunda Heimstra, and she got married to a man from India or a man who was an Indian - I never knew which. He doesn't seem to know any yoga. He speaks funny and I'm told that from the deep South where he's from, they speak funny. Gunda named him Ananda. They have names like that down there. That big snake they have is called an anaconda. Maybe that's where they got the name. He told us his father's Indian last name sounded like Moyer so that's what he wrote down as his official name. But Moyer is more German than Dutch! So I don't know why he decided to spell it that way. It's so confusing! Ananda Moyer met Saskia and then showed up here. Until that terrible business with Saskia's son, we all rather liked him. As the Pennsylvania Dutch say - they're German, by the way - 'We get too soon old and too late smart.'"

"Poor Saskia... to be so mistaken about someone. How did she take this awful situation?"

"Terrible, at first. But the next day her former brother-in-law came to comfort her. He was single."

"Is prune juice still a breakfast staple? I understand she favored it."

"Oh, she wasn't old enough to need prune juice. At her age a little shredded wheat will keep her regular."

"But she gave her four year old son prune juice every morning. Did he have some kind of problem?"

"Well, he surely did if she gave him prune juice every day."

Beryl did not want to push the topic any further into oracular ambiguity. At the moment, within arm's reach, Ananda's personal effects and some mail of his were in a brown paper bag that had been carefully folded and stapled at the top. Since it would be rude to open the bag, the contents would have to wait.

After tea and dessert, it was time to go. Beryl thanked her hostess and carefully picked up the bag. "I'll be back, I expect, within a few days," she said. "I have a few more brief interviews to complete. Is there anything I can bring you from Philadelphia? You've been so kind."

"Ah, I wish there were. But if it isn't my high blood pressure, it's my incipient diabetes. And if it isn't either of those there's my acid reflux or nuts and seeds that get into my dentures."

"Then I will do you a favor and not bring you something delicious."

"I'll pretend that you did," Karel called as Beryl walked to her car.

Particularly when they wanted to discuss a case, Beryl, George, and Sensei often had ginger tea and pastries after services in the small first floor utility kitchen at the rear of the temple.

Beryl reviewed the conversations she had had with Willem Van Kempen and Karel Hiemstra. "And now," she concluded, "you must hear the letters that Olivia wrote to Ananda Moyer just before she left Albuquerque. There is also a letter from a man named Tony deJong whose address is *Jack's Pink Dolphin Roadhouse* in care of the Cajana post office, Sipaliwini, Suriname, that seems to be significant. I'll read Olivia's two letters and then I'll read deJong's. The first is dated February 22nd from Olivia to Moyer.

"Bright Star...

I waited for your letter yesterday. None came. How I missed reading your beautiful thoughts. What was worse was the fear that perhaps deVries had laid a trap for you. And you, innocent lamb, walked right into it. As the hours dragged on I felt certain that you were not permitted to have outside contacts as punishment for rejecting him. I even worried that you were sick or injured and unable to write. Even your lawyer has let you down. All that money went for nothing! When it rains, it truly does pour.

Then, this afternoon, I waited again, and when the mail came with no letter from you, I telephoned the prison and the clerk said that your papers were being readied for transfer and that any day Federal Immigration agents were coming to take you to Baltimore, and from there you'd be deported back to Suriname. So I hurried and wrote this note to congratulate you on winning your freedom.

I expect escrow to close by Thursday at the latest. I hope nothing interferes and that I will be able to fly down to Paramaribo. I'll have the funds transferred as soon as possible so that we can get started building our church. My lawyer is preparing the documents now.

Take good care of yourself, my Bright Star, My Polaris who guides me home.

Your loving,
Bright Spirit."

Beryl passed the letter around. "We learn more in the next letter dated February 24th."

"My Bright Star,

I am living in a motel and find it very lonely. The escrow went through without a hitch and I received my Suriname visa. I still have a few things to clear up and then I will be flying down to Paramaribo on Tuesday, March 1st. I don't know whether you are still in Pennsylvania or Maryland. I don't want to call the prison again since the priest and his friends may find a way to use my calls against you. My telephone numbers at the shop and at my home have been disconnected - and my cellphone, too. I didn't want any troublemakers tracking us with my GPS or phone bills. We'll get new service as soon as we're settled.

I hope you are already in Suriname. As soon as I arrive, I will call your friend Tony at the desk. If you're not in Suriname yet, I'll be happy waiting there for you, so do not be anxious on my account. My dreams of decorating the old plantation house will keep me busy window shopping.

As I get ready to leave my house and my country, I think only of you and our future, building a church and school for the poor, and doing God's work together.

Forever,
Your Voyager."

Beryl looked up. "When Tracy Baldwin said she tried to reach her sister ten days or so after Valentine's Day, Olivia was getting ready to leave the country.

"The third letter, from deJong written on the same date, says:

"Hey Nandy,

We've got some good ideas about a place in Cajana that seems perfect. Things are moving right along. Tell us what flight you're coming in on and we'll meet you at the airport.

Tony.

"Tony deJong and 'us' seem to be waiting for Ananda," she said. "And what does the place in Cajana seem perfect for?"

George looked at the letter. "We know she's registered at the Hotel Tropical Haven in Paramaribo. But what 'things' are moving right along? I don't like the sound of any of this. And she obviously sent him money for an attorney."

TUESDAY, MARCH 22, 2011

There was something odd about the case that interested George Wagner. He decided to go with Beryl to interview Father Haas and the warden.

A receptionist, who couldn't have been less than ninety, smiled as she accepted Beryl's business card but did not look at it. Instead she kept looking at George. She began a smile that would have lasted a long time if Beryl had not intruded.

"I'm Beryl Tilson from Philadelphia," Beryl said softly. "My partner, the eligible bachelor George Wagner, and I are here to keep the appointment with Father Haas. Are you are the favorite receptionist of Father Willem deVries, Miss Violet Miniver?"

The receptionist looked sheepishly at Beryl and whispered, "I should get new glasses. You're very sweet. Beryl, you just come on and follow me." She got up and led the investigators into Father Anton Haas' office.

Beryl looked around in admiration, and, trying to put the priest at ease, she remarked, "All this furniture is made by hand, by an expert cabinetmaker. And none of it is varnished or shellacked. And the brass fittings! They've been polished without leaving a bleached area around them. Amazing."

"There's a trick to it," Father Haas said as he rose to shake hands with George. "For years I wondered about it," the old priest replied confidentially, "and then one day I came upon a box of wooden cutouts... wood as thin as veneer. Each one had a description of the piece it fit around. The polish only touches the cutout," he said as he gestured for them to sit down. "I understand that you're interested in Ananda Moyer."

"Actually," Beryl said, "we've been retained to locate a missing person, a lady by the name of Olivia Mallard who corresponded with him."

"Ah, probably through our *Skyspirit* program."

"Skyspirit?" Beryl asked. "I'm not familiar with any the program."

"They are a prison outreach ministry," Haas explained. "They help to find good pen pals for inmates. The men discuss their correspondence with the supervisor sent by the church - in our case that would be Deacon Samuel Faber. He gives Skyspirit's English grammar and composition course to help the men. Ananda Moyer, I believe, took the course. Our Church's prison ministry performs many functions. We don't proselytize, but we do render spiritual comfort to those prisoners who request it."

Beryl spoke softly. "The priest who served at the prison during Moyer's incarceration was also known to Ms. Mallard. He seems to have had something to do with Moyer. Father Willem deVries. He is of interest, too. We can appreciate that this is a delicate matter. We know that he has been dismissed from your Order."

"Yes," Haas nodded. "A sad affair. But tell me," he said with a cagey attitude, "do you know if Olivia Mallard ever corresponded with Father Willem?"

"Yes, she did. But I can attest to only one exchange of letters."

Father Haas went to the bookshelf and removed a book. He fanned the pages until he stopped where a hand written letter had been inserted. "This book belonged to deVries," he said. "We found it after he left. This had been inserted into it." He gave the letter to George. "Would you care to read it aloud, for the benefit of Miss Tilson?"

George read:

"Darling,

You say that I have brought sincerity into your life. Do you know what you've brought into mine? Do you know what it feels like for someone like me, someone cast aside, "the stone that was rejected," to be made the cornerstone of your beautiful life? I know what it means to be both needful and useful.

Yes, you are right. Those who truly serve God have no other desire but to serve in the name of Jesus Christ. Together we shall serve the poorest among us. The money I receive from the sale of my properties will be enough to start our Church and schoolhouse. I am overjoyed to think that you will preach the

Gospel to villagers and that I will do my small part teaching them to read and write and use a potter's wheel. What a perfect future awaits me in your arms and in your soul. We will stand as one, united in love. Oh, my beloved Star and companion, I cannot wait for our journey to begin. You are my Bright Star. My Polaris. I will follow you in perfect faith."

George looked up. "It is signed, '*Your Voyager.*' There's a few faint numbers at the bottom... 1/10. Probably January 10th. I recognize the handwriting. It's Olivia Mallard's."

Beryl asked, "What would a love letter to Ananda Moyer be doing in a book owned by Willem deVries?"

Father Haas looked surprised. "Why are you supposing that this letter was written to Ananda Moyer? Surely it is obvious that, though the letter is a bit on the florid side, it was written by an educated person. And an educated person, by definition, could not possibly imagine that a crude and depraved individual such as Ananda Moyer is qualified or even desirous of preaching the Gospel. Start a church with him? My dear Miss Tilson, if the author of that letter is indeed the person you are searching for, and if that letter, as you say, was written by her to Ananda Moyer, you should commence seeking her in asylums."

"He wasn't too crude and depraved for Saskia Deken," Beryl countered.

"I don't mean to be argumentative, Miss Tilson, but in this community we have slightly different criteria. Ananda Moyer was not an outsider. He had blood relatives here. Outsiders, no matter how impressive their qualities, are not easily accepted. We have Amish neighbors, and outsiders tend to gawk at them and some, regrettably, will make derisive remarks. We have also learned over the years that even though one outsider might fit well in our society, he or she will have friends and relatives whose behavior is unacceptable. Ananda Moyer did not speak good English or Dutch. We could not fault his language inadequacies since he spent his boyhood in the southern part of Suriname in which a native language is mostly spoken. He was a handsome man with a bright smile and a fetching kind of personality. His depravities, unfortunately, were not immediately visible."

Haas' error in believing that Olivia's letter was intended for deVries presented an opportunity to induce him to convey information about the young priest that ordinarily he would not have revealed. Beryl wanted to know more. "Very well," she said, trying to seem conciliatory, "I admit that it makes more sense to assume that Olivia was in love with deVries rather than Moyer. But I'm afraid that we've only deepened the mystery and the danger. Olivia Mallard has placed nearly a million dollars in a bank in Paramaribo. We know that Willem deVries was dismissed from your order for financial misconduct. We simply cannot return to our client without more information. We can obviate a full-scale investigation - contacting Amsterdam, canvassing the citizens here in Harderwijk, and so on - if you'll give us some details. We don't need much. For example, we know that they corresponded. Surely they spent time together. Were they ever seen together up here?"

Father Haas did not want an investigation of any kind. Reluctantly he answered, "As a matter of fact she did come to the prison last month... just before Willem was dismissed."

Beryl opened her notebook. "There's so much gossip about the embezzlement. Can you give us the truth about this? If you don't want to be quoted, that's fine. We'll keep your name out of it."

The old priest folded his hands and leaned forward. "You've brought up a sensitive topic."

"How did he engineer the theft?" George asked.

Haas sighed. "We have many sources of income. Donations come in for our various charitable programs, Sunday collection-plate receipts, tuition for our private school, our gift shop, rents from properties we own, and so on. As these funds come in, each is put in a separate envelope and then put in the safe. We have a rudimentary computer program. It's adequate for our needs. On Sunday night Willem would enter the cash receipts into the journal and they'd be posted to the various ledgers. He'd make up a deposit slip and on Monday morning, our deacon, Samuel Faber, who has been with me for twenty-two years, would take the money to the bank.

"The embezzlement could have involved most of these income sources, but the one that caught Willem deVries concerned our tuition receipts.

We have a small - but first-rate school system. Our tuition is expensive, but for a particularly gifted student whose parents cannot afford the cost, we offer an installment payment plan. If they miss a payment, we often issue a credit and forgive that month's debt without making an issue of it.

"Willem had kept the books for nearly two years. The number of tuition credits had increased, but there had been an economic downturn and we assumed that this was the reason. And then Deacon Faber learned that one family that had been on the payment plan had inherited a considerable sum of money. He happened to be looking through the tuition ledger when he noticed that they had been issued several credits. He brought the matter to me. For the next week I personally noted each source of income before putting the envelopes in the safe. Later, after Willem had completed the bookkeeping, we matched them against his recording. Sure enough, a check for a one thousand dollar tuition payment was received and yet a tuition credit had been issued and several cash receipts had evidently been exchanged for the check's amount. To put it simply, he deposited the check but first he cashed it out of currency received and then he pocketed the money.

"I confronted him and he denied it. He knew of the credits that had been issued, but he assumed that I had authorized them. In fact, I had done no such thing and it was his signature that authorized them. I could not understand why he would have done such a thing. As the French say, "*Cherchez la femme*." I had my answer when Olivia Mallard came to the prison all the way from New Mexico. The ecclesiastical council in Amsterdam determined that he should be dismissed. It was a sad end."

"Who had the authority to issue a credit in lieu of a payment?" George asked.

"Only Willem and I," Haas answered.

"Who else had access to the safe?"

Father Haas responded unemotionally. "Only four of us. Samuel Faber, Willem deVries, Miss Miniver who previously kept the books, and I. But regardless of who had access to the safe, Willem deVries signed the credit vouchers," Haas said, "and I verified his signature, although he denied signing them."

George shook his head. "Signatures are not always so easy to verify." He placed his notepad on the desk and pushed it towards the priest. "Please sign your name, Father."

Haas signed his name with a few more flourishes than usual. "Here," he said, pushing the notepad back across his desk.

It was an old trick that anyone in a normal world would recognize, but George knew that they were not in a normal world and that the trick would probably work. He turned the notepad upside down and pushed it towards Beryl and asked her to copy the signature.

Beryl took her pen and seemed to scribble beneath Haas' signature. As soon as she finished, George, without looking at it, pushed the notepad back to Haas. "Which one is yours?" he asked.

Haas was startled. He could not tell the difference between the two. "How did you do that?" he asked.

Beryl explained, "When a person is trying to copy something that has meaning for him... such as a signature... his own mind prejudices the formation of letters. But when the signature is upside down, it becomes just a bunch of squiggly lines and his hand is free to copy it without any psychological interference."

"But if it is this easy," said Haas, "why do people place value upon a signature's authenticity?"

"It is the reason why photocopied signatures are worthless. In order to prove that the signature was not forged in the manner we just demonstrated, a microscope is used to determine the direction in which the fibers in the paper were broken and also the direction of the flow of ink. My copy is backwards."

George asked, "Was the reason for the credit a multiple choice kind of voucher? Just check the applicable box?"

"As a matter of fact, that is the form."

"So only the signature was determined to be deVries's. I'm not trying to be confrontational, but a case could be made that deVries was not the intended recipient of that love letter. 'Darling'? My own mother used to call me 'Darling.' I verified that it was Olivia Mallard's handwriting. Until I did that, you knew only that it was an anonymous woman's love letter written to someone called Darling."

Father Haas responded quizzically, "Who else could have been the recipient? *My* concern with church property is the location I'd like my grave to be. So I am not intended as the recipient. Our cleaning lady and receptionist are too arthritic to be traipsing around a jungle. And Deacon Faber, while not vowed to celibacy, is not inclined to engage in dalliances with anyone... particularly with women."

"Ah, I understand." What George understood was that the cast of characters involved in Olivia Mallard's disappearance had grown even more diverse.

Father Haas' demeanor changed. "While I might wish that his desires were different, I cannot fault his disposition of them. He's forty-four; and I suppose that aside from being a solitary man of great integrity, time has dulled his appetite. He is a completely responsible man... one of the few I know who are without blemish."

"Is there any chance that we could meet him?" Beryl asked.

"You'll have to make an appointment with him. Please understand that he has been doing yeoman's service. Amsterdam has not yet sent me a replacement for Father deVries and all the prison duties as well as the bookkeeping chores have fallen upon Deacon Faber and me."

"I can imagine the work," Beryl said, standing up and extending her hand to the priest. "You've been under this strain for weeks. Thank you, Father. You have been kinder to us than we deserved."

The prison was an old stone and brick building that had been meticulously maintained and was overseen by a circular guardhouse that looked more like a lighthouse. At the entrance, the prison's high walls curved in on both sides, creating a funnel shape that led to the door. Clusters of tulips edged the base of the curved walls. Heavy glass doors opened into a vestibule and then other doors opened into a large reception area.

At the far end of the room, a prison guard sat behind a glass and steel partition. He spoke through a screened hole in the glass. "What can I do for you folks?" he asked.

"We have a one o'clock appointment with Warden Conner." Beryl pushed her card through the security slot.

The guard contacted the warden's office. He smiled. "He'll see you now." As he pressed a large button a foghorn sounded and a heavy door at the side of the room began to slide open. "Straight through and up the stairs on your right."

From his office window, the warden had watched them as they walked to the entrance. He stood to greet them as they opened the door to his office.

George handed him his business card. He used his right hand which had shriveled slightly as the result of a gunshot wound. The warden looked quizzically at his hand; and George explained, "I'm a private investigator, now. I used to be with the Philadelphia Metropolitan Police."

"Injured in the line of duty?" the warden asked.

"Yes," said George, "shoulder and knee." As he sat down, he gestured an introduction. "This is my partner Beryl Tilson."

As the warden shook hands with Beryl, he said, "So this is about Willem deVries and Ananda Moyer. I hoped I'd never hear that rascal's name again." He smiled. "I mean Moyer, naturally. We keep the prison administration separate from the religious volunteers. That is a Commonwealth mandate."

"Does the name 'Olivia Mallard' mean anything to you?" Beryl asked.

Warden Conner repeated the name to himself. "I know that I've heard it." He buzzed his secretary on the intercom. "Helen, do you remember the name of that woman who came up from Arizona or New Mexico and wanted to visit Ananda Moyer? I think he was with another woman and Faber had to tell her that he couldn't see her and she didn't take it too well. There was a bit of a ruckus."

George and Beryl glanced at each other, startled to hear the truth so casually spoken. They could hear the voice on the intercom answer, "Yes... her name was Olive..." she paused to check something. "Olivia. Her name was Olivia Mallard."

Conner said, "That's her. Thank–"

Helen interrupted him. "We did hear some gossip about Moyer. I'm not one to repeat gossip, but for you I will."

Warden Conner cocked an eyebrow as if to ask his visitors if they were interested in the gossip.

"Yes, by all means," Beryl exclaimed. "What was the gossip?"

Helen heard Beryl's response. "That an American woman - and I think it was Miss Mallard - was going to put a million dollars into a bank account in that country he was from. Suriname. They were going to build a church or mission in the jungle. That's all I know."

"Thank you, Helen," Conner said, closing the intercom. "Now don't that beat everything?"

"What kind of man was Ananda Moyer?" George asked.

"Do you know what got him arrested?" the warden inquired.

"Child molestation," George answered. "But the charges were dropped. While that matter was being resolved, his visa expired."

"That's it," said Conner. "We held him until our Federal brethren came and got him. But you asked what kind of man he was. Nice looking, well built on the slim, tall side. Dumb as a tree stump. He spoke English when he put his mind to it. Other than that nobody could understand him. But he had a lot of friends. Lots of letters, in and out."

"And Father deVries?" Beryl asked. "Did he get along with the inmates?"

"He got along with everybody. When we heard he was dismissed because he embezzled church funds, we couldn't believe it. But they never consulted us."

"Do you happen to know," Beryl asked, "if Moyer had an attorney?"

"A public defender came up from Lancaster when he was arrested. But when the criminal charges were dropped, he no longer needed representation. And usually in deportation matters, a lawyer is retained by those who want the person to stay. Nobody in this borough wanted Moyer to stick around."

"He doesn't sound like a man who could write eloquent letters. Yet that's how Ms. Mallard described them. That confuses me."

"No doubt he got help writing the letters from Deacon Faber. He's the man who taught the Skyspirit English course."

"What kind of man is Deacon Faber? Do you know him?"

"Sure, he's from the same church as Father Willem. They had different styles. DeVries went in for group activities. Organized basketball teams. Volleyball. We had one inmate who had been a professional tap dancer. Father Willem got him to teach a class. He'd play music in the yard and we'd see these guys who'd been in stir for years out in the yard learning to shuffle. They'd all be laughing. It was good to see," he paused, smiling as he remembered the dance lessons. "As for Faber, he prefers one-on-one contact. Not much in personality, but otherwise, a good man. Anything else I can help you with?"

"You've been very helpful as it is," George said as he stood and extended his left hand in a fist bump. "Thanks for giving us your time."

The warden laughed and returned the bump. "Any time," he said, as their knuckles touched.

Beryl stood up, too. "I have one last question. Is it possible to visit an inmate even if you don't know him? I'd like to talk to someone who knew Ananda Moyer, preferably his cellmate."

"He didn't have a cellmate. There was one fellow in the next cell who served his time - he was released in January. They probably talked through the bars. I'll check with Harrisburg to see if it's permissible for me to try to reach him for you, and if it's ok, I'll see what I can do. I'll contact you either way."

As they walked to the car Beryl said, "Now we know why Olivia was seduced by Ananda's letters. Faber wrote them. That puts him in the middle of this scam. No doubt he wrote the credit slip for the tuition and forged the old man's name on it and then deVries entered it. And before Faber went to the bank he exchanged the memo that he had forged Haas's authorization on, for one that he forged deVries's signature on."

"Call the son of a bitch. No! Let's just drop by the rectory. If he were in the prison, Conner would have mentioned it. If anybody asks, say you wanted to ask him something about Skyspirit."

Beryl drove directly to the Church rectory.

Violet Miniver greeted them as though she hadn't seen them in months. "You're that pretty private detective from Philadelphia. And is this nice looking fella' your beau?"

"I wish!" Beryl said, smiling. "He's too stuck-up to give me the time of day. I try..."

"Keep tryin', Girl. A faint heart never won a good plowman."

Beryl, surprised at the remark's suggestiveness, gulped and laughed. Then she bent over and whispered in the old receptionist's ear, "And how do you know he's a good plowman?"

"The more your senses fail, the more you can sense. What can I do for you today?"

"You are amazing," Beryl said. "I'll bet you can even get us in to see Deacon Faber."

"If you're smart you'll leave *him* out here. The deacon knows a good plowman when he sees one, too."

"I'll protect him." Beryl handed her a business card.

"Good. Then you two just follow me back. He's not a priest. I don't have to kowtow to him."

Deacon Samuel Faber glared at the receptionist as she opened his office door without knocking and walked a few feet into the room. "You have visitors," she said, gesturing to Beryl and George to enter. "Be a good boy," she said to George, "and fetch that Windsor chair." She placed the business card on Faber's desk.

"Yes, Ma'am," George answered as he placed the chair beside Beryl's.

Faber kept his eyes on the receptionist as she left. He glanced at the card and his anger morphed into a frenetic kind of frustration. He began to move his hands and head, initiating actions that immediately ended in failure at which point he would sigh deeply. He looked under his desk blotter, and finding nothing, straightened it and sighed. He picked up his ballpoint pen and clicked it several times and laid it down without having written anything, and sighed. His hairline had receded to the crown of his head, yet he brushed his forehead as if he were getting locks of hair out of his visual field. Again he sighed. George and Beryl stared at him.

"What do you find so interesting?" Faber asked George, his voice contemptuous. "I know you've been up here asking questions about Willem deVries and Ananda Moyer."

"How did you get along with Father deVries?" Beryl asked.

Again, Faber sighed. "More questions about deVries! I'll go through it one more time. I tried to befriend Willem. I really did. But he was so aloof? Yes, aloof. He was a clam, socially speaking, of course."

George pursed his lips. "Do you mean he had no social life?"

"Clam. Clam. To clam up means to stay closed and not to be open to people."

"So he had no friends?"

"None that I ever noticed." Faber looked at his watch. "Oh! Dear me. I've misplaced my free time. I had it around here someplace. Where has it gone? Is there anything else?"

George was accomplished at concealing anger, but he suddenly reverted to an authoritative manner of questioning. "What was your relationship with Ananda Moyer?"

"I taught. He learned. That was my relationship."

"What did you teach him?"

Faber then began to recite a robotized explanation of the Skyspirit creed. "I teach communication skills that benefit a man when he rejoins society. How to write letters of inquiry for jobs and such; how to fill out an application; how to request a letter of reference from some responsible person. Practice in such correspondence can be had by establishing pen-pal relationships or by writing to family members who might one day be asked to be supportive in the event of parole." He took a deep breath. "Are you satisfied?"

George tugged at Beryl's sleeve. He calmly stood up, replaced the chair, and, with Beryl following, walked out of the office.

As they passed through the outer office, the receptionist gestured that they wait a moment. "I know people," she whispered to Beryl. "Willem deVries was a man of God."

"Miss Violet, I find your candor worthy of your charm. I will probably be speaking to Father Willem again in the next few days. May I give him your regards?"

"Please do. Beryl, don't make yourself a stranger around here. And the next time you come by make sure you bring your friend with you. He's medicine for sore eyes."

Beryl laughed. "I know! I need a prescription just to look at him."

George grinned as they walked to the Bronco. As they drove through the town and headed for the Expressway, his attention was drawn to the little bursts of color given by the irises and daffodils that perforated the bleak winter border of farmland and road. "The season's changing," he said. His eyes searched for lilies but found none. George had a forbidden fondness for a pretty blonde girl named Lily and the thought of her made him smile. "Those yellow flowers are really pretty."

His remark startled Beryl. She took her eyes off the road for a moment to stare at him. "You... noticing daffodils?" She turned away and winced. She had forgotten about George's infatuation with the blonde girl.

"I'm an orchid enthusiast!" he replied defensively. "What the hell is so strange about me admiring daffodils and those other blue things?"

Beryl kept her face away so that he would not see that she was laughing.

Deacon Samuel Faber had been waiting weeks for Ananda Moyer to contact him. He had received no word at all.

More than a lover's rejection was involved. Moyer owed Faber half of the money they were scamming from Olivia Mallard. She had transferred nearly a million dollars to Suriname. Deducting for expenses, Faber calculated his part of the "take" at four hundred thousand. Other women, too, were in the scam's pipeline. They had been "hooked" and now needed to be reeled in. Had Moyer contacted them? Was someone else helping him to write to them?

Faber and Moyer planned to create a small but "select" spa for men whose tastes inclined to sado-masochism. Only Moyer had access to the money. How could Faber find out what was going on? His frustration grew into the reasonable fear that he was being shut out of the scheme he had created and worked so hard to develop. Deciding that he would not stand idly by and let a fool like Ananda Moyer make a fool of him, he bought a prepaid cell phone and tried to locate Ananda in Suriname.

The first time that he called *Springer's Roadhouse,* he was told by the bartender who answered the phone that Moyer was "back in the country but he hadn't seen him yet." Faber left his number and asked the bartender to tell Ananda that the "American church man" had called and wanted Moyer to call him back.

He knew that when Saskia Deken wrote or called Ananda at *Springer's*, she received quick responses. Two days later he called the Roadhouse again in the chance that Moyer had not received the message. Again, his message went unanswered. There was no other explanation. He was being shunned by Moyer; and where Deacon Faber came from, shunning was an extreme punishment. It rankled him to think that a man for whom he had done so much could be so ungrateful.

Moyer needed to be forced to pay, and the only pressure Faber could apply was to threaten to tell Olivia the truth about Ananda. And he had to exert that pressure before Moyer and his unknown partner completed their scam. Not wanting to leave his own name, he called again and tried to sound extremely happy when he asked that Ananda be given the message that he, Father Willem DeVries, was delighted to accept Ananda's invitation, and he'd soon be arriving in Suriname. Would Ananda call him so that he could give him details about his flight?"

The bartender suggested that he try to reach Moyer at Holman's Air Service in Paramaribo, a suggestion which the bartender repeated to one of *Springer's* managers.

To Olivia, lingering over a late lunch with Ananda there in the dining room of the Tropical Haven, the world took on the glow of one of Plato's Ideal Forms laid up in heaven. She experienced the certitude of meditative insight. She had just won a game of dueling index fingers with Ananda. He let his defeated finger go through a complete death scene, down to the final shudder and slump into a napkin shroud. She smiled and wondered why she was so lucky. "You know, my dear," she whispered, "you did write to me about getting married. I've been waiting to hear you ask me. Have you changed your mind?"

Ananda Moyer had not changed his mind, he simply had not made it up. He was sorry he ever got the whole scam started. He liked Olivia. He wanted to make love to her. And despite his grammatical errors, she loved him. She was pretty and she was respectable. He'd be rich and respectable. But the plan was set in motion. What could he do?

Then he thought, suppose he married her and let the scam go through. He'd be as shocked and hurt as she was. But he'd have $200K. They'd go farther south than Cajana - to his mother's village. They'd build a little church and school. He cursed his ignorance. How could he become a preacher? The first time he opened his mouth she would realize he had deceived her. But maybe not...

"Tell me somethin'," he said. "If you were stranded on a deserted island and you had ta' pick a man to be with ya. You had ta' choose between a stupid man and a bad man. Which would you choose?"

Olivia laughed. "Choose between a fool and a knave? Well, a knave can change his ways. He can be forgiven. But stupid is forever. I guess I'd choose the knave."

Suddenly he knew what he had to do. A door in his mind that had been closed opened. He had been bad; but of course, he was not stupid. He simply had never cared to learn the Bible, but he *could* learn. Let her lose the money. He'd be done with Hendrik and Tony and Jackel and any of his rotten so-called friends. He and his respectable wife would still have the mission. He would take a quick course in the Bible. Faber had told him there were children's editions of the Bible. He could start there and work up to the King James. He had seen how the really flamboyant preachers entertained their flocks. He could preach like that. People would come from miles around to hear him. He'd learn all those stories and tell them in his own "Ananda" style! He could see himself in a pulpit, making the Word wonderful and entertaining and inspirational, too.

He cleared his throat. "I haven't asked you," he said, "because I wanted ta' wait until you bought the land we need for our church. If we was married and then you bought it, in the eyes of the law, it would belong to us both. And that wouldn't be fair to you. I'm not gonna' take advantage of an angel." Before she could respond, he added, "Look... I want to show you something."

He got up from the table and walked into the lobby to buy a newspaper. He returned to Olivia and opened the newspaper. "I saw this ad this morning. I hope it's still here." He turned to the classified pages and found the ad Hendrik had placed. "Here! You read it for yourself!"

The ad was in the Commercial Real Estate section. Olivia read, "For sale: near Cajana. Plantation style house with 500 acres of cleared land. Completely enclosed house. Large conference room. 3 bedrooms. Asphalt tile roof. Veranda. Write to Wollenback Co. General Delivery, Paramaribo, for appointment."

Olivia was excited. "Let's contact them immediately!"

Ananda feigned being sad and spoke in a lilting creole kind of way. "Ah, no phone numba. You never know wit writin'. If he had left a phone numba, that would be different. But I knew you'd wanta' see the ad." Then he jumped up. "Surprise! I made plans! If you wanta' go, we can go Saturday morning. That's the only time I could get a pilot to take us. That is... if you wanta' go."

"Do I want to go? Oh, darling," she cooed, "This is perfect! But can't we go as man and wife? I don't care about the money or community property."

He pouted. "I want you to look like a bride," he said. "And I don't have the money to dress up like a groom."

"A bride?" Olivia asked. "All right. Let's go. Let's find a bridal shop and get me a long gown and you a nice tuxedo. You can rent one for the occasion."

"Tomorrow we can get the marriage license and see the preacher. But today!" he said as if the idea were all his, "Today is for weddin' dresses!"

"Well, then, let's go and get one," she said, summoning the waiter for the check.

Ananda ordered a tuxedo to be delivered to Olivia's room at the Tropical Haven and then he went to *Jacque's Creole Cuisine,* a nearby restaurant and dance bar, to wait for his bride-to-be.

Olivia Mallard's task was not an easy one. She had to find a dress that would fit her without requiring alterations and would not make her look foolish. She tried on two-dozen dresses before she found one, a white silk empire-style dress that both fit and conveyed mature respectability.

"I'll take it," she said, "and any veil and white pumps that go with this Napoleonic style."

Before Olivia left the shop she called the florist at the Tropical Haven and asked that a bridal bouquet be delivered to her room by nine o'clock the next morning. Then, carrying her parcels, she left the shop to have dinner with the adorable Ananda. Tomorrow was their wedding day. They had some celebrating to do.

After they had had their fill of *Jacque's* cuisine, Ananda made Olivia get up onto the dance floor with him and follow his lessons on local samba variants. He was charming, he was instructive, and with a little rum and Dutch gin in Olivia to assist him, he had her dancing as though she had been dancing all her life. In fact, she had not danced a step in twenty years.

It was ten o'clock when Ananda walked his bride-to-be back to the hotel and, as she insisted, left her at the elevator doors. "Don't forget," she said, blowing him a kiss, "tomorrow at nine o'clock sharp."

Ananda was feeling good. He hailed a cab, and all the way back to Hendrik's office he was still dancing with Olivia in his mind. He hummed the music and with subtle movements, kept the beat as he unlocked the office door and turned on Hendrik's desk lamp. On a pink message pad Hendrik had written with a black felt pen news that Ananda was unprepared to receive. Willem deVries called him *again* to tell him he was on his way down to Suriname. Hendrik printed in large letters - TAKE CARE OF THIS.

Ananda Moyer knew that it was Faber and not deVries who had called and that he had to get out of town as quickly as possible. He packed a few things in one of Hendrik's old overnight bags and went out to take the first bus he could find. That bus took him fifteen miles north to Nieuw Amsterdam on the coast.

When he was finally checked into the Seabreeze Motel, he began to think. Faber had to be desperate if he was using deVries's name. Faber was spiteful. He'd ruin the plantation house deal and tell Olivia how he had deceived her. Olivia would leave him. Holman and deJong would blame him, and they were not the kind of men who took disappointment well.

In the cabin, as Ananda lay upon the bed, he felt safer. Negative consequences to any of his actions began their habitual slide into oblivion. The mosquito netting shielded him against everything that at that moment sought to harm him. Time had once again ceased to be linear. Each of the cabin's wide hinged windows was pulled up, connecting him to the outdoors and giving him a sense of being open to the universe. He could see the lights of distant stars and of nearby fireflies. He could smell gardenias in the breeze. He could hear the soothing sounds of the Suriname River as it flowed into the Atlantic. All time condensed into a beautiful moment. He sighed. Without a clock or watch he would drift into "whenever's" freedom. "Whenever" he woke up, that would be the correct time to awaken.

Faber checked the time. The visit by the two private investigators commanded him to act. Since they were looking for Olivia Mallard, either the deal had not gone through or, if it had, Moyer had a share of the money - and Olivia was out of the picture.

Faber saw things clearly now. Moyer could be so easily manipulated. Betrayal came naturally to him. He survived because of his looks and his charm. "Why," he asked himself, "do I have to fall in love with such undeserving men?" He might have lost Ananda, but he would not lose his money even if it meant that he would have to go to Suriname. Yes, he would go. But if he failed, he needed a way to get back.

The distress he felt showed itself in his expression. Father Haas, standing in Faber's doorway, looked at him with concern. "Samuel," he said, "I came to ask if you were going to Lenten service, but I see that you look troubled. Are you ill?"

Faber put his hands to his forehead and said, "I'm fine. You go on."

As he heard Father Haas shut the rectory door, Faber, now both angry and bitter, called Holman Air Service. The call went to voice-mail. Faber said, "Would you kindly ask Ananda Moyer to call his church friend in Pennsylvania?" He waited twenty minutes and called *Springer's*

Roadhouse. The bartender answered and said that Moyer wasn't there. Faber asked, "Is Reinhardt Springer there?" The bartender gave him Reinhardt's office number.

Faber knew that Ananda frequented two roadhouses in the Cajana area: *Springer's* and *Jack's Pink Dolphin.* Ananda had said that the two roadhouse owners hated each other; and that he personally preferred *Springer's.* He had spoken about the notorious exploits of the "aristocratic" Reinhardt Springer, and Faber decided that Springer was "his kind of man," one who was worthy of trust and respect. Springer liked money. If Olivia still had the money, Faber would offer him Ananda's cut if he would help him to teach the perfidious Ananda Moyer a lesson in loyalty.

He called Springer's office number. Since he knew he would be speaking to an educated man, a man who was reputed to have the same prurient interests as he, Faber introduced himself and then made the mistake of speaking to Springer as an equal.

Reinhardt Springer listened as Faber listed his grievances about Moyer. "I set him up with a rich woman and half the money gained from that introduction - and thousands more that are potentially available - was to be used to open a resort 'up north' - a resort that catered to men of distinction, men who enjoyed sexual extremes."

Reinhardt Springer had heard many absurd stories about creating spas for sado-masochists, but he had never heard that they'd be located in the well-policed north. The beauty and the privacy of the Gran Rio made Sipaliwini's Southern District ideal. Every few years some misbegotten entrepreneur would do a feasibility study that always included the probable number of clients who would be lured away from *Springers* and even *Jack's Pink Dolphin.*

No doubt his caller was the "churchman" deVries, who had been calling Moyer. Springer did not like to be taken for a fool and it occurred to him that his caller was trying to do precisely that. Springer coldly asked, "Tell me... deVries, isn't it? Why is it that you think your tale of humiliation is worth five minutes of my time?"

Despite the contumelious response, Faber did not yield. He said, "The woman, Olivia, has brought nearly a million American dollars with her. I thought perhaps you might find some use for the trifling half million that would be yours."

Springer proceeded to ask a few questions that he thought were pertinent. "Where is the money now?" Faber did not know. "Where is the woman now?" Faber did not know. "What is her relationship to Moyer?" Faber did not know. "Do you know that you are an irritating bore?"

Faber was silent for a moment and then, deciding that he had had enough of Springer's insolence, he bit his lip and disconnected the call.

At the little Zen temple, Sensei stood at the altar in his priestly role as Shi Yao Feng. His back was to the congregation, and he did not see either the Reverend Tracy Baldwin or Father Willem deVries enter and sit in the back of the room.

Beryl, the official bell ringer, struck the small brass bell that indicated it was time for Sensei to begin his Dharma talk. After years of listening to them, Beryl had determined that Sensei's talks were structured like a sonnet. He would give eight minutes of exposition, then the volta's four minutes of shift in perspective, and then the final two minutes of summation.

She watched the clock. He had been speaking for eight minutes. It was time for Sensei to reach the volta. In the brief pause, she glanced around and saw Tracy and deVries.

Sensei's tone changed. "We think that we are responsible only for what we do and not for what we think. We also suppose that we will be punished in some way that is commensurate with an evil act. 'An eye for an eye; a tooth for a tooth.' This is Law of Like Retribution, *The Lex Talionis*. On both counts we are wrong. We kill in an instant and spend a lifetime in prison. And our evil thoughts are punished, too. *Honi soit qui mal y pense*. Evil to him who evil thinks. You may ask, 'Who knows our thoughts to be able to punish them?' We do. Our Buddha Self inside us knows our thoughts, and we punish ourselves for those thoughts that convey our evil desires.

"What we *do* is obviously an important societal matter," Sensei continued, "but what we *think* is infinitely more important. Our thoughts are what we most of all need to understand. Jealousy is a thought. Pride is a thought. Lust is a thought. Hate is a thought. Greed is a thought. And when these thoughts convey an evil intention towards someone else, we hold ourselves accountable for them.

"Our ego must by punished for the evil it wishes upon someone else. How do we punish ourselves? Is this a mystery? Do we not understand self-destructive behaviors? Ask a drunk... a drug addict... a reckless driver... a person who is depressed or suicidal. Ask someone who is 'accident-prone.' We think an evil thought and later that day we trip over something and fall. We may have walked over that object a thousand times without incident. Why then did we suddenly fall? The cause is not confined to wishing someone else would fall. We may have thought an ugly, jealous thought or mocked someone. We may have figured out a way to cheat or to seduce someone. Going home that day for some reason we accelerate beyond the speed limit and get a ticket. What made us depress the accelerator? The need to punish ourselves for sinful thoughts. Whenever such a thought arises, take it apart and see how unworthy it is. The man of Zen frees himself from jealousy... lust... anger... pride... greed... and hate. If he does not, his evil thought becomes a disease that spreads its contagion to all his thoughts.

"In Zen we illustrate this by the following story: there were two rival businessmen who hated each other, mostly because of jealousy and the prideful fear that one would be regarded as more successful than the other. One morning they met at a train station in Tokyo. Each bowed to the other. One asked, 'Where are you going?'

"The other hesitated and then answered, 'I'm going to Osaka.'"

Sensei suddenly raised his voice and with great animation finished the story. "'*You liar!*' the first one hissed. 'You tell me that you are going to Osaka because you think that I, knowing how deceptive you are, will then think that you are really going to Kobe! But I have made inquiries... and I know that you *are* going to Osaka!'"

After the congregation finished laughing at the priest's little joke, Beryl rang the bell. Sensei returned to the altar. Beryl rang the bell again and Sensei called out the final chant. Beryl looked around. Tracy was still there, but deVries had gone.

After the service, Tracy Baldwin joined George, Sensei, and Beryl in the Temple's utility kitchen.

"Did anyone notice that Father Willem deVries was here?" Beryl asked.

"Maybe he wanted to hear a Zen Buddhist point of view," Tracy suggested.

"Nah," George disagreed. "He's in solitary confinement... shunned by the people he served. Who's he got to talk to? The hospice patients? No. Beryl and Sensei talked to him as a friend. 'No man is an island,' except when he's been cast away by everybody he knows."

"I wish I had more free time. I'd go and try to lend him a hand," Tracy said.

"Take him to a hockey game. That'll do him more good." George shuffled some papers. "So where are we in this investigation?"

"We've reached a critical phase," Sensei said. "We've done all we can do up here. Decisions have to be made."

"Olivia is in Suriname with Ananda Moyer," Beryl began, "and there are indications that friends of his are conspiring with him in some sort of scheme. She took roughly a million dollars with her. Olivia is in love with him. He says that he loves her. And we don't have the right to damage any of Olivia's loving relationships. We can't assume that she's going to be hurt. Do we *think* it's probable? Yes. And if she's in trouble, we can't help her up here. We need to go down there - but not as 'the cavalry to the rescue.' We need to respect her choices and just be ready to help if she needs it. So, do we go down or not?"

"I'd like you to go," Tracy said. "Are you willing?"

"Yes, of course," Beryl replied.

"I'll go with her," Sensei said. "I'll get a karate teacher to sub for me in the dojo and–"

"I'll open the temple per your schedule," George volunteered. "Incidentally, for what it's worth, I tried to reach Olivia again at her hotel. She's still registered, but she wasn't answering the phone in her room."

Sensei added, "I've looked up Cajana, a river town in Suriname's Southern District that deJong said 'seemed perfect.' But he didn't say what it was perfect for. It's in the rainforest. We don't know where her trail will lead us. She wouldn't be starting a mission in an established area - which means she'll probably head into jungle terrain. We'll need some preparation... visas, shots, clothing. Suriname's new tourist system isn't in effect yet. We can get our shots, fly to Miami Thursday, get our visas, and then fly to Paramaribo on Friday."

Beryl nodded agreement. Sensei flicked through his phone and made reservations for the flight.

WEDNESDAY, MARCH 23, 2011

Dawn came and then sunrise and slowly it occurred to Ananda that this was supposed to be his wedding day. What time was it? He looked at his naked wrist and cursed the women of Ellington's. He had to find a phone to call Olivia. That he knew. What he did not know was what he would say when he reached her. He dressed and went to the reception cabin.

Olivia was frantic, waiting for him to arrive. It was nearly ten o'clock. The florist had delivered her bridal bouquet, and the tuxedo rental shop had delivered his suit. She stared at it thinking that it hung there in its plastic bag like a huge 'jack of spades' covering her closet door. Something had happened to Ananda. The chapel minister called to ask why they had not kept their appointment. Noting the strain in her voice, he told her that if she and her gentleman came by before six, he would accommodate them.

The phone rang again. It was Ananda. "I'm callin' from Nieuw Amsterdam over hea' in the Commewijne District."

"Where on earth is that?" she asked.

"I'm about... oh, I don't know... maybe ten miles away."

"When can you get here?"

"I was wonderin' if you could come here. We may not be able ta' get a marriage license in this district until tomorrow... if you don't mind waitin' a day or so."

"Oh, Ananda! I'm dressed. Your tuxedo is here. The minister at the Chapel said that he'd wait for us. Is there no way you can come here?"

Ananda was silent for a long minute. He was trying to decide on what he should do. He took money out of his pocket and counted it. Finally, he answered. "I can take a taxi ta' the hotel but we can't stay in

Paramaribo. I'll explain later. I'll come ta' the hotel in the taxi. You be outside with my tuxedo. We'll honeymoon here by the ocean."

Olivia would have agreed to anything. This, however, seemed like a wonderful plan. "Yes," she said enthusiastically. "I'll be out front waiting. When do you think you'll be here?"

"Forty-five minutes... but you be there in thirty in case I make good time."

It did not occur to Olivia that it would look odd for a woman in her forties to be sitting in front of a hotel in a snow white wedding dress, with a stiff white veil mushrooming around her head. She moved quickly to a bench near the entrance drive. As though she were watching a tennis match, she alternately looked to the right and then to the left. She did not know from which direction Ananda would be coming.

Finally, a cab pulled up to the front entrance, a rear window rolled down, and an arm stuck out and waved. She got up and jogged to the cab's open door.

The first stop was the marriage bureau. They obtained their license, and then the same Nieuw Amsterdam cab that had waited outside, drove them to the Chapel and continued to wait. Inside, the minister's wife continuously photographed them while they were married.

As man and wife, they returned to the cab and drove to the Hotel Tropical Haven so that Olivia Moyer could check out of the hotel and pick up the box that contained the treadle sewing machine, the bolt of mauve silk, and the rest of her luggage. The doorman carried the items to the cab. Olivia said goodbye to the staff, tipped the doorman for his kindness, and joined her husband in the cab for the ride to Nieuw Amsterdam.

Mr. and Mrs. Ananda Moyer got out of the taxi at the The Seabreeze motel and, at the insistence of the owner, transferred to a larger thatch covered cabin. The owner's eighteen year-old daughter made such a fuss about Olivia's bridal gown that Olivia gave it to her along with the veil and shoes. The girl was going to be married in May, and the wedding gown came to her as if God had answered her prayer. She confided to Olivia that she definitely did not want to be married in Hindu clothing. "I am so sick of marigolds," she whispered.

"What is the proper thing to wear for trekking through the jungle?" Beryl asked the Sporting Department's sales clerk.

"Hard ground or swamp ground, rainy season or dry, and which jungle?" the sales clerk sensibly asked.

"The rainforest just north of the Amazon... in Suriname. I'm leaving tomorrow."

"They've got mountains and swamps and the rainy season is just starting. Dress for the worst condition. Swamp land. You need everything waterproof or you will get a fungus infection. There are huge pit vipers called Bushmasters. There are coral snakes that have little fangs but deadly venom. There is malaria. Is there a limit on how much you want to spend?"

Beryl shook her head. "No, I don't want to come home in a body bag or in intensive care. Give me the best."

"That would be our *Swamptec* line." She produced a pair of space-age material wading boots that looked and fit like a scuba insulated wet suit or, Beryl thought, like leather pajamas with feet in them. The pants went up to just under the bust line. White 'saddle shoe' cut-outs were glued to the top of the feet and thick rubber soles were glued to the bottom.

"All anyone can see are these fake saddle-shoe bottoms. The boots are a single, no-seam whatsoever, unit. They are completely lined with a bulletproof material. If you get shot with a small caliber, you'll get a nasty bruise. A larger caliber bullet will penetrate and, depending on many factors, wound you. If a snake strikes, it will regret it. The knees, ankles, and crotch have lateral pleats for movement in any direction. These parts will re-form themselves immediately. Your foot rests on a platform over an absorbent pad to collect perspiration. A dozen extra pads are provided. Let's try them on."

Beryl looked at her legs in the mirror. "I look like I'm doing a guest shot on *Sea Hunt*... with 'white bucks' on. She walked around and squatted. "They feel fine and they're rather light weight. I'm surprised. How much are they?"

"Twenty-one hundred dollars."

"I'll take them. What else do I need?"

"You'll need street pants that can be worn over your skin or over the boots. These look like ordinary blue denim, but they have two layers. The outer one may be sprayed with mosquito repellent. The inner one prevents you from getting poisoned with the spray. It's also nearly impervious to the proboscis of a mosquito. The shirt that accompanies the pants is identically made. The slightly folded back shirt cuffs contain protective gloves made of the same material. Just open the zipper. Pith helmets are *outré*. We all know that. So we have a kind of sun hat... all cotton with an interior bulletproof crown." She picked up a hat. "Look at this! I just unzip the decorative brim and voila! A mesh veil descends. Killer bees could not penetrate this netting. The hem in the netting is for a chain you can thread through to give it weight and hold it down on your shoulders. There you are. Safe and more mobile than you could possibly imagine. If you have time, I would tell you to eat garlic until you despise yourself. It will saturate your skin and bugs will avoid you. People will too, but they are not likely to lay eggs in your skin or give you malaria."

Beryl purchased the wading boots, two pair of jeans, two shirts and a hat. She spent slightly more than four thousand dollars. When she got back to her apartment she put on the garments, expecting to howl at the "ensemble." Instead, she looked rather plump and ordinary except for the fake saddle shoe exterior of the wading pants' boots which looked, she conservatively estimated, ridiculous.

She called Sensei and told him what she had purchased and asked him if he were properly attired for the jungle. He laughed. "I've got hiking boots and some tropical fishing gear. I put them away in mothballs. I'll just unpack them and air them out. I'll let you handle the social affairs alone. I'll bring only street and jungle clothing to fight off all those bushmasters and wandering spiders. By the way, I called the American vice-consul in Paramaribo. We have an eleven a.m. appointment on Saturday. And, I got my vaccination. Doc Frasier has yours ready. Call him and get over there."

Perhaps it was the shot she had just gotten. Or, maybe it was that uncomfortable feeling that accompanied the purchase of so much protective gear. A 'doomsday' scenario began to play out in Beryl's mind.

Suppose she didn't make it out of the jungle alive? She had admired Father deVries; and before she left for Suriname and an unknown fate, she thought it prudent to inform him that Father Haas was holding, as evidence against him, a love letter that Olivia had actually written to Ananda Moyer. The letter was considered proof that deVries was having an affair with her, and the affair was considered his motive for the theft he had been charged with. Yet... he was also a handsome single man and it seemed too forward to call him. Sensei was teaching in his dojo, but perhaps George would let him know. She called George.

"I hate to sound melodramatic," she said, "but in the unlikely event that Sensei and I don't make it out of the jungle, will you be sure to call Father deVries and tell him about Father Haas's erroneous ideas about that letter and the person Olivia came to visit on Valentine's Day. I think he has a right to know."

"If you have the time to call me, you have the time to call him. I don't know the guy. Call him up and get some tips about Dutch travel expressions. Invite him for dinner. Make him some of your famous microwaved diet spaghetti entrées. Get a bottle of Chianti - the kind that comes in a basket that he can take home and use as a candlestick... for that hospice ambience. The 76ers are playing Atlanta tonight. Take him to the game. I'm not sure if they're playing here or in Georgia."

"Where did I get the idea that you would be helpful?" she asked.

She called the hospice. "Can you speak or have I called at an inopportune time?"

"No. I'm in my office. What can I do for you?"

"I'm leaving for Paramaribo in the morning, and I have something important that I want to discuss with you."

"I'm free after seven but I'm without transportation. My car is being repaired. We can talk here in my office."

The thought of being inside the hospice was nauseating. "We'd probably be more comfortable here, in my office," she said. "Why don't I just drive down and pick you up at seven?"

"Ok, but you do realize that if you take me somewhere, you'll also have to bring me back."

"I didn't intend to hold you prisoner or make you swim across the Delaware."

He laughed. "All right, then. At seven."

It had begun to rain and the highway down to Camden was slick and puddled. It took her an hour to get to the hospice. She was fifteen minutes late and found the priest standing on the sidewalk, holding an umbrella. She stopped in the middle of the street. He closed the umbrella and got into the Bronco. "Promise me you'll follow the Cinderella script." He was being playful. "You pick me up, take me out, we dance a little, and you get me home by midnight."

"I give you my word." As Beryl headed for the bridge, she said, "Father Haas has a love letter that Olivia Mallard wrote to Ananda Moyer. But their names aren't mentioned specifically and he assumes it is from her to you."

"Oh?" said deVries. "He never mentioned it to me."

"Faber and Moyer were running a con game through that Skyspirit program."

"What's done is done," said deVries. "I really don't want to talk about it."

Beryl clicked on the CD player and Mahler's *9th* began to play, eliminating the need for conversation while she concentrated on maneuvering through the traffic. Just as the symphony ended, she pulled into a parking place at the rear of her office building. The trash still hadn't been picked up, and the wide rear alleyway was filled with overflowing trash cans and bags. The slum-like appearance embarrassed her.

DeVries saw the look on her face. "I'm assuming this is the rear of your building," he said, "and it still looks classier than the front of mine. I won't discuss the rear of my building. Don't try to worm it out of me."

Beryl smiled, appreciating his attempt to relieve her embarrassment. She led him up the rear exterior stairs to the kitchen of her apartment. "Are you hungry?"

"No. I've already eaten. Mmm. Cabbage and potatoes cooked with fat-back."

"Selfish pig! And I bet you didn't save any for me!"

"What? And give you gas?"

She laughed as she put the teakettle on and piled some frozen pastries into the microwave.

She took her shoes off and placed them on the floor near the radiator. "You ought to do the same," she said. "Here," she said, tossing him a pair of hospital type slippers. "In the room we're going, we can't wear shoes."

"Ah," he said, "like the little temple. I went to hear Sensei's *Lex Talionis* sermon. Well done. And he probably doesn't even have a divinity degree."

"No. His bachelor's is in civil engineering." She grinned. "His master's is in Karate." She loaded a tray with a tea service. "Jasmine? Darjeeling? What's your poison?"

DeVries selected Jasmine. She filled the pot and put the plate of hot pastries on the tray which she placed in his hands.

She led him into the dimly lit hallway, past the bathroom, her son's empty bedroom, the storage room, and her own interior entranceway-bedroom and office. She flipped on a switch that illuminated the soft, indirect amber lighting of the front meditation room and that also started the shakuhachi flute music that softly played in the "repeat" mode. She took the tray from him. "I'll let you open the sliding doors," she said, and the priest deftly drew apart the shoji screen doors.

He looked into the room and whistled with surprise. "This is another world. It's really nice!"

He cautiously walked across the tatami platform flooring and sat on a pillow beside the low table on which Beryl placed the tray. As she poured the tea, she said, "You can loosen your collar. The Buddha over there–" she pointed to the statue of the Buddha on her altar, "will prevent me from attacking you. Regardless of your religion, you're under his protection, now." She grinned as she walked to the altar to light incense.

"You are too kind," he laughed and continued to look around. "I really like this room." The bay window had been covered by a continuous row of rice-paper screens that, illuminated from behind with tinted bulbs, cast a soft, late afternoon glow into the room. In the bay a circulating fountain let its water cascade down a stone waterway to a pool in which real lotus flowers grew and three goldfish swam. The gentle gurgling of the water, the Japanese flute music, the sandalwood incense, the jasmine tea, and the mellow light relaxed them both. "I'm glad we're in your office," he said. "What is it that you want to talk about?"

"As you know, I'm trying to locate Olivia Mallard. George and I went to the prison and the rectory. We've talked to Warden Conner, Father Haas, and Deacon Faber. We were particularly interested in Ananda Moyer's relationship with Deacon Faber–"

"Let me stop you there. I can't discuss Deacon Faber," he abruptly said.

The manner in which he spoke annoyed her. He seemed a little too righteous in his refusal to discuss Deacon Faber. Guessing that he was Faber's Confessor, she used a police tactic of converting a guess into a fact. "I'm not asking you to break priestly vows," she retorted. "I know he confessed to you and I respect that Seal. At the same time, I'm not bound by it."

"Ouch! You should put a 'Beware of P.I.' sign out there. I thought the big guy on the altar was going to protect me from your attacks. I didn't mean to offend you. Doesn't he protect you from me, too?"

She remained stiff. "I'm not having the best day today. I had thought it important to let you know that quite possibly I could produce evidence that would clear your name, and I even imagined that you'd be pleased to have your reputation restored! But, excuse me!"

"Are we having a fight? We've been married... what?... an hour and a half and already you want to castrate me... here... in this House of God."

"Lord!" she yelled, trying not to laugh. "Now you're attacking my religion?"

Willem deVries laughed with her and then he took a deep breath and sighed. He spoke softly. "Day in and day out I'm in that pit of pain and grief and its unbearable stench. Please believe me when I say this place is heaven. Here, there is not only sandalwood incense but really *good* sandalwood incense. Fresh flowers - not plastic - on your altar. The flute. Nobody dying. This jasmine tea is, for want of a better word, fantastic. I hate to complain. I'm no materialist; but I'm no Assisi, either. Our tea is vile. And yes... the bear claws. Yours were made with butter. Ours are made with lard. A vegetarian wouldn't be able to eat them. You may never get me out of here. Go ahead! Convert me to Buddhism! I'm game for anything tonight that doesn't violate the other nine commandments."

"Which one did you violate?"

"The first. 'I am the Lord thy God. Thou shall have no other gods before me.'"

"The Buddha is not a god. He was a man who woke up."

"In that case I can die in purity." He stretched out and put his head on the pillow. Beryl sipped her tea and watched his facial muscles relax and his breathing become slow and regular. Within five minutes he was sound asleep.

Beryl still felt feverish from the vaccination. It was only nine-thirty. She got a blanket from her bedroom and covered deVries with it. Then she closed the shoji doors and thought she'd rest awhile on her own bed. In less time than it took deVries to fall asleep, she slipped into unconsciousness.

At two o'clock in the morning deVries shook her awake. "Beryl," he said softly, "Beryl! It's late. I have to get back to Camden."

"Can you drive a stick shift?"

"Yes."

"Do you have a valid driver's license?"

"Yes. I'm still using my Pennsylvania license. Why do you ask?"

"Take the Bronco. I'm woozy from the vaccination for my trip to Suriname tomorrow. Your car is in the shop and I'll be gone at least a week. I'm fully insured. My car keys are on the kitchen table. I'll call you when I get back."

"Yes, but I hate to do this. I'd call a cab but frankly I don't have any money."

"You'd never get a cab in the rain. *Vaya con Dios,*" she said and rolled over.

DeVries went into the kitchen, put on his shoes and socks, grabbed the keys and his coat, and left.

THURSDAY, MARCH 24, 2011

On Thursday morning the manager's daughter brought Olivia and Ananda breakfast and a picnic basket in case they wanted to go to the beach. "It's such a beautiful day," she said, "I thought you'd like to see the sea."

Ananda was proud of Olivia. This was what the future held for him: a woman who brought happiness to all who came into contact with her. He thought again about his mother, sitting there singing without needing to fan herself or having to breathe the smoke of burning palm nuts that was supposed to keep the mosquitoes away but rarely did. He saw himself in the pulpit moving people with his colorful Bible stories. He would lift spirits up and guide people to righteousness! But at the moment, his earlobe began to itch. "I've gotta' see the Doc and get these stitches out."

Olivia looked at the stitches. "Here, I'll do it." She took some antiseptic mouthwash and wiped the area. Then using her cuticle scissors and tweezers she expertly snipped each suture and pulled it out.

Ananda looked at her and said in a flat emotionless voice, "You are the best thing that ever happened to me."

FRIDAY, MARCH 25, 2011

It was, by local time, 3:30 p.m. when Beryl and Sensei Percy Wong touched down at Pengel International Airport in Paramaribo. They had brought only carry-on luggage and were whisked through customs and out into the tropical sun in the great sweep of travelers who wanted to get to their destinations before the business day was over.

At the shuttle port, a line of people waited to board an already filled mini-van that bore the Hotel Tropical Haven name and logo. Beryl and Sensei jogged to the vehicle, tossed their bags to an attendant who loaded them in the rear of the bus and shouted, "That's it!" just as they squeezed in and the doors shut behind them. They stood all the way to the hotel.

As Sensei finished checking in, he asked to be connected to Olivia Mallard's room on the house phone. The clerk responded with regret, "Ms. Mallard is no longer a guest at this hotel. If you wish to leave a message for her I can put it in the general delivery message box. She might come by looking for a message. You never can tell."

"Can you tell me when she checked out?" Sensei asked.

"No, I'm sorry. We don't give out such information."

"Do you have a Mr. Tony deJong working here?"

"No, I'm sorry. He no longer works here."

"Do you know where I can reach him?"

"No, I'm sorry. I can't give any information about our employees; but you can call the hotel manager if you like tomorrow morning."

Sensei shook his head. "Thank you." He picked up the card-keys to room 822, the double room he had reserved.

In the restaurant, a strong breeze blew in from the veranda while they sat by a window and marveled at the beauty of the hotel's gardens and the broad Suriname River as the view shimmered in the light of the lowering sun.

When the waiter brought menus to their table, Beryl asked, "Do you happen to recall an American lady who was here for a few weeks?"

"We have many American ladies as our guests," he said, "but I cannot discuss any of them. I'm sorry. It's hotel policy."

"So I've heard," Beryl said dejectedly.

After they ordered, Sensei asked, "So what do we do now? Olivia is gone and nobody's talking."

"I'm still not a hundred percent after that shot I got. I'll be more efficient in the morning. We should wait for a male desk clerk to come on duty. I'll try flirting and if that doesn't work, you can try bribery. We can also talk to the chambermaids, the breakfast waitresses down here or, better yet, the room service waiter, and I can make an appointment with the hotel hairdresser and also get my nails done. They're human beings. They'll talk. We also have to get ready for our meeting with the vice-consul tomorrow morning."

SATURDAY, MARCH 26, 2011

The taxi returned for Mr. and Mrs. Ananda Moyer on Saturday to take them to Zorg en Hoop airport for the flight to Cajana.

The cab parked in front of Holman Air Service's office. Hendrik Holman, carrying a clipboard, came out onto the sidewalk to greet them. "Congratulations!" He checked the clipboard, "Mr. and Mrs. Moyer. There's nothing more rewarding than taking newlyweds on their honeymoon."

Ananda put his arm around Olivia and recited his lines. "We're already on our honeymoon. We're goin' down to Cajana to look at a place that was advertised in the newspaper. We're interested in starting a mission and the property seems to be perfect. The ad said to write, but we thought we'd save time by lookin' at it first."

"Ah, you must mean the place they call 'the plantation house.' It's a nice property, and as far as I know, it's still for sale, although I did hear that some people were looking at it the other day."

"We'll say a prayer that it's still available," Ananda said, following Holman into his office. Olivia had given him a thousand dollars of "spending money" so that he would not be embarrassed by having her pay. While Ananda paid Hendrik for two return trip tickets, Olivia picked up a Berg En Dal resort brochure on the desk. She read the brochure and as she returned it she saw a pink phone message slip addressed to Ananda. "Priest is flying down. Call him. NOW"

"Is this message for you?" she asked her husband who stared at her blankly.

"Oops! Yes," Holman answered. "I forgot to give it to you. I didn't think it was my business to tell him you were married. He's one insistent guy."

"Is that the same troublemaking priest from Ephrata?" Olivia asked.

"Yeah, I don't know what he's after. But the farther away from him I get, the happier I am." He turned to Hendrik. "He's a crazy guy. Olivia can tell you. He's got a mean streak a mile wide. But we won't let him spoil our trip."

"How did he know to call here?" she asked.

Hendrik quickly supplied an answer. "What? Did you call *Springer's* to ask if anybody knew about that place that's for sale?"

"Yeah, but that was a few days ago right after I saw the ad in the paper. I mentioned that I'd probably be flying Holman Air to come down and look at the property."

Hendrik Holman smiled at Olivia. "It's a small world down here. Sooner or later everybody knows your business. We'll be taking the big white Cessna that's parked at the edge of the tarmac. My smaller Piper is in the shop."

Faber understood that he had two choices: forget Ananda and the money that the ingrate owed him, or fly down and confront him. At the very least Ananda would pay him to keep him quiet. Maybe he wouldn't get all that was owed, but at least he wouldn't be completely cheated and mocked, deceived yet again by a perfidious lover. Faber was feeling the desperation of middle age. His "life's project" was beyond the planning stage. Still in debt from his last romantic disaster, he had no financial security. He was not an ordained priest and could not fall back upon retirement in some plain but pleasant country house for men who retired from service. Three women had sent Ananda $5000 each to pay for an attorney. Faber had Ananda endorse the checks, and then he deposited them in his own account and paid down the principal in an old loan he had made in the cause of a previous love affair. He had intended to explain the deposits by saying that he merely cashed them for Ananda; but he had no proof that he had given any cash to Moyer. He was as idiotic as the women who sent money to men in prison.

If one of those women complained, he'd never be able to lie his way out of trouble. He'd lose his job. He saw himself working in a gas station or slicing meat in a delicatessen. "I'm too young for Social Security and too old to start over," he muttered aloud. He decided to press on, but this time to use his wits and not be ruled by "amour and hope." It was time to play hardball. "I'd rather die standing in a jungle with a machete in my hand," he said bravely, "than wither away on my knees here, scratching out my epitaph with somebody's complimentary pen."

He still needed an ally and a proper excuse for leaving Harderwijk in case he was unsuccessful in the jungle. Perhaps Jack Donovan of the *Pink Dolphin* who was a competitor of that arrogant Springer fellow would be interested. Yes, that was the next logical move.

In the morning, after a late breakfast, Beryl and Sensei kept their eleven o'clock appointment with the American vice-consul, Bernard McCarthy.

The vice-consul tried to be helpful. "I understand that you're trying to locate Ms. Olivia Mallard. I spoke to her a couple of times. She was scheduled to marry a citizen here."

"Yes," Beryl said. "Do you recall what her purpose was in contacting you?"

McCarthy's eyes narrowed as he searched his mind. "Her case was rather unusual. She had put a considerable sum of money into the bank here and intended to establish a religious mission and trade school of some kind in the Sipaliwini District. If I remember correctly, she said that she knew the ceramics' business. She wanted to teach pottery making. They have some great clay down in the Southern District."

"Would that be the area around Cajana?" she asked.

"She never mentioned Cajana. I was under the impression that she and her husband intended to go farther south."

Sensei asked, "Her fiancé was being deported from the States. Do you know if she had met up with him yet? His name is Ananda Moyer."

"Oh, *him*. He's gonna be her husband? The deportee? I've heard about him. He has an unsavory reputation, but not for anything major. If she's involved with a character like Moyer, your best bet is to consult Suriname's chief criminal investigations' officer for Sipaliwini, Captain Jan Osterhaus. He would have the most complete information. Would you like me to call him?"

"Thank you. We'd appreciate it," Sensei smiled with relief.

McCarthy called Osterhaus's office and learned that he was meeting with Alcoa executives in the South. "Suriname," McCarthy informed them, "is a rather large exporter of bauxite... aluminum ore."

"When is he expected back?" Beryl asked.

"Later in the week. Apparently he just left this morning."

"Then I guess we'll be going down to Cajana. We have no other leads."

McCarthy suddenly became alarmed. "I would not do that, if I were you," he said emphatically. "You're not going as tourists. You're going as investigators who lack the authority to conduct an investigation. You need official sanction and even with it, you're quite likely to find more trouble than you can handle. I'm afraid that I'll have to insist that you wait for Captain Osterhaus."

As they left the consulate, Beryl said, "A week to get permission? Did I understand him correctly? We're stuck here for a week waiting for some cop to give us permission?"

"McCarthy said, 'within a week.' Osterhaus could be back sooner."

"We're not equipped to spend all this time up here in Paramaribo, but we can't go south without permission. I hate to tempt bureaucrats. If we go without official consent and then find that we need help, it might be slow in coming."

"So we wait," Sensei said. "What else can we do?"

"It looks like we're gonna be in civilization longer than we figured. Neither of us has packed business attire. If we have to meet with all these officials, we need to look presentable. Why don't we pick up at least one change of clothes and then head back to the hotel. Somebody there has got to be willing to talk."

As they walked through a shopping center, they each went into a clothing shop. Sensei bought a change of clothes in five minutes. He then went to the ladies' boutique and sat patiently as Beryl mixed and matched and posed in front of the mirror.

Unaccustomed to feeling exuberant from something as ordinary as a clothing purchase, and perhaps remembering how 'dumpy' she looked in her jungle togs, Beryl strutted happily as she walked back to the hotel. She felt festive in the lively streets of Paramaribo. Shops and stalls poured samba and reggae music onto the pavement. The rhythms, designed to seduce foot traffic, seemed to set her whole body into harmonic motion. Entrained, she felt the beat of Suriname; and she skipped a little, keeping the cadence of the sounds that came from each store they passed.

As they entered the lobby of the hotel, Beryl noticed a male desk clerk. "Maybe he knows something about the contact," she whispered. "You go ahead. I'll join you in the restaurant." She approached the desk and signaled the clerk. "I'm Beryl Tilson, Room 822," she smiled. "I could really use your help. I'm searching for a missing person, Miss Olivia Mallard, a former guest here. Do you remember her?" The clerk stared at her and said nothing. "She was to leave a message for her friend, Ananda Moyer, with one of your former employees, Anton deJong. I'm wondering if you knew where I might reach him."

"I?" The clerk looked at Beryl contemptuously. "I don't associate with either Ananda Moyer or Anton deJong." It suddenly occurred to him that the guest deJong had victimized might be her real client. His attitude softened. "I'm sorry. We don't discuss our guests or our employees."

"I appreciate your discretion, but this particular lady may be in serious danger. Her sister has engaged my firm." She handed him her business card. "I'm a private investigator. Her sister is frantic with worry."

"I can only repeat that we regard keeping the privacy of our guests as a sacred duty. I cannot help you." He turned and walked away. She went into the restaurant to join Sensei.

Sitting again at a window table, Beryl stared at the view, frustrated and depressed. She became almost mesmerized by the river. Sensei noticed and broke the spell. "We've got some hard work to prepare for. We should do an exercise routine and practice some katas up in the room. We can't afford to tighten up. I don't need the *I Ching* to tell me there's a jungle in our future."

They finished their lunch and as they walked to the elevator, one of the women desk clerks signaled Beryl. Asking Sensei to wait, Beryl approached the desk.

The clerk's tone was urgent. "Miss Mallard's sister is right to be worried. She was with a shady character, that friend of Tony deJong's, who's very shady, too. But she married that guy on Wednesday and checked out."

"Oh, God!" Beryl gasped. "We're too late."

"You may be too late to stop the wedding, but she could be in other trouble. It was crazy!"

"Crazy how?"

"She was here alone for a few weeks. Then, of all things, she went out and bought a bolt of expensive silk and an old treadle sewing machine. We kept them here in the storage room. This seedy guy had dinner with her. They were like a couple of lovebirds. Then last Wednesday she comes down out of the elevator dressed in a bridal gown, carrying her bouquet and a man's tuxedo that was delivered here for her. That was really strange. She sat out front on a bench by the street in that white dress for an hour. Then the doorman said she got into a cab that came for her."

"And this was Wednesday, the 23rd? Do you know who delivered the tuxedo or where the gown was bought?"

"I don't, but I can ask around. A couple of hours later, she came back and checked out. She took her silk, that sewing machine, and the rest of her luggage with her. The doorman carried everything to the cab for her. That guy was sitting inside the cab the whole time. He never got out to help."

"Oh?" said Beryl. "I guess he didn't want to be seen. It looks like she's planning to sew in a rural place, like... maybe Cajana, in the Southern District?"

"I don't know. It was expensive silk for jungle use. She might have mentioned something to the shop owner. Usually when a whole bolt of material is bought, a certain amount of gabbing is done."

"And where would that shop be?"

"Kanchipuram Silk Importers. It's near Julianastradt and Verlengde Mahonyaan."

"Would you happen to know how late they're open?"

"Yes. I'm the one who told her about the shop. You're too late for today. They don't do much retail except in silk and high-end saris. They're open from 7 a.m. to 3 p.m., but because of the tourist trade, they're open on Sundays."

As they flew south, Ananda directed Olivia's attention to various points of interest: the reservoir created by the dam; the neatly divided farmlands; and the long expanse of Bloomenstein Lake. They followed the Suriname River's gash in the green carpet, and then they followed its tributary, the Gran Rio, passing over *Springer's Roadhouse* and landing at the bumpy dirt airfield at Cajana.

Holman said he'd be "getting lunch and some shut-eye" while he waited for them at the Vandermeer Lodge. "The place that's for sale is down the road that runs beside the creek. It's only a mile or so." He pointed to the road and said he'd see them later when they got back.

Olivia, wearing new galoshes, was happy to walk. She wanted to see the land that surrounded the property.

After they had walked a mile, they passed a sign that announced *Wollenback Mining Ltd.* Half a mile farther, the house came into view. "It's had some work done to it," she said, noticing the different roof tiles that had been used to repair it.

"Yep," Ananda agreed, "even from here you can see the place is in good shape."

They climbed the stairs to the veranda and knocked on the front door. The shutters on the windows were open and Ananda peeked inside the house just as deJong opened the door and smiled, "I wasn't expecting any company," he said. "What can I do for you folks?"

Ananda was surprised to see how different Tony looked wearing glasses, his hair and beard rinsed brown. He also sounded different, speaking in a refined and 'intellectual' tone. "Ah!" Ananda said, looking up, "my wife and I are here to see the property that's for sale. Is this the house? We read an ad in the paper."

"I'm afraid the place is taken," deJong said, and then slowly corrected himself. "I shouldn't say that as if it were cast in bronze. The prospective buyer wants me to make improvements to the road as part of the deal.

I'm not inclined to do that, but money is money and I've got to sell the place quickly."

"Maybe we can do business," Ananda suggested. "Let's see if my wife likes the place, if that's all right with you. Incidentally, I'm Ananda Moyer and this beautiful lady is my wife, Olivia."

DeJong extended his hand. "I'm Brian Longwood, Chief Engineer, Wollenback Mining."

Olivia looked around, "It's lovely." The door to the conference room was open. She peeked inside. "This conference room would be perfect for a little church until we got one built."

"You're missionaries?" deJong/Longwood asked.

"Yes... well, not precisely," Olivia explained. "We're here to do the Lord's work but we're non-affiliated."

DeJong/Longwood produced the documents that evidenced his right to negotiate the sale. Then he showed them through the house. He took them outside and pointed to the earth moving equipment. "The excavator, loader, and crusher will be removed within a couple of weeks. They're valuable and are needed elsewhere. There's a bulldozer, too, but it's around the other side being cleaned up for the trip downriver. Well," he said with finality, "that's all I can 'show and tell.' If you want the place, it's $800,000 U.S. dollars."

Ananda looked at Olivia. "I'm not gonna' try ta' influence ya'. If you like it, that's good enough for me. I like it, too. I think you'd be perfect here. People would come from Cajana and from all the little villages you can't see on a map. And that conference room? It's enclosed for an air conditioning unit." He lowered his voice. "And I like the master bedroom too."

Olivia agreed. "We'll take it. How will we handle the sale?" she asked.

"I've got to be in Paramaribo this afternoon," deJong/Longwood said. "What airline did you use to get down here?"

"Holman Air Service," she answered. "Mr. Holman is waiting for us at the Vandermeer Lodge."

"Is he waiting to take you back to Paramaribo? If so, and there's room in the plane, I'll go with you. We'll need witnesses who know us both to put their signatures on the documents. We can ask Holman if he'll be available on Monday morning when we transfer the property and money. We can meet at his office in the morning, if that's suitable, and go to the bank from there."

At three o'clock, Tony deJong/Longwood and Mr. and Mrs. Ananda Moyer stepped onto the veranda of the Vandermeer Lodge and greeted Hendrik Holman. It was a festive meeting. They had a quick drink and began to walk back to the airfield.

Two men, Kaza Ross and Chico Chavez, stood by a high fence outside the hangar's office. They had seen the three: Moyer, a man, and a woman, walk out of the road that went back to Granger's Mining and enter the Lodge. Now, a few minutes later, they watched four come back to the airfield. Kaza, who was chief of security at *Springer's Roadhouse,* recognized Ananda and Hendrik. "Who's the woman and the guy in glasses, and what were they doing back at Granger's?" he asked Chico, his Number Two man at *Springer's.*

Chico Chavez could contribute only one piece of information. "They covered the mining company's sign with a new one that said 'Wollenback.' They've got something going on. Maybe that's the church guy who keeps calling Ananda Moyer."

Kaza suddenly noticed a well-groomed native get out of a motorized canoe and approach Hendrik Holman. "Who the hell is that?"

Chico did not recognize him. He turned to a native boy who was working nearby. "Who's that dressed up native? And who's that woman?"

"That's Jackel Mazumi," the boy answered, "wit' a haircut. He fly in couple days ago with Tony. And that lady be Nandy's new wife. That guy wit' glasses and hair on his face, that's Tony deJong."

"Son of a bitch," said Kaza. "Something is definitely goin' on down here."

He took a dollar from his pocket. "Boy! Go ask the cleanin' gal what she knows about Tony and Jackel and about Nandy Moyer gettin' married. Why are they back at the mining place and what's Henny Holman got to do with anything? Here's a dollar. Hurry up." Kaza grabbed Chico's sleeve and gently pulled him back into the shadows of the bougainvillea that cascaded over the fence.

They watched as Jackel shook hands with Tony, Ananda and Olivia. The five headed for the Cessna.

Olivia innocently said, "I guess it's lucky that we had such a big plane."

"I was annoyed with my mechanic," Holman explained, "for not having my Piper ready. Now I'm glad we had to take the larger plane. Everything works out in the end."

The boy returned with the information. "The cleanin' gal says that the maricon Tony deJong is pretendin' to be somebody else, but he still stays wit' Rubem, that Brazilian singer at *Jack's Pink Dolphin*. And she says Nandy Moyer gotta rich wife now. They buy the Granger place. It called Wollenback now. Maybe Moyer's wife name is Wollenback."

Kaza shook his head. "Tony the Hustler Fag, Henny Holman who'll fly babies to hell, Ananda Moyer who's never done an honest day's work in his life, and a rich broad who's supposed to be his wife? Why the hell would they be buying that place? Opening up a little competition, maybe?" He called to the boy and asked him if he knew any of Jackel's kids. The boy knew them all. "You find out what they're up to," he said, "and I'll pay you for your trouble. But keep it quiet. Bring the information to me at *Springer's*."

SUNDAY, MARCH 27, 2011

At the Kanchipuram Silk shop, the owner, resplendent in a peacock blue sari, remembered Olivia Mallard well. "Douppioni silk, mauve. Beautiful fabric. I gave her a good price on that bolt of silk," she said, "I can tell you that. And the old sewing machine, too."

"A bolt is a lot of silk," Beryl said, pretending to be impressed by the quantity. "What on earth was she going to do with it?"

"She was going to buy an old plantation house somewhere down in Sipaliwini District. The place needed renovation, she said. And since she was going to be married soon, she thought she'd start with the bedroom and make draperies, pillowcases, a duvet... upholster some chairs. We had a nice conversation. I told her dark wood would look best with it. She agreed."

"Oh, yes," Beryl cooed. "Dark walnut with mauve. I can see it now. Perfect."

With a professional's eye, the owner estimated Beryl's size and said, "Since you have good taste, let me show you something that will dazzle you." She walked towards the rear of the shop, signaling Beryl to follow with an upraised wave of her hand. "This black silk sari just came in. I put it on the manikin yesterday. It is edged completely with dangling sterling silver beads. There is not another one like it in the western hemisphere. And it is your size."

Beryl sighed. "It's a magnificent garment. But I have no place to wear such a dress. I wish I did."

Sensei had followed her back to the manikin. "It would look great on you," he said. "How much is it?"

"Four thousand dollars American," the shop owner replied. "But I will sell it to you for thirty-five hundred."

Beryl laughed. "A bit out of my price range," she said, looking at the dress with an expression that indicated that it would be a long time before she could banish the vision from her mind.

"Take a look at that bamboo print over there," Sensei pointed to the side of the shop nearest the entrance. "I want to buy some for my bedroom." As Beryl walked towards it, he gave his credit card to the owner and said, "Charge it to my account and deliver it to Room 822 of the Tropical Haven."

The owner completed the transaction before Sensei had time to join Beryl at the front of the store. As they examined different bamboo prints, the owner tapped Sensei on the shoulder and, when he turned around, gave him his credit card and had him sign the sales receipt.

Beryl, fascinated by the pairing of solid colors with bamboo prints did not notice.

As they returned to the hotel and walked past the registration desk, a clerk summoned them. "There's a message left for you." He handed Beryl an envelope.

The note said simply, "The cab that picked her up was from Nieuw Amsterdam. I'm still looking." Beryl asked the clerk, "How far from here is Nieuw Amsterdam?"

"It's just across the river, but you have to go down to the bridge to cross. So in miles," he calculated, "about a dozen. A bus that goes there stops in front of the hotel at 8 a.m."

Beryl thanked him. She turned to Sensei. "If we don't hear anything from the captain, we can go there tomorrow. Meanwhile we can start calling."

They started with the motels in the Nieuw Amsterdam area. The second one that Beryl called, The Seabreeze, was the right one. "Unfortunately," the girl who answered the phone said, "they're not here now. They went to the beach and then they were going dancing. We don't know when they'll be back."

"Ah," Beryl said, "but they didn't check out, so I guess they'll be back soon. Do you know where they planned to go dancing?"

"No," she whispered. "It's their honeymoon so it isn't polite to ask."

"The wedding chapels are open today," Sensei noted as he checked the brochures on the desk. The first chapel he called refused to give him any information on the phone. Sensei said, "Thank you." Turning to Beryl he said, "We have to go in person. We'll get no where on the phone."

The desk clerk gave them a printout of the city's wedding chapels. They went to the cabstand. "Nothing about this case is easy," she said. They made the rounds for two hours until they came to the Paramaribo Wedding Chapel that was presided over by the Reverend Girard Thompson who warmly welcomed them.

Beryl gave him her business card and showed him photos of Olivia. "We're trying to locate Miss Olivia Mallard who may, by now, be Mrs. Ananda Moyer. Were they married here?"

"Why, yes, they were. Last Wednesday." He opened a registry book. "I had the certificate recorded on Thursday. Why do you ask?"

"As you can see, we're from the U.S. Mrs. Moyer's sister is trying to locate her. She's not involved in any crime, so please don't think we're searching for any such purpose."

"Yes," Thompson said, looking at the pictures. "This is the lady. And the other lady is her sister? They look alike."

"Could you give me your impressions about the bride and groom, and did you possibly overhear any plans they might have spoken about?"

"Around noon they arrived by taxi. He put his tuxedo on and then my wife took photographs. We sold them the memory stick at the end of the ceremony. Plans? Yes, I overheard them mention Holman Air and some kind of appointment on Saturday. She asked the usual questions about piranhas and mosquitos. Evidently they were going down to Sipaliwini, to Cajana, I think. They kept the taxi waiting because they were first going to Nieuw Amsterdam for a short honeymoon and then they were going down south. I have pictures. Do you want to see the photos?"

Beryl was surprised. "Of course!"

"I load the pics into my computer when I sell them since they're evidence of my charge for the work. But mostly, I keep a copy because more often than you'd imagine, the couple loses the memory stick."

He clicked onto the "Moyer-Mallard" wedding file and one after the other images of the happy couple filled the screen. Beryl was fascinated. "Olivia and the mysterious Ananda."

Sensei looked. "She's beautiful!"

Beryl studied the photographs. "Nobody can *act* like that. That man is... well... gorgeous. And he is in love with her. Look at them. Just look at them. Did you get the impression that they were in love?"

"Oh, definitely. You can tell, you know." Thompson spoke with authority. "The ones who are in love touch each other and smile with their eyes. The others are more formal... stiff. Sort of business like. These two were in love. Her dress had a zipper down the back and he kept trying to pull it down... playfully... then she would pull his bow tie and it would come undone. Finally, I gave him a clip on. You can see the difference." He pointed to the first three photos in which the bow tie was clearly different from the rest of the photos. "And they wouldn't stop laughing. I told them to just smile, but they couldn't just smile. They were too happy. It was genuine." He closed the file. "I hope you don't ask me for a copy of these. I could not do that. But if the request were official..."

"I understand." Beryl thanked him and told him what a big help he had been.

As they left the Chapel Beryl announced, "It is not possible to be more confused about anything than I am about Olivia and Ananda."

MONDAY, MARCH 28, 2011

"I'm starting to feel like a slug," Sensei said as they waited for the bus that would take them to Nieuw Amsterdam. "Too much rest and getting nowhere."

They boarded the bus and observed the landscape as they crossed a bridge and traveled north. Sensei approached the bus driver. "When we near Nieuw Amsterdam, could you tell us when we're near the Seabreeze motel?"

"Sure," the driver said, smiling in a man-to-man way. "That's the best one for you and your lady to stay in. I'll let you know when we get there."

Sooner than he expected, Sensei got the signal from the driver. "Come on, my love," he said to Beryl, "we have an assignation to keep."

Beryl laughed and followed him to the exit door.

The motel manager knew the Moyer bridal party. "Did you come for the wedding?" he asked Sensei.

"We did, but I'm told that we missed it. We'd like to drop in and perhaps take them to lunch or brunch."

"They've still got their room, but they went out this morning and I don't know when they'll be back. You're welcome to sit in here to wait or rent a cabin."

"Ah, no," Beryl replied. "We have to get back to our hotel."

"The bus will be making its return run in a few minutes. Do you want to leave a message for the Moyers?"

"No," Sensei said as he pulled Beryl's arm towards the door, "we want to surprise them."

Reinhardt Springer listened carefully to the report about the strange occurrences at the Cajana dock. DeJong posing as someone named

Longwood? Hendrik Holman flying two people down in his Cessna and going back with four? Moyer and his new wife going to the Granger house - now named Wollenback? And Jackel going about dressed like a businessman?

Springer wished he had listened to more of the priest's amateurish attempt to con him into believing the resort they planned to build was up north. Well, Granger's was not up north. He decided that if there were eight hundred thousand dollars in Suriname that needed direction, he was the rightful one to direct it. The *Pink Dolphin* was enough competition. He did not need more. He needed money and the removal of any obstacle that stood between him and it. The challenge lay both in getting the money and in destroying the competition.

He spoke with due urgency to Kaza Ross and Chico Chavez. "We have no time to lose," he said. "There are four or five people involved in trying to move in on my business. This, no doubt, is the deal the idiot deVries tried to cut me in on. Find out whatever you can about an American woman who is trying to buy property in our area. Of the five, who is in town now?"

Kaza answered. "If by the five you mean deJong, Moyer and his wife, Holman, and Jackel Mazumi, then only Jackel. He just got a ride back with Kenyon Air."

Springer knew what he must do. He had "an arrangement" with a renegade group of Brazilian natives who had been semi-civilized by missionaries who then became too authoritarian. They killed the missionaries and fled in a northeastern direction, continually being harassed by local natives until they entered land privately owned by a group of investors which included Reinhardt Springer. They made a deal with Springer. In exchange for living without any interference on private land, they removed some tribal markings and performed unpleasant tasks for him. To protect them, he referred to them as renegade Yanomami Indians, Indians who lived nowhere near Suriname. He called them his "Yanos."

"I want the Yanos to keep an eye on the Granger place. Describe to them the people we're interested in. I don't want anyone killed in case we need signatures or something. But they can't ever be released, either. If the woman shows up acting like she thinks she's bought the property, then she's already laid out the money. We don't want her to rescind the deal and tie up the money. So keep her out of the mix. Take her to the Annex. Bring the men here to my private offices."

Kaza raised his eyebrows. "The Annex? Isn't that extreme?"

"That's what she gets for trying to steal my business. Besides, when the bitch is humbled, she'll automatically cooperate."

"You're the boss," said Kaza.

Jack Donovan, owner of *Jack's Pink Dolphin,* did not welcome the arrival of the short rainy season. It always came around Easter, and business would suffer. On the other hand, the Passover Moon would inspire Jack to wax philosophical; and Jack enjoyed waxing philosophical.

He compared the kind of people who frequented his establishment around the Christmas holidays to those who came at Easter. He opened his notebook and wrote, "Christmas heralds the short dry season when heaven infiltrates the exquisite mountains of Suriname. Patrons happily leave the crèches and the carols behind, along with all the ungrateful people they know, trading them for the sight of brilliant parrots flying overhead and orchids nestled in the tree branches."

He turned the page and continued, "But at Easter, even the most ardent sinner is raised up by triumphant Palm leaves before being struck down by the defeats that follow. They know that they will end up by being hauled up, nailed and dying, on their own made-to-order Cross. It makes them not want to visit the *Pink D.* The Bastards!" They always wanted to be home or someplace other than his Roadhouse during Easter.

He closed his notebook. Someday, on the shelves of deep thinkers, there would be a book entitled, *The Wisdom of Jack Donovan.*

Meanwhile, there were bills to pay. He could let the local workers go. They expected seasonal work. But key employees - the chef, certain croupiers, the good whores, the bookkeeper - had to be kept on and given a salary even though they had less work to do. To let them go was to have them work elsewhere and then to badmouth him. They were a stupid and ungrateful lot who didn't understand economics or loyalty. "Betrayal!" he exclaimed. "The theme of the short rainy season!"

In such a gloomy mood did he find himself that he could barely get up to close the casement window and shut out the rain that was blowing in. His phone rang. He answered and a voice he did not recognize said, "Jack, I'm calling from the United States on a prepaid cell. If we run out of time, please call me back. I'm calling to see if you're interested in a scam that's being run near Cajana." Faber waited for an answer.

"Go on," Jack said, as he wondered what kind of idiot would call from the U.S. on a prepaid cell.

"I had a partner who double crossed me. I connected him with a woman who put over eight hundred thousand U.S. dollars in a bank in Paramaribo. My partner is somebody you know... Ananda Moyer. He was in prison here in the States. That's where I got to know him. Half of that money was supposed to be mine for an investment in a gentlemen's BDS&M club to be built up north. I keep trying to reach him at *Springer's* but he ignores my calls. The last hint I had of where he might be trying to scam the woman was in a plantation house somewhere near Cajana. I was told to try to reach him at Holman Air up in Paramaribo. This led me to believe that the money probably hasn't changed hands yet. I can come down there but I need an ally. We'll go 50-50 on the money we recoup. Are you in?"

Jack Donovan had heard that a good customer of his, Tony deJong, was involved in a scam that was supposed to net eight hundred thousand U.S. dollars to be split four ways. "Before I tell you anything," Jack said, "I want to know who the hell I'm talking to. What's your name?"

Faber said, "Don't give out my name to anyone. Don't even write it down, but it's Samuel Faber. I'm the church deacon who works with the prison here in Harderwijk, Lancaster County, Pennsylvania."

"Is your phone listed?"

"Yes." Faber gave him his landline number.

"Hang up," Jack said, "and I'll call you back. It may take a few minutes so be patient."

"All right. I'll wait for your call." Faber sat on his bed feeling like a punished child. He reached for the water pitcher on the table beside him, filled a glass, and sipped it, repeatedly clearing his throat, readying it for action.

Jack Donovan got the information operator and asked for the number of Samuel Faber. He saw that it was identical to the one the caller had given, and he put the call through. Faber answered.

"Let's talk," said Jack. "Who is the woman with the money?"

"Olivia Mallard. There's a religious group that furnishes pen pals to prisoners. Moyer is an idiot. He couldn't write a laundry list. So I composed the letters he sent her and she fell in love with the letters and the man she thought wrote them. You know the play *Cyrano de Bergerac*? It's one of those deals."

"Who else knows about this?"

"Reinhardt Springer. I spoke to him a few days ago. He's an ignorant man who's got delusions of grandeur. I'm sorry I called him first. My apologies."

"So Moyer is going to scam this woman out of nearly a million?"

"Yes. That's what she had told him she was bringing with her. But Moyer and I wrote to *other* rich women who are also in the money pipeline."

Donovan considered this last comment. Was it some sleazy enticement? If it were puffery he wouldn't appreciate the little trick. He disliked deceit both in kind and in degree. Four hundred thousand dollars would solve many of his problems; but to be gullible and taken "for a ride" would only add to his troubles. He decided to test Faber's veracity. He had detected a feminine note in Faber's voice which, if Faber acknowledged it, would explain much. "Tell me, Faber, what's your personal relationship with Moyer?"

"Not that this should make any difference, but we were lovers. We planned to live out our lives running a resort that catered to men of distinction. You know, men who appreciate pleasure and pain. I suppose that that is no longer possible. He seems to have 'dumped' me, as they say."

As quickly as Donovan felt relief at hearing Faber admit an awkward truth, he formed the basis of a plan that could use "unrequited love" as Faber's motive for killing Moyer or any other male. Yes, here was a possible "fall guy." Eight hundred thousand dollars was a lot of money. Twice as much as four hundred thousand. Donovan heard the desperation in Faber's voice. He would know how to manipulate him. "How soon can you be here?"

"I'll need a visa, shots, and plane reservations." Faber felt a rush of relief.

"Call me back with the flight information in exactly one hour."

Donovan ended the call and left his office. He noted the time as he headed for the bar to ask his bartender for details on the scam that was supposed to net deJong $200K. "Tell me more about that deal that Moyer and deJong are running."

Gus, the bartender, leaned on the bar. "The scam they're runnin' with Henny Holman and Jackel Mazumi?"

"Yeah, with those two." Ah, Donovan thought, so there were four of them. Faber didn't seem to know that. Three of them had worthless lives; and while he liked Jackel Mazumi, he wouldn't put much of a price on his affection.

"I can try to find out more, but what I just heard is that as soon as an eight hundred grand deposit clears the bank in Georgetown and Jackel gets the business checks he ordered, they're gonna go and write checks to the four of them."

"Who told you this?"

"Rubem told me. He was high. He can't keep nothin' to himself. Lover-boy Tony was gone for a week doin' something secretive and Rubem went nuts, thinkin' he had somebody else on the line. So Tony got back and told him about some scam they were pulling that would net each of them two hundred K, which is why he was gone. The bank was in Georgetown. Then he disappeared again for a couple of days and Rubem went nuts again. But people said Tony was seen in Cajana sportin' a dark beard and glasses. He left with Henny Holman to fly back to Zorg Airport with some other people. He's staying up there with Henny in case he's needed for any loose ends."

Jack Donovan began to consider the timing of the scheme. "So when the checks come in to the bank in Georgetown, Tony will go get them and write the checks?"

"That's what Rubem said."

"Then I need Tony down here so I can determine exactly when the checks come in and he gets ready to go to Georgetown again."

"I could give Rubem something that will make him sick - then call Tony up in Holman's office. Rubem won't be able to sing," he grinned, "but he will be able to groan. I'll just tell Tony that I think it's really serious. He'll come runnin'."

"Do it! There's a bonus in it for you."

Donovan did not have to wait long for the phone to ring. Samuel Faber said that he would be flying to Miami the next day where he'd get his shots and visa, and stay overnight at an airport motel. Early Wednesday morning he'd fly to Paramaribo. His e.t.a. was 2:10 p.m. "Will you meet me at the airport on Wednesday?" Faber asked.

"No. Why the hell would I go all the way up to Paramaribo to meet you at the airport? Write this down. On Wednesday, after you go through customs at Pengel International, go to Zorg en Hoop airport and find one of the small airlines that cover eastern Suriname and book your flight. One of the pilot owners, Hendrik Holman of Holman Air Service, is involved in the scam. Moyer let some other guys in. So don't trust anyone. Keep your mouth shut. Pretend you've got motion sickness. Kenyon Air also comes down here. There are others, too. Just find one that can take you to Cajana on the Gran Rio in Sipaliwini. Got that?" Jack paused for some kind of affirmation.

"Yes, yes… I'm getting it."

"I'll have someone meet you there. How will he recognize you?"

"I'll wear a red scarf around my neck, one of those square cowboy handkerchiefs. I speak Dutch."

"Good. When you get to Zorg don't act like a tourist. Move like you know where you're headed, like you know all about these hops. Tell people, especially the pilot, that you're Surinamese. Don't give your real name or occupation. Speak Dutch to them. Don't tell anyone you're coming from the U.S. Tell them you've just spent a couple of years in The Netherlands. What name will you use?"

"How's Edwards? Jeffrey Edwards, a mining engineer?" There was a Bible on Faber's bedside table. Mr. Jeffrey Edwards de Grasse was the man who donated it to the church.

"Good. I'll have you picked up at the Cajana dock at 4 p.m. Wednesday. Donovan out."

Sitting back in his chair, Donovan sought to identify the problems and to find solutions to them. There was only one reason that anyone would include Jackel in a Guyana bank scam: Jackel was a citizen of Guyana - which meant he was vital to the account. Taking his wife and maybe one of his kids hostage would force him to do anything Donovan wanted. As far as deJong was concerned, Donovan could simply go to Guyana in his place. Donovan was not too different in appearance. True, his waist was larger than deJong's, but one of his whores had a waist-cinching corset he could use. He'd get it when he got one of their wigs that looked like deJong's long hair. Then he could wear deJong's clothes. Would that mean he'd have to get rid of deJong permanently? Probably. And who would guard the hostages? Why not Faber?

Jack Donovan thought of the perfect place to hold hostages. There was an abandoned mill house half a mile from the *Dolphin's* main building. The house was situated just below a small waterfall. An attempt to harness the power by using a waterwheel to generate electricity had been made years before by an engineer who knew more about engineering than he knew about tropical waters. In the dry season there was not enough water to turn the large wheel. In the rainy season, the torrents of water washed down, splashing over the riverbank and into the mill house. Caiman and fish clogged the machinery.

The engineer had attempted to correct the problems by building a coffin dam around three sides of the mill house. He then constructed a lever-operated headrace gate that directed the falling water into a sluice that dropped water onto the wheel. After the wheel turned, the water flowed out a ground-level tailrace gate that was also lever-operated to prevent caiman from crawling inside the coffin construction. In heavy rain, water would accumulate inside the coffin dam but it would safely rejoin the river. The whole system, however, was so noisy and erratic that very little electricity was ever generated. A gasoline generator proved to be much more efficient. The mill house and the coffin dam panels and pilasters were still there, covered with vines.

While Jackel Mazumi sat at the counter, Tony deJong/Longwood, Hendrik Holman, and Mr. and Mrs. Ananda Moyer sat down together in a cafeteria booth. All the faked documents were in order.

Hendrik announced, "Longwood, here, is probably too polite to tell you, but his boss is eager to have him in Caracas. He's got some big business deal going. Yours truly has been asked to fly him there. All this is another way of saying that we can't waste time."

DeJong/Longwood contradicted him. "A purchase of this magnitude can't be rushed. My boss is a nervous-nellie. He can get along without me. We don't need to rush anything."

The waitress came for their order but they delayed service so that they could keep the table clean for signing the papers. Hendrik pretended to be uninterested in the details of the house and its environment, in particular the nice helpful people that deJong invented as he went along.

As they had anticipated, they needed a second witness. "Mr. Mazumi's at the counter," Holman said. "He's a nice guy. I told him he might be needed, and here he is. That's the kind of people you'll find down there." He got up and went to the counter and brought Jackel back. "Would you mind witnessing some signatures?" he asked.

Jackel said, "No problem." Everyone signed the documents, and then Hendrik signed as a witness, and with grueling care, Jackel, taking what seemed to be a full minute to write each letter, inscribed J-a-c-k-e-l M-a-z-u-m-i on the witness line beneath Hendrik's signature, and then he returned to his place at the counter.

Olivia, Ananda, and deJong called a cab and waved goodbye to Holman. DeJong/Longwood called, "As soon as I'm finished at the bank, I'll come right back. Go ahead and file a flight plan."

At the bank, Olivia signed the transfer documents; and as soon as the transactions were completed, she went to the counter and asked that her present account be closed and the eighty thousand dollars that remained in it be placed in a new account opened in her and her husband's name. She asked Ananda's advice on selecting the style of checks that should be printed for their new account. He chose the ones that had pictures of animals in the background.

She turned to deJong/Longwood, "I suppose the proper thing now for us to do is to go and record the deed."

"Yes, of course," he replied, "but you should have a schedule of items attached - things that go with the sale. We didn't have time to do it before, but when I get back from Caracas in a few days, I'll have a better idea of how long it will take me to get the heavy equipment out. Then I'll contact you at your motel and we can get together and do it right. What's more important is that you get your vaccinations... in particular the new malaria vaccine. I think it's called Mosquirix. You'll have to call the hospital and order it. There are other shots you can get, too. And be sure to get yourself a supply of anti-venom for snakebite." He shook hands. "Good luck," he said and pointed to his new Longine wristwatch. "I've got to get to the airport. Holman's waiting."

Sensei and Beryl were almost finished a full series of 'forms' when the phone rang. Out of breath, Beryl answered. "Is Mr. Percy Wong available?" a man tentatively asked. Beryl, breathing heavily, said, "Yes... just a moment." She handed the phone to Sensei who also answered with a heaving chest.

Jan Osterhaus was apologetic. "Sorry to disturb you, Mr. Wong. My secretary told me that Vice-consul McCarthy was looking for me. I called him, and he said you needed some information and told me where to reach you. My business down here wasn't as complicated as I expected. The problems have been resolved and I'll be back in the capital tonight. Do you want to meet me in my office tomorrow morning at, say, 10 a.m.?"

"Of course," Sensei replied. "Tell me where your office is."

"Anybody can give you directions. See you tomorrow." He disconnected the call.

Deacon Samuel Faber had enough credit available on a credit card to pay for his airfare down and back to Suriname, but he needed an excuse to go and, if his mission should fail, to return to Harderwijk. He worked on the problem and found an answer.

When Father Haas returned to the office, Faber feigned the most amazed but suffering expression into which he could contort his facial muscles. Alarmed, Father Haas asked him what was wrong.

Faber tried to explain - Oh, he did not know how to say it - he had had an epiphany! No, two of them! "Please don't think I am boasting about this," Faber covered his face, bit his lip and looked up, pleading, "I do not understand the ways of God or of angels. But I can no longer keep silent."

He finally yielded to the old priest's entreaties and slowly related the strange events. "I had the first epiphany last week. I was asleep. I awakened hearing my name being called. I looked around and then very steadily a light on my bureau began to glow. It grew brighter and brighter until I saw the perfect figure of an angel. I was terrified." He stood up and walked to the window.

Father Anton Haas knew from sad experience that usually, when people report epiphanies, they want money or attention. The words, "God spoke to me and told me to do this or that," invariably were a prelude to a pitch. Haas believed that Faber was an honorable man but not a particularly spiritual one. He waited to hear the rest of the story.

Faber faced the old priest. "The angel said, 'I am here to deliver a message from God. You are to go to Suriname and there you will find proof that Willem deVries is innocent of the charges made against him.'" Faber paused to watch Father Haas's startled expression. "I could barely believe that I was the recipient of a holy message. And then the angel asked if I understood my assignment. I said that I did. I agreed to do as God commanded me to do. And then the light faded. I couldn't get back to sleep. By the morning's light, my excitement seemed foolish. Like the coward I am, I dismissed the experience as a dream. I am utterly ashamed." He turned his face away again feigning humiliation. "This is why I've been troubled lately."

"I did notice that you were upset, Samuel. I had no idea why."

"Earlier, after you went to the Lenten service, I went up to my room to mend one of my socks. It had a hole in it. As I sat on my bed, darning, the glowing light reappeared. I fell to my knees. I knew that I had failed to keep my word. 'Please forgive me,' I said. It did not speak kindly to me. 'Why have you done nothing?' it said." Faber created a look of terror. "I couldn't speak. I was too ashamed." He began to speak in a helpless whine and sat down, covering his face with his hands in shame. "I know only that I must go to Suriname as God has commanded me." He looked up at Father Haas with a pathetic expression. "Father, how am I to arrange this?"

Father Haas appreciated the delicacy of the request. He spoke cautiously. "Are you asking for money, Samuel?"

Faber recoiled from the words as he would recoil from a striking mamba. His eyes widened and he leaned back to get out of the range of such a venomous suggestion. And it then occurred to him that he might gain more from the epiphany story than he figured. He had wanted only an excuse to leave and get back, but now he might gain the means to pay for the trip. He looked at Haas as though he were preparing to shout, *J'accuse!* "Money?" he repeated the word as if it were a criminal charge, "You misunderstand, Father! I am to go to Suriname to redeem the reputation of Father Willem! Money is not my problem. I have enough, just enough, to do it. I am a frugal man as you well know, but I will manage. I did not come to you for money but for your blessing and for your forgiveness in advance of my leaving you at a time that you are already so burdened with work. I know only that I must go and I must not delay a moment!" He could barely contain his indignation.

"Samuel," the old priest begged, "please forgive me. I meant you no insult."

"All I ask is how I am to do this when I know how difficult it will be for you to manage without me!"

Father Haas was ashamed. "Samuel," Haas said in the measured, reassuring tone of a Holy Man, "you have never asked me for anything. I see your poverty. I see the frugal way you live. And I know that though you have little, you happily share what you have with others." Haas began to put two and two together. Suriname. It was not so farfetched after all. Didn't the detectives think that the love letter was actually written to a man who had been deported to Suriname? "Of course, you must go to Suriname; but you must let me share in the expense of the trip. I will go to the bank first thing tomorrow morning and from my retirement account I will give you three thousand dollars. Would that be enough to get you down and back with the proof that our beloved Willem is innocent?"

As if drawn from a transcendental state, Faber stood up slowly. "Oh, thank you, Father. I don't know the cost or the time it will take but with your prayers and God's help, I will succeed; and the good name of Father Willem deVries will be restored. Thank you." He expressed gratitude as a wave of resentment engulfed him. He remembered years of financial difficulties during which the old man had offered him nothing. Yet, for his precious Willem, three thousand dollars was such a trivial sum. The old son of a bitch probably had the hots for Billy Boy.

TUESDAY, MARCH 29, 2011

Beryl felt a change in the status quo... in herself and in the case. It had depressed her that after several days in Paramaribo, nothing much had happened. Finally they were getting somewhere. She would have to charm the chief of Sipaliwini criminal investigations if she needed his permission to go to Cajana. Her mood lightened. She dressed with new enthusiasm and confidence.

Sensei noticed the change. "It shows. You look like a different person in your new dress and hat."

It was true that Beryl looked better than she had looked in days. The effects of the vaccination had vanished, and she was rested, made up, and wearing a new blue dress. Her hair had been swept up under her wide-brimmed sun hat, and looking both contented and ready for action, she took Sensei's arm as they walked to the office of Captain Jan Osterhaus. A bystander could have mistaken them for a couple going out on a date.

In Beryl's light-hearted mood, she expected that Jan Osterhaus would be an overweight bureaucratic sloth. She would flatter him and "wind him around her little finger." With the self-assurance of a runway model in a Dior gown, she entered the government office building and sauntered down the hall to his office.

One look at Captain Jan Osterhaus and Beryl's visions vanished along with her professional demeanor. He was handsome, tall, slim, with wavy brown hair, hazel eyes and rather long dark lashes. His complexion was warm beige, and she guessed that he must be of mixed ancestry, possibly Dutch and one of the indigenous peoples. As she sat there studying him, she thought that his face, when relaxed, seemed to settle into the slight smile of omniscience, as though he possessed an oracle's secret. When he spoke to Sensei, his voice conveyed the velvet mystery of tropical nights. She stared at him and noticed that he was not wearing a wedding ring and that his shoulders were wonderfully broad. Vaguely she heard her name being called.

Sensei repeated, "Beryl…*Beryl!*"

Slowly she directed her gaze to Sensei. "Yes?"

Jan Osterhaus had been looking at her as if she were Percy Wong's girlfriend, an amorous appendix whose only function was entertainment. He was certain that when he called Wong's room the day before, he had interrupted them in some sexual activity. He had even questioned Wong's professionalism for bringing the woman to an important meeting. But now Wong was saying, "Didn't you want Captain Osterhaus to give you information about Moyer and Olivia?" Osterhaus was confused.

"Why, yes," Beryl responded, and then she remembered why she was there. "Yes!" She sat back, crossed her legs, and put her fingertips together in the manner of a psychiatrist conducting an analysis.

With her eyes fixed on the captain's eyes, she began to speak in a gentle but authoritative voice. "Ananda Moyer, while in prison in the U.S., began a romantic correspondence with Ms. Olivia Mallard, who is the sister of our client. When Moyer was deported, he arranged to meet Olivia here at the Hotel Tropical Haven. She had transferred nearly a million U.S. dollars into a Surinamese bank. We recently learned that Ananda Moyer and Olivia Mallard were married on March 23rd.

"Olivia's intention was to found a religious mission in Sipaliwini. She would teach pottery making and elementary education. Ananda Moyer would preach the Gospel at the mission church. We've been told by those who knew him in the United States that, aside from Sodom and Gomorrah's colorful events, he is totally unqualified to preach anything remotely associated with the Bible.

"Olivia's sister fears that she is in danger. We are proceeding accordingly. If she is dead, as she may be, we'd like documentation to that effect - if not her actual remains. Her sister's interests are entirely sentimental, but Ms. Mallard has property in the U.S. and her heirs cannot lay claim to it if she is merely missing." Beryl extracted a business card from her purse and placed it on Osterhaus' desk.

Even before he looked at the card, Jan Osterhaus' expression had changed. Prior to her definitive little speech, he had assumed that she was Percy Wong's girlfriend. Now he wondered if Percy Wong was *her* boyfriend. What the hell were they all about? Momentarily unable to adjust to this shift in authority, he blurted out, "Please explain the reference to Sodom and Gomorrah."

Beryl maintained her sterile businesslike composure. "I take it that you were not informed of the circumstances of his deportation."

"Only that he had illegally remained in the U.S. after his tourist visa had expired."

"Ananda Moyer allegedly was caught in the act of molesting a four year old boy. The child would not break his promise to Moyer to keep secret what had occurred, and his mother declined to subject her son to a judicial ordeal. The complaint was withdrawn, but during these legal proceedings, his visa expired and the INS simply deported him for the visa violation."

"Those are serious charges," Osterhaus said.

"Yes," Beryl agreed. "Moyer denied the allegations; and I personally find his denial credible, but the judgment is not mine to make." She uncrossed her legs and leaned forward. "What can you tell us about him?" She smiled with a kind of "mind-reading" seduction that was intended to challenge him.

Osterhaus returned the smile. "Well..." he began, "since he hasn't broken any laws that we know of, I can offer only gossip. From time to time we hear that someone wants to create a fashionable resort for all kinds of unusual sexual behaviors. We've heard his name associated with such a scheme in the Cajana area, which, incidentally, was the general area he resided in."

Beryl knew nothing about any such resort. "Yes, Captain. There were many possibilities. I did not say 'Sodom and Gomorrah' idly. I would imagine that his business associates considered many sordid enterprises."

"Do you know the names of any of these associates?"

"Only one at the moment. Ms. Mallard and Moyer were supposed to exchange messages through a clerk named Tony deJong who used to work at the desk of the Hotel Tropical Haven."

"Yes... I know of Tony deJong. The connection to Sodom and Gomorrah is clearer now."

"I think I can assure you that Ms. Mallard's sole interest was in the mission and little school. She knew nothing of these licentious activities which, of course, is why we are so concerned. They, Moyer and his associates, need her money. They do not need her."

Captain Osterhaus pursed his lips and shook his head. "I begin to get the picture."

"What kind of sleeping accommodations and restaurants are available in Sipaliwini?" Sensei asked.

"There are essentially two kinds of accommodations. The expensive ones for the tourists, scientists, and the executives of the various logging and mining companies, and the rough roadhouses, those all-purpose establishments for the manual laborers or for those who don't work at all... the fugitives, the poachers, and so on. These roadhouses are common throughout the rainforest. Each one functions as a general store, a restaurant, an inn, a brothel, a pawnshop, a casino. And life is always very cheap."

"It sounds like the Old West in the U.S." Beryl said. "Can you give us directions and advice about the best way to travel to Cajana? We'll leave tomorrow, if that's possible."

"Oh, no! No. No." Osterhaus slammed his hands on his desk. "Mr. Wong can go at his own risk. But you absolutely cannot go. It is no place for a woman much less a woman who is asking the wrong kind of questions. Have you ever been in a jungle, Ms. Tilson?"

"I've had some experience in Central America... the Peten."

"Still..." Osterhaus stood up and shook his head. "I agree with Vice-Consul McCarthy. I cannot let you go. It is too risky."

Sensei quietly said, "May I ask if she absolutely requires your permission?"

Before Osterhaus could answer, Beryl tried to reassure him. "We respect the dangers of such a trip. We're not fools, Captain. As a great American once said, "There are old pilots and there are bold pilots, but there are no old, bold pilots."

"Chuck Yeager, I believe," said Osterhaus as he stood up, walked to a window and stared into the distance.

"Right," Beryl said, sizing up his height and shoulders. Catching herself in this distraction, she resumed her rigid pose. "You're a professional, Captain. And we are professionals. We've been hired to do a job. If Moyer was headed for Cajana, that must be the first place we look."

Osterhaus approached Beryl and sat on the edge of his desk, trying to seem reasonable and friendly. "Look, give me a day to ask around to see if anyone has heard more recent news about Olivia or Ananda. For all I know they're here in Paramaribo. Let me ask around. Please, before you make any plans, let me make inquiries. Promise me *that* and I'll take you both to dinner tomorrow night. Your hotel. Seven o'clock?"

"That will be fine," Sensei said, relieved to avoid a confrontation.

Osterhaus extended his hands and took Beryl's, pulling her up. "The jungle in the rainy season? Look at you," he said. "You won't last two days down there. You are too...too... delicate!"

"Don't let her fool you," Sensei said. "She's tougher than she looks." Sensei had detected the chemistry. Beryl's toughness surprised even him at times. To some men it might even be a turn-off, he thought. He stood up and looked at Osterhaus. "Much tougher," he repeated as a gentle warning.

As they left his office, Beryl whispered, "I saw the most divine dress in one of the hotel's shops. It'll be perfect!"

Deacon Faber looked ahead to his destination and wore garments that he thought made him fit in: cowboy boots, boot-cut jeans, western shirt, and a cowboy hat, all of which he bought in a farmer's supply store in Ephrata. He affected a John Wayne lope when he boarded the connecting flight to Philadelphia and again when he connected to the flight to Miami.

In Miami, he checked into an airport motel and took a cab to the traveler's clinic, obtained his shots, continued on to the Suriname consulate, obtained his visa and then directed the cab driver to take him to one of those ubiquitous but, to him, mysterious Golden Arches. While the cab waited, he went in and ordered something he had always wanted to taste: a Big Mac. He also bought fries and a Coke.

He sat on his bed and ate his dinner as he watched television - cable channels that he did not have on his TV in the rectory.

WEDNESDAY, MARCH 30, 2011

Olivia and Ananda, after enjoying a sunny day beach combing and making plans for their mission, returned to their cabin to find a loose-leaf page stuck under the door. The owner's daughter, functioning as Olivia's personal assistant, had sent her a note.

"I have been meaning to tell you in person that a man and a woman, nicely dressed people, called for you on Monday morning. They were Americans I think. They were sorry they missed you. They didn't leave their name. My dad says that he also received a call for you today from a man who didn't leave his number. I wanted to tell you in person but you were gone Monday morning, and Monday afternoon I had to go to my Grandmother's house. And then it just slipped my mind until my dad told me about the call he got."

Olivia read the message and laughed. "She's got a lot on her mind, planning her wedding. It couldn't have been important or they would have left their names."

Ananda read the message and did not laugh. "Who is looking for us? Why didn't they say who they were if they were friends? Americans came here looking for us? They must be your friends." He took the paper from Olivia's hands. "She doesn't say when her father got the message from the man. Did he call today? And that's three different people. Why are three different people looking for us?"

Olivia tried to pacify him. "If it's important, they'll call again or come here. Don't worry so much. They're probably salesmen. There's no secret that we bought the Wollenback place. If you don't want to be bothered by them then tell the desk to tell anyone who calls that we're out."

Samuel Faber took his seat in the plane and began to daydream, concocting a variety of ways to tell Olivia what a fool Ananda had made of her. He thought about seeing Ananda for the first time in more than a month and he hoped he wouldn't still be so handsome. He planned that when he saw him, he'd tilt his cowboy hat forward in a rakish angle and walk with a bit of a swagger - one that indicated independence. He now had a new and exciting persona. Rugged. Indomitable. Howdy Pilgrim!

He had never been to Suriname but it felt to him as though he were going home. When the clerk at the consulate had asked what his purpose was in going to Suriname, he said, "Pleasure, Ma'am. Just pleasure." Somehow he knew that his heart would be happy there.

A few hours later, Faber deplaned in Paramaribo and speaking a quaint but natural Dutch, passed through customs. He did not go immediately to a taxi station as Donovan had instructed. Faber had been thinking about the acquisition of his half of the money. He went to the first bank he found in the busy airport and opened an account in his own name, making an initial deposit of one thousand dollars cash.

And then he went to the taxi station. "Zorg en Hoop" he said simply; and the cabbie took him there.

There were several small planes parked at the side of the tarmac. The Holman name was printed on each of them. He entered Holman's office and asked, "Are you free to fly to Cajana one way?" he asked in Dutch.

"I'll have you there in an hour," Hendrik responded, picking up a clipboard. "I just need a little information and the fare. Your name and nationality?"

"Jeffrey Edwards. Suranimese - but I've spent much of my life in The Netherlands." Holman wrote down the information, collected the fare, and led Mr. Edwards to his four-seat Piper Tomahawk.

Before they could climb in, another cab pulled up and a still slightly bearded Tony deJong ran up to them. "I got Rubem everything he needs at the drug store. You going to Cajana now?" he called.

Holman shouted back, "Yeah, get in. I'll go add you to the manifest."

As soon as they were airborne Faber pretended to be ill and kept his face turned away from the pilot and the passenger who, he noted, was called "Tony" by the pilot. He listened to their conversation which had something to do with Moyer and others named Rubem and a bartender named Gus.

When they landed at Cajana, Faber put his cowboy hat on and, with his chin up to show as much of his neckerchief as possible, awkwardly proceeded to the dock.

"Mr. Edwards!" a boatman called. Faber hurried to the boat. He handed the boatman his suitcase, but he was too unsteady on his feet to board without assistance. Finally, he sat down in the narrow craft.

Tony deJong, recognizing the boatman, called, "You goin' back to *Jack's*?"

"Yeah," the boatman answered. Tony deJong got in behind Faber.

Nobody spoke and Faber, with fear and fascination for what the water contained and admiration for the beauty of the waterway, went upstream to meet his new partner. The boatman turned into the stream that ran by the *Pink Dolphin*.

DeJong called to Faber, "You here for business or pleasure?"

Faber forced himself to smile as he looked back and answered, "Both. I'm here on family business."

Donovan came down to the dock and made a great show of welcome to Faber who cued him to the identity he had given to Tony by calling him "Cousin Jack."

In the privacy of Donovan's office, the details of the scheme and counter-scheme were made known to Faber. As if it meant nothing, Donovan said, "So Moyer married the broad." He then remembered that Faber had said that he and Moyer were lovers. Donovan was effusive in his apologies. "I strive to be refined in spirit," he said. "What I just said was so insensitive that I can hardly believe I said it."

Faber had turned cold at the news that his beloved Ananda had married the very woman his own letters had wooed and won. What a dreadful irony! He forced himself to inhale and then to sigh. "Life goes on," he said. "So," he picked up the thread of Donovan's presentation, "we clearly have no choice but to pressure Jackel to cooperate."

"That's how I see it," Donovan answered.

Faber asked, "By the way, where is the office of the international transfer agency?"

"From what I understand, it's in the same building as the bank."

"That's good. And I agree. You're a little heavier than deJong, but you can pass for him. A few touches would do it. If you do go in his place, I'd recommend that you watch the bank around the lunch hour until Jackel tells you that the man who waited on him is now going out to lunch, and then go in and deal with his lunchtime replacement."

"That's a really good idea! I mean it. That is one fine idea. When my girls were out of their dressing room I went in and stole a wig that's nearly identical to his hair and a lace-up corset. Tony has no gut. I can use his clothes and aviator sunglasses. A substitute teller wouldn't know the difference.

"But you'll have to guard the hostages - Jackel's wife and maybe one of his kids - while Jackel and I are at the bank. I think I have the perfect place a half-mile from here. It's an old mill house. I'll take you there and you can tell me what you think. Don't we need to find out when the Wollenback account checks are due to arrive?"

"No. We need to find out when the money will be available for Jackel to use counter checks to effect the transfer. The moment the account is cleared, we can move on it right away. Reinhardt Springer knows about that money and he'll be laying plans to get it. He'll probably think he needs to wait for the printed account checks to arrive. No doubt he'll use the same hostage strategy."

"Olivia, Moyer's wife," Jack continued, "thinks she owns the real place. And naturally Springer will be watching. If she shows up and finds out that she's been conned, she'll screw-up everything. Springer won't let that happen. I wouldn't give you a nickel for her life if she shows up down here before the con is completed. He's a cruel man. He'll force the information about the check arrival out of one of them."

Faber nodded. "Here's what I suggest. Let's make sure the bank will allow him access to the money using counter checks. Is the bank open now? If so, let's get them on the line."

Donovan looked up the phone number of the bank, called the number and handed the phone to Faber. In flawless business English, Faber asked about the bank's policy with respect to new accounts and counter checks. He asked his questions in a professional way, as if he were comparing bank services in order to make a selection.

The clerk who spoke to him was cautiously informative. "Under the hypothetical conditions you've outlined, an account opened on March 21st should be accessible in ten banking days... that would be Monday, April 4th. Counter checks would be fine - particularly if the money were going to be disbursed through an international transfer agency. The printed checks would probably arrive no sooner than April 7th." Faber thanked him and then relayed the information to a jubilant Donovan.

"We can have the account cleaned out by the time Springer starts calling to see if the checks have arrived," Donovan said. "This is beautiful. He's such a stupid ass. Counter checks won't even have occurred to him."

Jack Donovan took Faber to the guest room which looked regal to Faber. Above the bed was an iron ring from which yards of mosquito netting hung gracefully over the edges of the bed. The bedspread was green linen - not that wretched chenille he was used to at the rectory. The floors and cabinetry were native hard wood and he had a private bathroom. "All the comforts of home," Faber said, as Jack opened a bathroom cabinet which contained a full array of toiletries.

Faber thought of his bedroom and the bathroom he had to share at the rectory... the hideous black blotches of worn areas in the linoleum flooring, the roll-up window shades, and the thin hard single-ply toilet paper he detested. He said, "Yes, it will do nicely."

"Let's go down and have some dinner. Have you ever eaten piranha?"

"No! Is it good?"

"The way our chef prepares it, it is. And next you can have snake. Constrictors have to be cooked with finesse... but you'll like them. They're really tasty - when he cooks them, anyway. He's going to extremes to please everyone tonight."

"Why tonight?" Faber asked.

As Donovan ushered Faber to his private table, in a low voice he said, "You'll get a kick out of this. Before you found out that we could access the Wollenback account with counter checks, I thought I needed to get deJong down here so that I would know when to intercept him and go to Guyana in his place. But I didn't know how to get him down here and keep him down here. DeJong is having some sick fag thing with our cabaret singer, Rubem, so our bartender, Gus, says that he can make Rubem sick; and Tony deJong will come running and he can keep them both sick enough for us to keep them under our control."

"How will he do that?" Faber's spine tingled at Donovan's use of the adjective "our."

"Ipecac and laxatives. He mixes ipecac into Rubem's after dinner drink, and drizzles chocolate laxative over the sugar cookies that he eats with his creme de menthe after dinner drink. The chef had to be bought off. Chefs are the most conceited assholes in the world."

"I get it. Rubem threw up the food and it cast aspersions on the chef's cooking. Is that why deJong came running up here this afternoon?"

"You got it. Rubem's throwing up and shitting and tonight Tony will be shitting, too!"

"Is their toilet near mine?" Faber laughed joyfully. "It may keep me awake."

"Between the vomiting and the shitting I'll be forced to call the old souse of a doctor we have in Cajana who thinks everything is cholera. We may be able to do our work in the privacy of quarantine."

The two new friends were still laughing when the waiter served the piranha house special.

After dinner, Faber asked, "What will deJong do when he finds out you've accessed the money?"

"Sam, I've been wondering about that, too. You're the guy with ideas. What would you suggest?"

"Is cholera a terminal disease?"

Donovan raised his glass. "It certainly could be. And contagious, too." They laughed again and ordered more drinks.

Faber was thinking constructively. "I think we should just concentrate on Jackel and his wife. Once we have them, there's nothing Springer can do. But first the money issue. To whom will you and Jackel be writing the checks?"

"I was gonna say the engineer from Wollenback leased some of my land that had gold on it, but how do you want your half sent?"

Faber had an answer. "Let Jackel wire $400,000. to me at my Suriname account."

Donovan was surprised. "You have a bank account?"

"Yes, in Paramaribo. I'll give you the account number when you're ready to go. Have Jackel mark the explanation as 'Repayment of loan in full.' I can worry about accessing my own account. He can do the same for you. I'll get my $400K and you'll get your $400K. Is your conscience up to disposing of some of these people?"

"I need the money more than I need a course in ethics."

"What about Jackel and his wife and kids?" Faber asked.

"We can tell him there'll be trouble with the police if we don't get the money back to Moyer's wife and that she'll give him a reward. We could each give him $10K How's that?"

"Sure. Sounds good." Samuel Faber suddenly realized how casually he had suggested murder.

"Let's make a wish," Donovan laughed.

Faber nodded dejectedly and sighed. "If wishes were horses, beggars would ride."

"That's a great line!" Donovan said, envisioning it inscribed among his parables. To himself he said, "Jack, my boy, this guy is a real asshole, but a smart one. He's also got a mean streak." He concluded the meeting. "As soon as the time is right, we'll get Jackel and his wife and kid and keep them down here until I can go with him to Georgetown on Monday morning."

In the waning daylight, Samuel Faber and Jack Donovan, carrying spades, pruning shears, machetes, and a can of WD40, took a small boat upstream to the waterfall and the abandoned mill house. Faber could see nothing but impenetrable jungle, yet Donovan nosed the boat into the shore and hopped out onto a tree root and then jumped onto dry land and proceeded to tie the bowline to a tree. Faber followed him but he had such a quizzical look on his face that Donovan again felt obliged to apologize. "I ought to tell you as we go along what we're doing. There's two kinds of jungle. The first is the canopy jungle. All the trees are like an umbrella and it's kind of dark in there and there isn't much vegetation on the ground because the sun can't get to it. But when you bulldoze a road, or a river runs through it, there isn't an umbrella over it any more, and the sun hits the sides of the road or the river and the shit grows like crazy. You drive down the road and ask yourself how the hell you're gonna get through all that. But all you have to do is cut your way through a short distance until you're under the canopy and then you can walk with no problem. Watch..." Donovan slashed at the foliage for some thirty feet and the world changed.

The stream had curved and ahead of them, no more than two hundred feet distant, Faber saw something that transported him to childhood wonder. There was the mill house and the wheel, like a painting in a fairy tale book, appearing in the nick of time to shelter a lost child. Pale green vines, some with pink flowers, embraced the doorway and curled around the eaves. Faber gasped. All thoughts of banks and confidence rackets and sado-masochism vanished from his mind. There in the improbable distance waiting for him to enter was a child's dream dwelling... a haven, eternal and enchanted. A blue crowned motmot flew past him. Its dazzling feathers tantalized Faber's eyes as it disappeared into the brush. "Faber!" Donovan called. "Come on! We've got work to do."

The spell was not broken. Faber continued to be awed by the reality of a place that no one ever imagined could exist outside a Disney movie or a book of fairy tales. "It's bigger than I figured it would be. How come no one lives in it?" he asked.

"Who the hell would want to live here?" Donovan answered. "Let's clear the path to the door."

The vines clung to the woodwork; and tearing them away seemed more like tearing parasitic veins away from a living body. Faber, identifying with the building, pulled and hacked at the vines, and murmured encouragements. "We'll get these blood-suckers off you. Don't you worry. Just a little more..." He got down on his knees and with his fingers dug away the dirt that had accumulated on the threshold, preventing the door from opening. He could smell the flowers that grew around the building. The vines were their enemy too. He ran his finger along the bottom of the door. Donovan squirted WD40 into the door lock and knob and into the three hinges on the side. He inserted the key and miraculously it turned. He turned the knob, put his shoulder to the door, and shoved it open.

"That was easier than I figured," Donovan said. "I'll get some men up here to clean it out and put some furniture in it for you and the hostages. You ought to have another guy in here with you... just in case." He slammed the door shut and tested its interior bolt. "It's still good."

"This building was meant to last," Faber said.

"Maybe it was and maybe it wasn't. It ain't been used so how can we tell?" He led the way out. "Let's go back and make some plans."

"When will you get Jackel and the hostages?" Faber asked.

"On Saturday, Gus and a man will go down to Jackel's house. Gus will give spiked soft drinks to the family and pretend they're there on business with Jackel, something that has nothing to do with Georgetown.

"They'll get Jackel and his wife and one kid and bring them here to the *Pink D.* His hair and clothing have to be attended to. We have to be ready to leave by 6 a.m. on Monday morning. Say... can I borrow your cowboy hat?"

"Sure," said Faber, feeling the warmth of belonging to a partnership, of having a friend.

At seven o'clock Captain Osterhaus called at the hotel desk and received a note from Sensei saying how much he regretted not being able to join them for dinner. "But if you call room 822, Beryl will answer and come right down."

Beryl took a moment to dab perfume behind her ears, on her wrists, and in her cleavage. She had gotten her "perfect" dress and, though it was much too expensive, it fit her perfectly. It was, after all, she rationalized, absolutely necessary to make a good impression on the handsome captain.

Jan Osterhaus was waiting at the elevator doors when Beryl emerged, her hair styled and freshly renewed in its ash blonde color, wearing a dark silk chiffon gown, the neckline of which plunged to the waist.

"Ms. Tilson," he said, "please tell me that you are single... even if it is a lie."

"I'm a widow with one son... and that's the truth, Captain Osterhaus. And you?"

"I am also single. But divorced. No children. The orchestra is playing tonight. Will Mr. Wong be angry if I bring you home late?"

"Tomorrow I will be sure to ask him."

When Osterhaus had first entered the hotel, he had not yet decided whether he would tell Beryl that he had a week's vacation time coming and that he could escort her and Percy Wong down to Sipaliwini. He was not used to being wrong about anything; and he had misread her. She fascinated him; and now, after seeing her dressed so beautifully - obviously for him - while still continuing to be so strangely independent, he decided that he wanted to protect her and, of course, Mr. Wong. "If it is necessary to go down to Sipaliwini, I intend to go with you. But it may not be necessary. Olivia and Ananda were there, but it's my understanding that they're back here, possibly in Nieuw Amsterdam."

"Yes, we were told that they were staying there days ago, but we haven't been able to ascertain if it's true. We called but they weren't in their cabin. We went to their motel on Monday morning, and again, they were out. We called yesterday and today and were told they were at the beach. The pastor who conducted the wedding ceremony described them as exceedingly happy. Olivia didn't seem to be in any distress. Yes, if she's being conned, her life could easily be in danger. But if she's not being conned, we're invading her privacy. Our focus, at the moment, is the validity of the deal she's negotiating."

"My focus is a little different. It's not just that I suddenly have the urge to be your escort - however pleasant that prospect is - but the fact is that women have disappeared in the Southern District; and the rumor is that they've been taken into the flesh trade. Sipaliwini is an enormous chunk of our country and they could have entered any one of the hundreds of roadhouses we have down there. Most of the time they seem to have gone willingly. Miners, particularly, have the kind of sudden wealth that gets spent on female company.

"But one persistent rumor is that unwilling women are taken into the trade in the Cajana area. The problem is complicated by the absence of missing persons reports. The women are said to be from Venezuela, French Guiana, Brazil, and Guyana. They're supposed to be prostitutes, but we have no way of knowing whether that is true. The jungle is vast and fraught with problems; and we have a limited amount of resources to commit to its many problems. We believe in equal justice for all, but I doubt that I'll shock you when I say that some people are more equal than others. If a tourist lady of some importance disappears in that area we can justify a much more thorough investigation.

"I also learned something that may make sense to you. Apparently someone from a church in the U.S. has been calling Ananda Moyer at *Springer's Roadhouse*. I have no idea what he wants. You mentioned Tony deJong as Miss Mallard's contact. DeJong has a lover, a Brazilian singer who performs at *Jack's Pink Dolphin*, and he is bragging about a windfall that is coming his way. I should add that the singer is a male. Moyer and deJong used to frequent both of these roadhouses, *Springer's* and *Jack's Pink Dolphin*.

"In the Amazon River," he explained, "there is a species of fresh water dolphin that is actually known as a pink dolphin. At any rate, both of these roadhouses are in the general Cajana vicinity, in particular, the mining areas. *Springer's* is on one hill and *Jack's* is on the next. There is an unpleasant valley swamp between them. Can't I induce you to stay up here?"

"Captain Osterhaus, Olivia committed herself to moving to your Southern District. The rumors we heard concerned a plantation house in the Cajana area that you say doesn't exist. DeJong wrote to Moyer and mentioned Cajana, and Cajana is where we have to start. But I agree. Let's check out their motel in Nieuw Amsterdam first."

Osterhaus looked at the ceiling and sighed. "All right. You will need weapons. I could expedite permission to get you side arms, but the thugs down there will kill you for your weapons. Killing me would bring government forces on them, so I'm reasonably safe."

"What about knives?" Beryl asked.

"I know a good place to buy them. Before we leave, I'll see that you get good knives. Also, you need proper clothing."

"I think we have the clothing problem solved," Beryl said. "Let's enjoy the music. I did not buy this dress to sit and worry about weapons."

"I will consider that my vacation time has just begun. Mr. Wong was right. You are tougher than you look."

They dined and exchanged their favorite stories about unusual criminal cases. Then they danced. For an hour and a half straight they danced.

Close to eleven o'clock, Osterhaus grew serious. "We've been having a lot of fun tonight. I'm really enjoying myself. But it ends tonight. I want you to realize that we won't be going on a tourist jaunt. This trip to the roadhouses is entirely off the track and dangerous. I need time tomorrow morning to clear my desk. I can take you shopping for knives tomorrow afternoon. Friday, if we still haven't located Olivia, we can go to Cajana.

"But what we're looking for may lie farther south. Our southern border is not too far north of the Amazon River and the more we descend toward that great waterway, the more dangerous it becomes. Electric eels, piranha, caiman. Suriname is blessed with altitude, but it does have swamps."

"Will you be bringing anti-venom?"

Osterhaus sighed. "Yes, and antibiotics. And by the way, don't touch any blue frogs."

"I promise I won't touch *any* frogs. But tomorrow, would it be possible for you to ask the Paramaribo Wedding Chapel to email you copies of the photographs he took of the Moyer/Mallard wedding? He said he would give them only by official request."

"Yes, of course. We can stop there in the afternoon when we get your knives at the martial arts' store."

"Perfect. A good martial arts' store is just what we'd prefer."

He affected a frightened look. "You're not planning to throw those star things at me, are you?"

"No. Can I intimidate you with a knife?"

Osterhaus laughed. "What are you planning to force me to do?"

"And spoil the surprise? What time will you be free to call for us?"

"I can't say precisely... around noon."

"Good. By the way, we won't be checking out of the hotel when we go south with you on Friday. We'll use it as our base and leave everything we won't be carrying with us in the room. Do we need reservations for the airplane?"

"No. Don't worry about the plane. I'll take care of that."

Close to midnight, Osterhaus escorted Beryl to her room. He took the plastic key card from her hand and opened the door. "Are you going to invite me in for a nightcap?" he asked.

"No, my dear Jan. We'd wake my master."

Osterhaus was puzzled by the remark. "Well, in that case," he said, trying to pull her close. But she had stepped over the threshold. She kissed her fingertips and pressed them against his mouth. "Call me tomorrow," she said, quietly shutting the door.

THURSDAY, MARCH 31, 2011

Ever since they concluded their business at the bank, Ananda's behavior became incomprehensible to Olivia. At the beach, he was fine; but the moment they were back in their cabin, he became jittery. In the manner of nervous lapdogs, he alerted to every outside noise.

Life, in the confines of the cabin, was becoming increasingly difficult. Every day, the number of mosquitos increased in direct proportion to the amount of rain. And it was beginning to rain nearly every day. Olivia's body was covered with daubs of calamine lotion; and she had begun to eat, sleep, and read inside the aegis of their bed's mosquito netting. She tried to content herself with making sketches of rooms in the Cajana house, but she could not estimate the dimensions of the rooms.

A lack of details of both the purchase and the house's physical aspects became a worsening source of distress. It wasn't just the big items - the appurtenances - but smaller things and pieces of furniture... dishes and pots and pans... curtains... cleaning supplies and kitchen utensils. What were the measurements of the windows into which they'd install air conditioners?

She wanted to take a quick trip down to Cajana, but Ananda always objected. He was certain that they'd just be in the way of the extremely complicated work of shipping the heavy mining equipment down river.

She had tried to place a call to Wollenback Mining in Cajana but was told there was no such listing. Ananda reminded her that the engineer had a satellite phone on his belt, and there was no way of knowing how he specifically listed it.

"Why," she reasonably asked, "are we living here, imprisoned by gauze, when we could be in our own home or at least in the Vandermeer where the rooms are completely screened?"

"Ya' need patience," Ananda repeatedly reminded her, "if ya' wanta live in the rainforest." Olivia understood the difficulties of jungle communication, of having to depend on radio, outpost mail, or unreliable cellular reception, but Cajana was easily reachable. She didn't need to talk to Longwood. She could go in person. "Perhaps," Olivia ventured to say, "some of these calls we've been receiving were from him. Why not ask the desk to put through any calls from Mr. Longwood or if we're not in our cabin, to get his phone number?"

Ananda thought this was a good idea; but just as he arrived in the manager's office, a call came in. The manager answered and hesitated, signaling Ananda that the call was for him. Before he could ask who was calling, Ananda wagged his head and his finger, indicating that he did not want to talk. The manager's confusion could be heard in his voice as he said, "I'm afraid you just missed him… again." He turned to Ananda, "He hung up. No message. I recognized his voice. He's called before. But, earlier you also got another call from a man who spoke Dutch. No message, either."

Ananda's confusion spiked into fear. He had no doubt that Faber was pursuing him. There was nothing he could do but go to Cajana and let her discover the fraud. He would give the performance of his life. He'd blame himself for having led her to that plantation house. He'd fall apart with guilt. She'd console him and wouldn't do anything that could make him feel worse; and if he put on a good enough show, hinting that the crooks would kill them if they complained to the authorities, he might be able to delay her from taking any action until the checks went through. Yes, they'd go south and forget the whole goddamned bunch of his greedy rat friends. Maybe this was just God's way of testing him. Meanwhile, he had to get Olivia out of their room.

Ananda's voice was firm as he entered the cabin. "Mrs. Moyer, ya've married a fool. I'm worried about money and every mosquito in Suriname wants ta take a bite outta ya. Kenyon Air Service flies down at noon, or maybe Holman's back. We can get a flight. We can stay in our own house over night or, if you want to get back here to go shopping, we can stay at the Vandermeer and take the 6 a.m. flight out." He put his arms around her. "You, my lady, are the only thing that matters. You finish gettin' dressed. If we hurry, we'll be at Zorg before noon."

Tom Kenyon had been hoping to get return passengers. He filled out the manifest and ushered Ananda and Olivia into his Cessna Skylark. Promptly at noon they were given permission to take off, and the Cessna revved up its engine and bolted down the runway.

Not wanting Olivia to speak to the pilot, Ananda engaged her in spirited conversation that he thought conveyed enthusiasm, but which disturbed her by its unmistakable nervousness. He called her attention again to every feature of Bloomenstein Lake and the Suriname River he could remember, forgetting that he had recently called her attention to the very same features. She was relieved when the Suriname River bifurcated into its tributaries; and Ananda remembered something he had not told her before: "the big branch is called the Gran Rio - but the folks they call it, 'the Glan Lio' and the little river that goes southeast, that's called, 'the Pikin.' My folks are from down that way - sort of between the Gran and the Pikin." He tweaked her nose. "Pikin, Pikin." They continued to follow the Gran Rio, seeing settlement after settlement notched into the riverbank. They flew over the cleared land and buildings of *Springer's Road House*, and then Cajana's airstrip came into view.

As they walked off the airfield, Olivia asked Kenyon, "Do they have regular boat transportation up to the Wollenback house?"

"Where?" he answered.

"The mining house... a mile or so west along the creek."

"Oh, you mean Granger's. The boatmen have a station at the end of the hangar."

Olivia thanked him. She wanted to ask Ananda why he had called the place "Granger's," but an uneasy feeling had seeped into her mind and would not drain away until she got some needed reassurance. It was possible, she thought, that the place was called Granger's before Wollenback bought it, and yet..."

Ananda took her arm. "Let's go to the Vandermeer for lunch."

Olivia hesitated. "Everything's quiet now. Let's just take a quick look at our house. I won't intrude if they're busy, but I'd like to get a better idea of the size of the windows and sills... for ordering the air conditioners."

When they engaged a boatman she specifically asked that they be taken to "the mining house."

They docked and began walking up to the house. Olivia asked the boatman to wait. "We'll pay you for your time," she said. "We won't be long."

Olivia tried to put the keys deJong had given to her into the front door lock, but none fit. The front door opened and a tall thin man whose eyeglasses were pushed up to his hairline stood in the doorway. "What are you trying to do?" he asked Olivia.

"Get into our house," she answered.

"Where did you get the idea that this was your house?" The man was annoyed.

"We just acquired title to this place," said Olivia, as she reached into her tote bag and removed the envelope that contained the documents. Placing the bag on the wooden floor, she removed several papers from the envelope and tried to show them to him.

"This is nonsense," he said, glancing at the documents. "You two have been victimized in some fraud. This building belongs to Granger's Mining. It has been Granger's mining for months now. We bought this place from Devers Lumber. Check up at the Lodge. Call our headquarters. Check with the Sipaliwini District authorities. I don't care who you call, you'll get the same answer. This is Granger's office. I'm Leighton, the chief engineer. I'm truly sorry that you got your wires crossed, but I have to get back to work. Your problems are your problems. I have my own." He noticed that their boatman had turned the canoe around. "You better call your boatman while you can." He hesitated as Ananda ran towards the landing. "I've got so much to do before the heavy rains arrive," he said to Olivia. "I'm sorry." He closed the door, leaving her standing on the veranda.

Something had frightened the boatman and he no longer cared to wait or even to be paid for having brought them to the mining house. Ananda called the boatman by name and was sure that the man heard him, but the boat sped away. He rejoined Olivia. "Why he leave in such a hurry?" Ananda asked, genuinely puzzled by the boatman's sudden departure.

Olivia's face had turned deadly white while Ananda's face flushed. She stood staring at the keys in her hand. "Not our house? What is he talking about?" she asked. Ananda was still trying to understand why the boatman had left so abruptly. He knew the man. Why had he turned back without them? Olivia tugged at his sleeve. "What is going on?"

Ananda suddenly felt afraid of whatever it was that had frightened the boatman. "Let's just start to walk back to the Vandermeer. Maybe we're being punked... you know... a big trick is bein' played on us. There's probably cameras pointed at us right now. Let's start walkin' back."

"This is no joke!" she said grimly. The lunch hour was over for the men who worked behind the house. A calliope kind of whistle sounded and then a motor started and as a large piece of earth moving equipment backed up, the warning beeps sounded. "Men are still working this mine!" she said, rushing down the steps to look at a hardhat workman who was guiding a backhoe into place. "What about the sign?" she exclaimed. "Let's look at the sign." Without waiting for her husband to reply, she hurried down the dirt road until she came to the sign that had once read "Wollenback Mining Operations." It had been removed, leaving fresh nail holes in the slightly worn sign that read "Granger's Placer Mining Operation."

Ananda had followed her. He looked at the sign. "Just a few days ago it say 'Wollenback,'" he said. "What is goin' on here?"

Olivia did not speak. She did not intend to inquire further into the problem. She had been swindled. Her husband was part of it. She knew that now. My God, she thought, *all this*... months of all this... all that she had uprooted to clear the way for them to defraud her. The letters and documents she had seen... the lies she had heard. She became stiff and breathless, as if her body could not move while her mind processed the terrible truth of all those sensory deceptions.

Ananda implored her to speak to him. He began to pull on her sleeve. "Olivia!" Finally she turned and looked at him, expecting to see another performance, but he seemed genuinely alarmed. Jackel Mazumi, carrying a basket of fish, was hurrying towards them, yelling words of warning to Ananda.

Olivia thought about a flight back to New Mexico. With a little luck she could be home tomorrow. Her adventure in South America was over. She realized that her tote bag was still on the veranda. She began to walk back to the house. Ananda followed her, pulling her arm, begging her to listen to him. She turned to the stranger, jerked her arm from his grasp, and continued to walk back to the house.

Mazumi ran alongside Ananda, whispering to him. Ananda replied in a loud voice, "We thought we bought the mining house. Turns out we were tricked."

She scoffed at her ears as they heard Jackel Mazumi say, "The Granger place? You thought you bought the Granger place? Man, I wish you said somethin'. I come every day with fish. I'm sorry. I didn't know you thought you got this place." He lowered his voice again and whispered news that sharpened Ananda's voice. His rehearsed surprise became comical.

"Yes," Ananda announced. "Maybe there's some mistake we can fix. We gotta' find that guy. Right away!" Olivia kept walking.

Jackel's voice was now loud enough for her to hear. "You gotta make her listen. Get back to Cajana. It ain't safe out here. Springer's been talkin' to that church man. He's got Kaza and Chico and his Yanos lookin' for you. It ain't good."

Ananda implored her, "Olivia, listen! That's why the boatman had turned back. There are thugs out here after us!"

Jackel, unable to get them to turn back, looked around, seeking another way. "Better we take long way round to my house. By now your boatman tell everybody you back here."

They continued to follow Olivia back to the house. She reached the steps and slowly climbed them, holding on to the railing as she went. She retrieved her bag and turned to see Ananda's ashen face. She knew fear when she saw it, and she saw it then in her husband's face.

"Olivia. Listen to me. *Please.*" He stopped at the bottom step. "The men who cheated us hired thugs to get rid of us. We're in real danger. Mr. Jackel will help us. Olivia! We gotta' move. Come on!"

She descended the steps determined to walk back to the airfield. Jackel Mazumi lay the basket of fish on the porch and grabbed her left arm as Ananda grabbed her right arm. She resisted, but Jackel's terrified look convinced her that quite possibly even more trouble awaited her than she had realized. She allowed them to pull her in the direction that was opposite to the town.

"We cross stream up there," Jackel said. "It's maybe one mile."

They jogged along a footpath until a planked rope bridge came into view. "In the dry time," Jackel explained, "we cross on stones." He pointed to large stepping stones that were now a meter beneath the surface of the water.

The bridge was formed by two pairs of long ropes that were tied to a single tree on either side of the water. The pairs of ropes were kept apart by the planks that formed the steps of the bridge. Each pair of ropes was knotted at a notch on either side of a plank, securing the plank-step in place. A single rope, strung a meter above the steps, provided the only railing.

They crossed the bridge, one at a time. Jackel stopped and looked back at the direction they had come from. He raised his arms, pointing straight ahead. "Down this rio is Granger place on my right hand. Straight down this rio is airfield and Vandermeer Lodge on my left hand." He extended his left arm straight out to the side, indicating a perpendicular. "We keep walking that way, we at Springer's. Six mile maybe." Then he moved his left arm to a 45 degree mid-point. "That way, maybe two mile, we find my place. Let's go. It gettin' late."

They had followed a footpath about half a mile into the bush when suddenly Jackel slapped the back of his neck and shouted. Immediately, Ananda and Olivia were struck too, Ananda in the right upper arm and Olivia in her left thigh. Olivia pulled a dart that looked like a small knitting needle from her leg. "What is it?" she asked.

Ananda and Jackel exchanged a look of terror. "Curare," Ananda said. "A tranquilizing dart. It all depends what else they put on it. It could just paralyze us for half an hour or it might have poison on it and kill us." With that he felt himself sinking to the ground, soon to be joined by Jackel and Olivia.

They were awake but unable to move when a group of natives suddenly materialized from the green shadows, carrying blowguns, nets, dagger style knives in scabbards at their waists, and blindfolds. The natives covered the eyes of their victims, rolled each in a long net, and carried them away.

Thanks to Gus's innovative recipes, Tony and Rubem continued to experience intermittent vomiting and diarrhea. "You two may be seriously ill. I'm calling the doctor up in Cajana so I want both of you to be as cooperative as possible," Jack Donovan said with convincing concern.

The old doctor made house calls only. There was a small clinic in town and if a person could drag himself or be carried, that is where the person went. But if transportation to the clinic was impossible, Doc Rutger Van Bommel would be summoned; and he would go, drunk or sober, his condition being somewhat irrelevant since his diagnosis for anything except snakebites, cuts and broken bones was invariably the same. Doctor Van Bommel had correctly diagnosed cholera twenty years earlier in Peru. Since vomiting and diarrhea were symptomatic of but one disease according to his diagnostic acumen, his critics cited the global incidence of the disease and claimed that like a stopped clock, he was bound to be correct somewhere. Nevertheless, the good doctor rode his Peruvian triumph through every *taberna* from the Andes to the Amazon basin as far north as Suriname, stopping only when he encountered real *Jenever* Dutch gin and his own native language with which he could order it.

He came to the *Pink Dolphin*, examined his patients, and pronounced them both victims of cholera.

Within what she estimated to be half an hour, Olivia still could not move her muscles but she was able to breathe more deeply; and slowly, as the net rubbed the blindfold loose, she began to be able to focus her eyes. In an immobile panic, she began to realize that Jackel and Ananda were no longer being carried nearby. They had been separated from her. She was alone with her captors.

The dirt path ended and she saw that she was being carried on a paving stone surface. She heard a knock on a door and muffled voices as the door opened. She was carried inside and dropped onto the floor. Olivia lay helplessly as a woman who had open sores on her face and arms removed the net while two other women pulled off her shoes, slacks and underpants. They opened the front door to examine the slacks in bright light and were pleased to see that she had not urinated in them. Another woman with pocked skin carefully unbuttoned her blouse and removed it and her brassiere and handed the garments to the women who held the slacks. All the items were put on a hanger and taken into another room. A woman, Doña Elena, who was treated deferentially by the others, knelt beside Olivia and began to tug at her earlobes, removing her earrings which she dropped into an envelope. She removed Olivia's gold chain and cross, her watch, bracelet, and wedding ring, and put them into the same envelope. The women were speaking to each other in what Olivia guessed were two different languages, Spanish and Portuguese. At least three of the women had no front teeth and it was difficult to recognize syllables much less to grasp their meaning. Finally, one came and put a large metal collar around her neck. A padlock on one end of a chain was inserted through the collar's buckle and Olivia, naked, was picked up and tossed onto a bed. The other end of the chain was secured to a metal ring under the bed.

Dusk melted into dark, and soon someone struck a match and lit an oil lamp. Not until then did Olivia turn her head and see that she was not the only chained woman in the room. The curare's lingering effects were not severe but they did serve to make the sounds in the room seem like distant echoing murmurs. When the lamp was lit, she quickly became alert and could hear the other women whimpering, begging, and even praying. She raised her head up to see that there were two other beds. In one of them there was a girl who could not have been more than twelve - if that. In the other there was a woman with full pendulous breasts.

The half dozen working women, all who appeared to have pocked, blistered, or oddly scarred skin, moved freely throughout the building. They wore sarongs that were printed with tropical flowers. A corridor went back - how far she could not tell - but there were women in rooms accessed from that corridor. Olivia could hear the footsteps and their voices. She heard a few men laughing and she heard their lumbering footsteps as they passed her on their way out. They spoke, but Olivia could not understand the language. She knew where she was. It was a brothel, and the physical condition of the attendants admitted no other explanation: it was a brothel that catered to the diseased. Prayers and Biblical passages filled her mind. She had not cried once. Instead she silently begged for mercy.

Another woman entered the building. She was clean and hard, a blonde European of some kind. Her hair was braided and circled into a bun at the neckline. She had a long sleeved blouse on and yellow rubber gloves. Three of the women in sarongs backed away from her - but not from fear since they seemed to joke with each other. It could only be because the blonde woman would not risk contagion. Her right hand rested on the holster of the gun belt she wore; but the stance was more of a pose than an act of readiness. In her left hand she held a bag which she turned upside down, emptying many plastic packets of white powder into a bowl. The women counted the packets.

The blonde woman came to inspect Olivia. "*U bent nieuw,*" she said. Olivia understood that she had said something to the effect that Olivia was new. Then the woman pointed to the table and made a guttural laugh. "*Coca*" she said. "*Heden is donderdag. Enkel enkele mannen zullen komen. Morgen zullen vele mannen komen.*"

For the first time, the foreign words were spoken directly to her, and with the tone and gestures that are vital to comprehension. She now understood much of what the woman said. "Today," "Thursday." "men," "come," "tomorrow," "many," "men come." It made its unthinkable sense. The cocaine was for the busy weekend trade... for the men who didn't have to work the next morning. Friday and Saturday would be the busiest nights for these women.

The front door opened and a burly man entered. The blonde woman joked with him as he disrobed and was examined. She led him to Olivia's bed and Olivia could see the sores on his body. He put his knee on the bed and said something to the woman. Olivia's eyes opened wide with fear and she gasped, sucking in staccato segments of air that could not fill her lungs.

"Ah! Ah! Ah!" the blonde woman cautioned her and pointed to a ball gag that was hanging on the wall. Olivia swallowed her scream.

Silently she recited the 23rd Psalm.

Ananda and Jackel, their hands bound behind them, were taken to an upstairs room in the original stone building of the complex, the owner's residential wing of *Springer's Roadhouse*.

In the 1930's, a gentleman named Franz Springer who, in the western hemisphere at least, claimed to be related to the House of Orange, became president of an ornithology society that specialized in tropical birds. The society's office and collection point, a building that had been made in the native thatched roof "hut" style, had been blown apart during a "sibibusi" or violent "forest broom" rainstorm, resulting in the death of many valuable birds. Springer, distressed by this loss, went to the opposite extreme in construction and created a two storey fortress-like stone building. The walls were thick, the shutters strong, the diamond shaped glass panes of the casement windows mullioned in hard wood.

The society dissolved during World War II along with Springer's fortune. Franz favored the aspirations of the Third Reich to such a degree that he enthusiastically pledged what remained of his wealth to the *Wermacht*. That he later could be declared *persona non grata* by his own countrymen perplexed him even as it broke his heart. As a matter of necessity, the stone building became his residence and commercial address. He repaired to the odd shoe-box shaped stone building. Eventually he was joined by another relative, a great grandson, Reinhardt Springer, who had been dismissed from his school for infractions that were deemed unforgivable. Reinhardt, unfortunately, had not the slightest interest in feathered creatures beyond the price that people were willing to pay for them.

As time passed wooden additions to the original building provided accommodations for tourists and businessmen. When international treaties curtailed traffic in rare birds, his ornithology business ceased to be profitable. Old Franz Springer died, and Reinhardt, scion of the Springer clan, looked to the Roadhouse to provide the money he required to keep himself in an acceptable style of living. All that he had gained from his first-class education he put in the service of one unassailable truth: vice was profitable. The Roadhouse flourished in tandem with its unsavory reputation.

The market in hardwoods, herbs, mineral deposits, and tourism increased, and the roadhouse expanded. Inured, then, to supporting itself by any means necessary, the enterprise became a haven for poachers, fugitives, remittance men, gamblers, an assortment of adventurers in the flesh trade, as well as businessmen, scientists, and tourists. It was said that many sado-masochistic events were held in the fortress-like security of the owner's wing; but no one ever cared to try to prove it.

At the edge of a clearing, Ananda and Jackel were dumped onto the ground and rolled out of their nets. They were no longer blindfolded but they were still visually impaired. Men who wore leather boots picked them up and in a "fireman's carry" slung them over a shoulder and carried them into the "forbidden" stone building of what they now realized was Springer's residence. They were taken upstairs and, as soon as a special mat was laid on the floor, their hands were tied behind their backs and they were pushed down onto the mat. A man removed their shoes and placed two carpenter's "horses" at the edge of the mat. He left the room and Ananda and Jackel sat up. "We in Springer's house," Jackel said. Ananda looked around. "I always wondered what it looked like in here."

The room was strangely beautiful. All of the furnishings were made of shaped and polished hard woods or intricately woven wicker, upholstered with cloth made from coconut fibers, cotton, linen, and other plant materials. There were no animal pelts on the walls and no crude spears and shields of native warriors. Instead, the objects, all made of clay, stone, or other natural materials, bore a modern design and were expertly finished and polished. Several oil lamps had wide shades that were reminiscent of Tiffany leaded glass, except the seams or lead lines supported brightly colored bird feathers, artfully arranged. There was nothing "stuffed" in the furniture's upholstery that could get soaked and moldy; and even the large rug over which the mat had been placed, had been woven from many different plant fibers each of which created an element in the intricate Indian design. The decor was so organic that it gave the impression that if the ocean were to wash over it and then retreat, a week or a month later, the furniture might be moved about, but the sun and a few opened windows would restore the room to precisely the condition it had before the flood.

The door opened and men entered, carrying a metal-framed curtain partition of the type seen in hospitals - a temporary shield designed for visual privacy. They placed the curtain near the door and put a chair behind it.

Ananda's and Jackel's ankles were tied and a rope hoisted their feet to the top of the carpenter's horses.

The door opened again and someone entered the room and sat behind the curtain.

For the occasion, Springer had elected to speak with an electrolarynx voice changing apparatus. As he gave orders to his two workers, the device gave an unearthly monotone to his voice, a weird and sinister emotional indifference that terrified his prisoners.

"Gags and rods," the voice said. The workers went to the side of the room and from a chest withdrew two gags and two lengths of slim, hard, and flexible bamboo. As though they were testing sabers, they whipped the air with the bamboo, making the unique whooshing sound of air slicing.

Ananda asked, "Where is my wife? What have you done to her?" He was too frightened to realize that this was the first time in his life that he thought of someone else's well-being before he thought of his own.

The mechanical voice asked, "What were you doing in the miner's house?"

Instinctively, Ananda answered "Nothin'!" A metal cricket sounded once from behind the screen. The bamboo rod whipped across Ananda's feet as a boot pressed on his mouth, choking off his scream. A gag was then put into his mouth.

"Now, you, Jackel," said the hidden Reinhardt, "tell me what you, Ananda, and the woman were doing in the miner's house."

"We work a scam, that's all."

"A scam for what?"

"For the house."

"Why did you want the house? What did you plan to do with it?"

"Sell the house. That's all."

"To whom did you intend to sell the house?"

"To us."

"We are having trouble communicating, Jackel." Two clicks of the metal cricket were heard.

Immediately, Jackel's feet were whipped twice. He suppressed his cries of pain.

"Bastinado," said the voice. "It is a lovely word. Do not tell me that you planned to scam yourselves." He ordered the men, "Take the gag out of Moyer's mouth." Then he said quietly, "Moyer, who is the woman?"

"She's my wife. I married her just to get the money for the scam. She knows nothin' about it. I swear."

"Who has the money now?"

"It's in Georgetown, in a bank."

"How much is in the bank?"

"Eight hundred thousand dollars."

"Who put it there?"

"Jackel."

"Jackel? Jackel put eight hundred thousand dollars in a bank in Georgetown?" He hissed, "Gag!" Immediately the gag was shoved into Ananda's mouth and three clicks of the metal cricket were heard. Three times the bamboo thrashed the sensitive soles of his feet. Again the cricket sounded three times, and Jackel's feet were also thrashed.

"Put extra towels under the horses to protect the rug," Reinhardt Springer ordered his men. "Mr. Springer would not like blood to drip on this superb example of native craftsmanship."

"Tony deJong help me," Jackel answered. "We follow Henny Holman plan. We go together to Georgetown. We register new Wollenback company and open new bank account. I am resident agent. When checks come back from printer we go again and write checks."

"When will the checks be ready and who will sign them?"

"Tony figure April six or seven. Either one of us can sign checks."

"Can Holman sign checks?"

"I don't know. Tony give him papers when we got back. Tony stay up there extra day or two with Henny Holman, but I come back here."

Springer had to think. He could accompany Jackel to the bank and get him to write the checks to Reinhardt Springer... yes... in payment of a gambling debt. But Tony deJong could sign checks. And for all he knew Hendrik Holman also was a signatory. Maybe the date of April 6th was a lie. "When did you open the account?"

"We start account on Monday and come back on Wednesday to finish paperwork. We ordered checks then. It was March 23rd, I think. They say it take time for new style check printing... minimum of two weeks."

"Where is Tony now?"

"I hear he is sick... Rubem too. Cholera. They at Jack's place."

Ah, Springer thought. So that was it. Jack Donovan was trying to steal the money, too. He was keeping Tony deJong there until the checks were ready.

The interrogation continued. Reinhardt learned the identity and function of all four original members of the con. Finally, Reinhardt grew tired. He wanted one more piece of information.

"Moyer, who is the church man who has been calling you?"

"I haven't talked to him. I'm not sure."

"Who is deVries?" he demanded.

"He was a priest at the prison I was in."

"Why is deVries calling you?"

"I don't know why Father deVries would call me. The only church man I had anythin' to do with was Deacon Faber. He had big plans for me... a scheme to get my wife's money."

"Why do you think that?" asked Reinhardt in his mysterious voice. "Do you think Faber is a swindler?"

For a terrible moment Ananda thought that perhaps the man with the changed mechanical voice might be Faber himself. He began to whimper. "I don't know. I don't know. Please, just tell me where my wife is. Please... is she all right?"

No one answered him. Kaza stepped behind the screen and whispered to Springer, "There's a new guy staying at Jack's. He dresses like a cowboy and he speaks Dutch."

Springer nodded and directed Kaza to follow him out into the hall. "That cowboy must be deVries," he said. "How many assholes can this stupid con hold? Well, we might be needing Jackel to walk into the bank next Wednesday, so tell the men not to hit his feet anymore. Leave them both here and make sure they're gagged properly."

It was nearly one o'clock before Jan Osterhaus arrived at the Tropical Haven. Beryl and Sensei were waiting for him on the patio. "We haven't had lunch yet," she said. "We thought we ought to wait for you. Are you hungry?"

"As a matter of fact I am. I've been trying to get everything re-arranged in my office so that I can take this time off without everything coming unglued."

Sensei signaled a waiter.

"After we have lunch, we can go to the Martial Arts' Supply place. I called the Chapel and asked Mr. Thompson to email both you and me the photo file of the Moyer/Mallard wedding. I used the email address that was on your card."

"That's fine," Beryl said. "They'll go to my office."

"I've got them in my phone. As long as we're here in the city with good reception, I'll send you the file."

Beryl gave him her iPhone address. He leaned towards her and said, "Now you have my personal address. Never hesitate to use it." He turned to Sensei. "You'll like the martial arts' store and dojo. They sell knives, but no guns. I doubt that we'll be needing guns."

Sensei wasn't so sure. "We can only hope."

After lunch, Osterhaus escorted them to his Land Rover and headed for the store. He drove down a wide street and then turned onto a smaller one and finally parked in front of an impressive old style Japanese building.

They entered the shop and a uniformed clerk pulled back a shoji screen to greet them. He stared at Sensei. "May I help you?" he asked.

"What a beautiful dojo!" Sensei murmured as he admired the building's interior.

The clerk suddenly recognized Sensei. He smiled, "Thank you, Master Wong."

"This country is filled with surprises," Beryl noted.

"Yes," the clerk said, "we often surprise even the most famous of karate masters."

As if on cue the shoji screen opened again and a mature man dressed in a blue kimono entered the room. The only identifying mark on him was the 'three hollyhock' mon of the Tokugawa shogunate that had been embroidered in gold thread on his garment's right shoulder. The top of his head had been shaved in the old *Chonmage* samurai hairstyle, and the sides had been pulled back and knotted. The man and Sensei bowed deeply to each other.

"Who would have thought it?" the man exclaimed. "The Chinese master of karate-do here with us. He clapped his hands. "We met in Osaka years ago. You visited Soke Hayashi for katana and sword... some tonfa... I can't remember the karate, but I definitely recall your skill with a sword."

"You are too kind," Sensei said simply. He gestured towards Beryl and Jan. "May I present my companions, Miss Tilson and Captain Osterhaus." The master bowed deeply. Beryl nudged Jan and then she put one foot behind the other - which Jan thought he was supposed to copy and did likewise until he realized that she was going to curtsy. Then he stopped and looked down at her, his face registering the question, "What the hell is going on?"

Master Nakayama was still addressing Sensei. "Your demonstration of straw-cutting at the tournament in Fukuoka was wonderful. Such clean cuts! Such footwork! The newspapers called you 'The Dharma Sword!' And here you are today!"

Sensei didn't recognize or remember Nakayama, but he smiled, bowed, and said, "I am undeserving of such praise."

Nakayama returned the bow. "Please come into my office, Master." He slid the shoji screen open and led Sensei back into a room in which dozens of high quality weapons were displayed. The clerk bowed slightly to Jan and Beryl and followed the two men into the office, quickly shutting the shoji screen behind.

Jan and Beryl stood alone in the shop, feeling strangely invisible. Jan said, "What are we? The porters on this safari?"

Beryl began to giggle. "Bring water, *Gunga Din*!"

Osterhaus began his impression of Edwardo Ciannelli as the Thuggee priest, "Kali... Kali... Kali..."

They looked at each other and without realizing that it was the chemical attraction they felt for each other that was making them giddy, they struggled to stifle an outburst of laughter until the urge became uncontrollable. Jan opened the door that led to the street; and the two of them, bent over and giggling hysterically, escaped to the pavement. When they stopped laughing, Jan asked, "Who is Sensei? I wondered when you called him your master. Is he some sort of martial arts star?"

"Yes," Beryl said, still gasping for breath, "but not in the way you might think. He'll be mad as hell when he gets out of there. Watch."

Jan put his arm around her waist and pulled her along the pavement until they came to the street corner and could sit on some steps. "Ok," he said. "I surrender. Why is Wong special? And you call him your master? What am I missing?"

Beryl laughed again, "He's known for two reasons: first, because he's of Chinese descent and yet he practices Karate and though he was ordained in a Chinese order, he follows the Japanese liturgy. That makes him unusual and therefore, newsworthy. Second, he can get into a trance-like state when he's on the mat or in competition. It's called 'Wu wei' and he had mastered it before he even started to learn karate. It's 'actionless action.' Action performed subliminally. No ego. Archers or any martial arts' practitioners will train for years to acquire it. Anyway, Sensei is both my karate teacher and my Zen priest. I belong to his temple sangha."

"All right. Wong is Chinese. Why not Gong Fu?"

"He was rebelling against his Chinese father. He started out doing yoga and meditation, and in college he became good enough in fencing and gymnastics to be a varsity team member. Do you know how some oriental men push their wives around? Well, even though they lived in the States, his father was a tyrannical Chinese husband. Sensei adored his mom and as soon as he was old enough to stick-it to the old man, he began to favor 'Nippon" in everything he did. It really got the old man's goat. Karate never had a more enthusiastic student.

"After he won a few tournaments some public relations' people made him a celebrity. He decided to stay home and teach, preach, and dabble in private investigation."

"I never thought my life was boring, until this week," Jan sighed. "How am I going to survive without these surprises?" Arm in arm, they returned to the shop.

Sensei finally emerged from the back room, carrying two boxes that contained the knives he had selected. "Wakizashis," he said to Beryl. "These are really wonderful weapons. It will be a crime to use them. The belts and scabbards are also first rate."

Jan stepped forward and thrust his credit card on the counter. "Allow me," he said. The clerk swiped the card and handed Jan the receipt to sign. He did not look at the amount as he signed his name. Instead he looked at Beryl who smiled sweetly and whispered, "You do know that you may have pledged your firstborn son."

Jan looked at the amount. "I hope that's not U.S. dollars," he said. He bowed and walked to the door.

Nakayama bowed to Sensei. *"Arigato…dozo arigato goziamasta, Sensei."*

Outside, Beryl said, "You have to let Sensei reimburse you for those knives. Otherwise, I'll be blamed for distracting you or embarrassing you into using your credit card."

"We'll see," Jan said. "Maybe I'll give you yours as 'a token of my affection' or something to remember me by."

"A sharp knife? Darling, you care!"

They got into the Land Rover and buckled their seat belts. Sensei was angry. "Great knives, but what a load of bullshit comes with them. If I were Japanese, nobody would know my name. Next time let's just go to a sporting goods store."

FRIDAY, APRIL 1, 2011

Beryl packed her *Swamptec* garments in her backpack and wore jeans and a western shirt as she and Sensei, who carried the boxed knives, went out to meet Captain Jan Osterhaus.

At the airport, Jan parked the Land Rover and the three of them walked towards the row of offices occupied by small airline companies. Near the hangar, Tom Kenyon stood outside his Cessna, overseeing the loading of cargo into the fuselage. Jan called, "Kenyon! I think we're your noon fares to Cajana."

"Hop aboard. We'll be on our way in another fifteen minutes." He signed the freight handler's manifest.

"I've got a question," Jan said. "What can you tell me about an American lady named Olivia Mallard Moyer and a local guy named Ananda Moyer."

"I took them down to Cajana yesterday. They're still there. Is there a problem? Something's goin' on. She asked me about a mining company I never heard of. She said that it was a mile down the creek road, and I said, 'Oh, you mean Granger's.' And she got a funny look on her face. Scared."

"Did you notice anything else?"

"No... but they were down last week, too. Henny Holman took them down and back. They were with Jackel Mazumi - the native who created quite a stir with his new hairstyle and manicured fingernails. Yeah, they got somethin' goin' on. Tony deJong is involved in it, too."

Jan acted as a tour guide pointing out places of interest as they flew over them. When they were airborne and still over the city, he asked, "Did you know that the first synagogue in the Western Hemisphere was built here in Suriname?"

"I had no idea," she said.

"I'm pointing out our cultural features... the genteel side of life... to prepare you for the dark side, the soft underbelly we'll likely find in the outposts."

"Jan... as we say in Zen, 'Folks is folks.' All the nice farms look like Amish country in Pennsylvania. Everything is so clean and neat. The Lake is beautiful."

"Berg En Dal is a really nice resort. I'll have to take you there for a weekend jaunt. Pick a date."

Beryl laughed. "Have your girl call my girl."

They followed the course of the Suriname River as it led through the rainforest and turned slightly west towards the interior and split into its tributaries, and soon they passed over a cleft in the green carpet. "That's *Springer's Roadhouse,*" Jan said. "A creek runs alongside it. It's actually a mile back from the Gran Rio, but Springer keeps motor canoes at the dock to shuttle the patrons back and forth if they don't have their own canoes." Cajana was in sight. "*Jack's Pink Dolphin* is on the other side of town, same side of the river as *Springer's*. Granger's is on that side too."

By noon, the staff of *Springer's* knew about the two prisoners upstairs in the stone wing. The boy who worked for Kaza was the first to learn of it; and when he talked to two of Jackel's sons and learned that their father was missing, the conclusion was inescapable: Jackel was one of the two men.

Jackel's wife Lola spoke to one of the cleaning girls and she, in turn, went to Kaza Ross and said that guests would probably be coming between Passover and Easter, and if the men in that room vomited, urinated, defecated, or perhaps even died and were left until some decomposition occurred, no one could rid the place of the stench before the guests arrived. Kaza told the girl to go back to work and then knocked on Springer's door.

"What do you want?" Springer asked as if he were dying of ennui.

"How about if we move those two birds outside to the dog shed. We can secure them there until you're finished with 'em. You don't want them stinking up your rooms."

"Yes! Get them out of my domicile."

In a few minutes, several men dragged Ananda and Jackel to an outdoor shed, the former residence of two now-deceased guard dogs. Their hands were bound behind them and their feet were so lacerated that they could not have walked away no matter where they had been put. A padlock was brought to the shed and the door was locked.

The dog shed, made from planks of cheap tropical pine, had many knotholes in its sides. Silently a long reed slid through one of the knotholes until it poked the back of Jackel's head. He turned and a trickle of water came down the tube and into his mouth. He drank for a couple of minutes. Then he put his head down as far as he could and the tube extended into Ananda's mouth. Jackel's son had brought them water.

Sensei, Beryl, and Jan checked into the Vandermeer Lodge in Cajana. The only room available in the central building contained two queen-sized beds. They still hadn't eaten lunch and it was after two o'clock.

Jan and Sensei dropped their gear onto their bed. "Why don't we confine our search today to a trip to the Granger place," Jan suggested. "It's getting too late to try to fight the bush. Most of the creatures we have to worry about are nocturnal. We can eat and still have plenty of light to get out to the mysterious mining house and have a look around. I don't think we need weapons."

"Will we encounter swampland?" Beryl asked.

"Miss City Girl," Jan teased, "you are in the general area of the Amazonian rainforest, and it is the rainy season. Where won't you encounter swampland is a better question."

Beryl told him that she would then change her clothes while they went to the restaurant's screened veranda to order lunch and have a few cold beers. "I'll be back in ten minutes."

Jan reviewed the menu with Sensei, explaining the various dishes. Finally, they decided to get the waiter's advice. "What do you recommend?" Jan asked.

"We've had good comments about today's chicken masala and vegetables."

Sensei nodded approval. "All right," Jan said. "Give us three orders... with some peppers. And two more Heinekens and a Coke for the lady."

Beryl, appearing in her *Swamptec* "ensemble," was greeted with laughter.

Sensei whistled and slapped the table. "I am not the father!" he shouted. "I demand a DNA test."

Jan put his head back and laughed. "And don't look at me! What is the e.t.a? I've got an alibi. I was fishing in the Zuider Zee nine months before that."

Beryl stood there with her hands on her hips. "And I thought you liked plump women."

"Did we order enough food?" Sensei asked. "She may be eating for two."

Beryl, glad that the two of them were getting along so well, pretended to be insulted.

When the waiter brought their food, Jan asked, "Have you heard any rumors lately about a plantation style house for sale... a place that is really Granger's? Or anything unusual about Ananda Moyer or his wife? And what about Hendrik Holman, Tony deJong, or Jackel Mazumi?"

"That's a tall order," the waiter responded.

"Pick anyplace you want and start there."

"Tony deJong is supposed to have cholera. Let's just say he and Rubem up at *Jack's Pink Dolphin* are both very sick. Ananda and Jackel Mazumi are supposed to be at Springer's place, tied up in a dog shed, if you can believe that. I don't know where Henny Holman is."

"What about Moyer's wife?"

"I really don't want to repeat that rumor."

"I'm not going to quote you. It's important. What rumor?"

The waiter hesitated for a long minute as he stared at the river. "All right. I heard she's at the Annex."

Jan squinted. "What Annex? Is that the whorehouse for people with sexually transmitted diseases?"

"Yes."

"Jesus! I was hoping that the rumors about that place were some kind of urban legend. How do we get to the Annex?"

"Nobody respectable will admit to knowing the way there. But tonight when the working guys come into the bar, you can shoot darts and get friendly. Maybe somebody can give you directions. Just don't wear your uniform and leave the lady back in the room."

"If she's not here and she's not with her husband," Beryl said, "it may not be so crazy."

"Well," the waiter countered, "what we heard was that the Yanomami Indians captured Moyer, his wife, and Jackel. There are no Yanomami Indians around here. Springer has a few renegades that he calls his 'Yanos.' They do favors for him and he lets them hunt on his land. There's always so much exaggeration with everything that happens around here."

"Where did they capture the three of them?" Beryl asked.

"I don't know. Moyer and his wife came down yesterday to look at the Granger place and that's the last anybody around here saw 'em."

"Granger Mining is legitimate," Jan said. "They sure as hell don't have anything to do with Springer. We'll have time to walk back there and see if their resident manager can give us some direction."

Beryl stood up. "If Olivia is possibly in that kind of trouble, we shouldn't delay."

Jan paid the check. "If we come up empty at Grangers, Sensei and I can do some barroom snooping tonight. And you can behave yourself, alone in the room. No hissy fits. Promise?"

Olivia Moyer awakened on Friday morning barely able to see. She had been slapped so severely during the night that her eyes were badly swollen. Her nostrils were stuck together with dried blood. Her wrists were still tied to the headboard and her ankles were lacerated. They were not bound now, but she vaguely remembered that they had been tied during the night.

All through the night she had heard the woman with the pendulous breasts weep and cry a singular word that Olivia could not understand. It was like the pathetic whimpering of a dog.

Towards dawn, a Chinese man who had been with a woman in one of the back rooms, stopped to snort a line of cocaine on his way out. He sat on the edge of Olivia's bed. He whispered, "You from England?"

"No," she answered, "The U.S. Where am I?"

"You in Annex. *Springer's Annex*. Dirty girl annex."

She groaned. "What does that woman who's crying keep saying?"

"She call baby's name. Most women here speak Spanish or Portuguese. She speak Portuguese. Every day two, three men come suck tits. She make lots milk. *Springer's* give her soy milk. You know soy milk?"

"Yes. Have you heard anything about two men who were captured when I was?"

"No... I not welcome in Roadhouse. I hear nothing. You get sleep. You got bad eyes."

"Can you get me water? They let us have water."

He got up and brought a bottle of water to her mouth and held her head up so that she could drink it.

"When will you be back?" she asked him.

"I come Thursday night. That's all. I see you next Thursday night."

"My husband's name is Ananda. If you hear anything about him, please let me know."

"Ok. You go sleep now. Nobody in line. You get sleep." He opened the door and went out into the morning sun.

She thought that he was the kindest man she had ever met. She had entered an altered reality and her judgments changed accordingly. Olivia was the newest citizen in Reinhardt Springer's hell.

The water she had been given relieved some of the physical tension she had been experiencing, and the futility of crying depressed even her ability to think. She quickly fell asleep vaguely aware that her legs had open wounds and that her ankles were bleeding.

At eleven o'clock in the morning, the padlock that held Olivia's chain to the floor was unlocked, and one of the women who spoke English told her to do as some of the others were doing and remove the sheets and the two pillow cases from her bed. Those who had been issued long white dresses to wear to wear as protection against mosquitos added these soiled garments to the laundry.

Women carried their laundry into the courtyard. The dresses and bed linens, each with its bed-number written on it in indelible ink, had to be washed by the woman who had used them. A row of six washtubs had been placed under an awning; and old-fashioned washboards and naptha soap had been placed inside the tubs. Each woman placed her dirty laundry in the tub and knelt to complete an initial scrubbing. When she was finished, she took the laundry to a large tub that contained detergent and bleach and let it soak while she went to bathe, shampoo her hair, and get rinsed off by a forceful hosing. The remaining group of women would come out to repeat the same routine.

After the women completed this phase of the daily cleansing, they put on fresh long-sleeved, full-length white cotton dresses and sat on several rows of benches under a different awning and helped themselves to coffee, pastry, fruit, and protein and nut bars. Olivia was astonished to see and hear the women laugh and talk as though this were a coffee klatch anywhere in the western world. However bizarre the routine was, it had become to them a normal occurrence.

When they finished breakfast, they took off their white dresses, folded and laid them on the benches, and went to the big soaking tub to remove their numbered laundry, place the pieces in net bags, and carry them to a small waterfall at the rear of the property for rinsing. A short chain link fence ran along the far side of the stream, preventing caiman from sliding down the bank into the water. Another chain link fence with a gate protected the courtyard on the brothel side of the waterway. During the laundering period, neither fish nor caiman entered the area beneath the waterfall since the water contained so much detergent and chlorine. It was safe for the women to enter.

In sunny weather, the bed linens were hung outside on clotheslines. In rain, the sheets were hung in a small shed that contained a stove. In either case, the women would remove a second set of numbered linens from a closet and go to re-dress their beds. If no one was waiting for service, the women returned to the yard, put their white dresses on, and sat around drinking coffee and chatting.

Olivia performed the routine and was given a white dress. When it was time to go outside again and sit in the sun, she began to speak to a woman from Guyana who spoke English.

To her surprise, four of the washtubs were now being used by men. The girls joked with some of them. "Where do they keep the men?" Olivia asked her companion.

"The long building beside us is just for women. But that building down there by the creek is for men. Two of the men are like female slaves," she explained, "and the other two are like macho masters. They do a lot of business. Mr. Springer says that there are half as many men, but they do twice as much business. They can entertain with wine and canapés."

Olivia nodded. "Oh… I guess that's why."

"You're still in front... new... But you'll graduate to your own room in a week or so. They'll take your collar off by then. Just be sure you don't get on anyone's wrong side. Doña Elena will have you put in a contraption they use for whipping and let the attendants teach you a lesson you won't forget."

"Is Doña Elena the blonde woman?"

"No, that's Greta. She's Springer's assistant. She's a boss." She looked around. "That's Doña Elena," she said, pointing to a dark haired woman who wore a caftan.

"Oh," Olivia said, glancing at the woman and then turning her attention to the men at the washtubs. "Their building isn't connected to ours," she said. Then she suddenly realized that she had made a casual observation. "My God!' she said. "I'm talking about this nightmare as if it's a perfectly normal place."

"Yes," her companion noted, "that's how it goes. You wake up in Hell and then you look around and see that the only friends you've got are also in Hell. This is your new normal."

"How many men and women are trapped in here?"

"Nobody's sure. I think it varies. When we're done with the laundry, the men come out and do the same. Usually there are four or six men and ten or twelve girls. The turnover is terrible." She did not say why the turnover was so high, and Olivia did not want to ask her.

"You can't see it from here," the girl said, "but at the very back is a sick room, 'The Sick Shed.' That's where you're taken when you've got a fever or something. A nurse comes and examines you."

On one side of the courtyard, bright yellow bulldozers were positioned in front of a rocky outcrop that had been painted. About ten meters of railroad track ran up to one large painted rock. Olivia could see that beneath the topcoat of yellow paint the bulldozers were useless and broken. "What are those bulldozers for?"

"For planes that fly over. The rocks are painted to look like a mine opening and the railroad tracks are supposed to look like those dumpsters ride the rails in and out of the mine. The heavy equipment makes the place look like a mining site. That's why nobody knows we're here. If you hear the sound of an airplane engine, you'd better get your ass under the awning quick, or it's the whip for you."

Soon the girl began to speak with pride about the cleanliness of Springer's Annex. Olivia learned that Doña Elena saw to it that no client brought crabs, lice, bed bugs, ticks, or parasitic infestations onto the premises. "It's bad enough," the girl said in her glowing review, "to be a victim of disease. You don't want crabs on top of it. We set a high bar here for cleanliness."

She also confided to Olivia that nobody with AIDS was allowed in the Annex. "There are independent houses somewhere in the bush that service AIDS people. Thank God."

"What happens if someone runs away?" Olivia asked.

The girl knew only that the one time anyone had tried this, a tattoo machine was employed to decorate the runner's face and neck with obscene expressions. "Besides," she said, "the girls are all city girls. Most of Springer's men are natives, and if they don't catch you, a snake, croc, or spider will."

"Things are different in the big Roadhouse. There," she said with some resentment, "the girls are well-paid. They get their hair styled and their nails manicured, and they wear make-up. A real doctor examines them once a week... not like here."

Their conversation was interrupted by Doña Elena, who ordered the end of the lunch and laundry break. Some of the women who had been up all night along with the three newcomers who had not yet earned yard privileges went inside. The rest of the women remained to chat amiably.

Olivia had not known that such a place as the Annex existed. There was so much she did not know. She did not know why she had been "delivered into such evil hands," or why she had allowed herself to be duped so cruelly in her attempt to preach the Word of God. What had happened to her husband? There was only one faint light in the abysmal darkness. She had seen the unmistakable look of fear on his face. Whatever his involvement in the fraud had been, he was not involved in her present predicament.

She prayed that he was safe. She also prayed for her own salvation, for the salvation of the other women, and for Providence's prompt intervention.

Chico Chavez hurried into Kaza Ross's office. "Head's up! There's an NBI officer who just checked into the Vandermeer. He's got a woman and another guy with him. They've been asking questions about everybody involved in that Granger con."

"Have one of the cleanin' girls go up to Mr. Springer's rooms and make sure there's no trace of Moyer or Mazumi. The boss may want to entertain the NBI officer up in his rooms."

Jack Donovan and Samuel Faber had just returned from overseeing the placement of furniture in the mill house when they heard a motor canoe approach. As they walked to the *Pink Dolphin's* landing, the canoe stopped, and one of the two native men who occupied it jumped out and rushed to tell them the news.

"Springer has got Jackel and Nandy Moyer locked up in a dog shed."

"Where?"

"Behind Springer's place."

"How long have they been there?"

"Somebody say they was put there this afternoon. They got bad beaten feet. All cut up."

"Who's guarding them?"

"Nobody. That's a metal roof on that shed. They gonna fry in there. Jackel's boy been given 'em water."

"Is the shed locked?"

"Yeah. It gotta' padlock on the door."

Donovan told them to wait. He signaled Faber to follow him to a short flight of stairs that led from the landing up to the roadhouse. "Let's sit down and do some serious talking."

Faber sat down and nodded. "I think I know what you want to talk about. How far are we prepared to go to solve the problem of the two sick birds upstairs?"

"Exactly. Sam, I wish I could think of another way, but I can't. You're the guy with problem solving skills - with insight. Can you think of another way?"

"From what you told me about the way you learned about the scam, Rubem can't keep his mouth shut. And you know what he'll do if Tony tells him he was cheated out of his $200K."

"Yeah, he won't believe it and he'll sing like a canary. How are we going to handle it?"

"I've thought about it. Is it possible that you can say that Doc Von Bommel's treatment made them worse and you happened to get a call asking about room rates or something business like... not a friend or anyone you knew well. And the caller was a pontoon helicopter pilot, parked on the river farther south from here, at some settlement. He was Brazilian - like your singer - and you told him that you had a couple of men, a Brazilian and another guy, who were in desperate need of hospital care, and you'd be willing to pay double for the flight to Manaus. The guy said that he was contracted exclusively to a company - but that he could use the extra money if you kept it quiet. So to keep him out of view, you and I carried deJong and Rubem down to the river in one of your motor canoes and delivered them to him someplace between here and Awarradam. We helped put them in his chopper. You paid him and that's all we know. How does that sound?"

"Fantastic. Perfect. That's why we don't know his name. And naturally I didn't want to use any of my workers because of the contagion. You and I were already exposed. What's our next move?"

"Give them some kind of knock-out drops."

"Right. Right. I've got ketamine, GHB, chloral hydrate, Rohypnol... a bunch of stuff."

"Use whatever you think is best. When they're asleep, we can carry them down, and when we get them upstream in some quiet place, we can feed the fishes."

"Sam, you're a genius. Let's get started."

"But first, Jack, you've got to be sure you have a copy of Tony's signature that you can use. You not only have to look like him at the bank, you've got to write like him. Do you have his signature anywhere?"

"Bar tabs! Casino markers! But let me look right now and make sure that I've got good specimens. You tell the boatmen they can go. Give 'em a few bucks for the information."

Donovan thought that if this were not a criminal matter it would make a great entry into his wisdom collection... something along the lines of "Look before you leap." His whole attitude toward Faber was changing. Here was a guy who had something to offer. He had a good brain."

Faber paid the boatmen. "Keep up the good work," he said. "We appreciate it."

Donovan gathered five samples of Tony's signature, placed them under his desktop blotter, and casually went into Tony and Rubem's bedroom to inquire about their health. "I was gonna bring you some herbal tea, but you're looking better. You're supposed to take a lot of fluids. What can I bring you?"

Both wanted gin and tonic with lots of lime. "Gus is busy at the bar. I'll get it myself."

Jack went to the bar and made the spiked drinks. After he served them, he put a DVD movie into the player and told them both to relax deeply and try to get some sleep. "The crisis is over."

Half an hour later, Donovan and Faber entered the bedroom to check on the two unconscious men. "Find deJong's driver's license and passport. You'll need them," Faber said.

Donovan looked in a bedside table drawer. "Everything's here." He opened the passport. "Uh, oh. He doesn't have a beard in this photo!"

"Neither do you," Faber said. "And since you can't grow one in two days, you can just say you shaved it off when you're at the bank - in case you don't get to deal with the clerk's replacement. Just keep the rest of your hair brown."

"But I stole a blonde wig!"

"So, rinse it with coffee. That's what he probably did."

"Sam, what would I do without you? Come on, let's wrap up these two and get them onto stretchers and carry then out to my motorboat."

Steering against the current, Donovan moved the boat through the midline of the Gran Rio and approached Awarradam, a few miles south of Cajana. He cut the motor and dropped anchor.

Simultaneously they each slipped a wire noose around a victim and tightened the noose, chatting with each other about the best time to fish for piranha. Under the blankets, they removed the clothing and jewelry from the dead men. Faber carefully lowered Tony deJong's naked body over the side and held him by his hair until Donovan could cut him. Then Faber released him and he slipped beneath the surface. Immediately Rubem, too, was lowered over the side, held, cut, and released.

They held their breath and watched as the water began to roil violently in the feeding frenzy.

When it subsided, Donovan said, "Sam, we've lessened the criminal element around here. We've got to think of it that way."

Reinhardt Springer's 'Yanos' had been alerted to the motor-canoe's presence on the stream that ran to Granger's landing. They got their blowguns, darts, knives, and nets and set off to see if the strangers looked suspicious. They watched as the boat tied up at Granger's, and two men and a woman walked up to the house.

Jan knocked at the door. Leighton answered and immediately recognized the uniform. "When trouble comes, it comes," he said. "I see that even the National Bureau of Investigation is interested in the phony sale of our building. I'm Leighton, the chief engineer."

"Do you have a few minutes to answer questions?" Leighton held the door wide and asked them to come in. Jan made the introductions. "Anything unusual happen lately?" he joked.

Leighton could not give much information. "All I know is that today Jackel didn't bring me any fish. I asked some of the native workers and they said that the Yanos got him. But they blame the Yanos for everything."

"What about the people who were swindled?"

"Yesterday around 1 p.m., a man and his wife were here. Jackel wasn't with them when they first knocked, but he arrived immediately after. He left his basket of fish on the porch. After I told the woman that she had been cheated, the three of them - she, her husband, and Jackel - ran in the opposite direction, not back to Cajana. I don't know why they went that way. One of the miners said there's a bridge across the creek up there about a mile."

Jan looked puzzled. "I don't know what's up there, but there's one way to find out. Thanks for your time, Leighton."

They returned to the boat and asked to be taken up to the rope bridge. "I can't do that," the boatman said uneasily, "cause there's a bunch of big rocks stickin' out the water."

Jan spoke to him in an authoritative voice that intimidated the man. "You can take us up to the rocks. We won't be long. You'll be well paid."

"I'll take ya' as far as I can. About thirty meters above the big rocks is where the bridge is. People can cross on stones in the dry season."

They followed the stream west and did not see that in the shadows on the north side of the river, Springer's "Yanos" were silently keeping pace with them.

Since the north side of the stream was filled with jagged rocks, they had to climb up onto the south side bank, which meant that they had to use the bridge to cross to the north side. Jan asked the boatman to wait.

At the rope bridge, they saw immediately that there was nothing on the south side that could possibly have been Olivia's destination. They looked at the bridge and had to make a decision. "This bridge looks too flimsy to support a grown man," Jan noted.

Sensei agreed. "I think it would also sway."

Jan twisted the hand woven hemp cables. "And those ropes look frayed."

"No engineer designed this," Sensei said.

"And the stepping stones are too far below the surface," Jan estimated. "The algae on them looks slippery."

The discussion irritated Beryl. "Olivia came this way and the only thing that's up there is this bridge. I'm not waiting while you guys circle-jerk. *The Annex? Have you forgotten the Annex?*" She jumped into the water, electing to walk across the stony bottom of the water since the stepping stones were, as Jan noted, filled with green slime that waved like long hair in the current.

Beryl's *Swamptec* wading boots performed as promised. She walked with slow deliberation across the current and climbed onto the opposite bank. "You can try parting it like the Red Sea," she taunted, "and after that doesn't work, maybe you can walk across it without getting your shoes wet."

Five feet behind her, standing erect with his blowgun and net slung over his shoulder, a native warrior stood behind a tall shrub.

"We can do without the sarcasm," Sensei shouted as he and Jan emptied their pants' pockets to put their money and papers into what they hoped would be dry shirt pockets. They descended into the stream.

Only one path led away from the creek. They followed it. Beryl smelled something cooking. Jan could only say that it wasn't the smell of palm nuts. "There's still plenty of light and we're apparently nearing somebody's residence," Sensei noted.

"Please, God," Beryl whimpered, "Let her be safe in there."

They continued to follow the path north. Beryl was in the lead. Sensei and Jan, walking side by side, followed. Suddenly a dart struck her in her left hip and glanced off into the path.

"Get down!" Jan shouted. Sensei instantly slid beside Beryl, pulling her down.

"I've been hit!" Jan shouted, as he pulled a dart out of his leg. "Are you ok?"

Beryl wanted to ask what was happening, but Sensei saw men moving towards them and he put his hand over her mouth.

"It's curare," Jan whispered. "And I hope that's all it is. Do CPR on me if I stop breathing–" he stopped speaking as he, too, saw the men approach. As if in slow motion, he collapsed onto the ground and slipped into an open-eyed paralysis.

Three natives, each carrying a nearly two meter long blowgun, emerged from the bushes. Beryl and Sensei remained motionless, while Sensei furtively looked to see if they were carrying other weapons. He knew that since the blowgun's indispensable feature is its straightness, no native would risk damaging the shaft.

Not knowing how many men were in the attacking group, Sensei lay still, as though he were stricken. Beryl followed his lead and also did not move.

The senior member of the group poked Sensei with his blowgun and grunted, indicating that he doubted that Sensei was really stricken. He loaded another dart and lifted the blowgun to his mouth, pointing it at Sensei, preparing to shoot. Instantly, Sensei grabbed the blowgun, fiercely thrusting the mouthpiece back into the man's mouth and throat, hurling him backwards as pieces of broken teeth shot out and scattered on the ground. Sensei was now on his feet. Beryl jumped up, too, and aimed a frontal kick at the second man's groin. He had carried a net across his left shoulder and arm, and as he bent forward from the kick, the net slid down his arm. Since the blowgun was useless in hand to hand combat, he dropped it and tried to reach for his belt-knife. The net had covered the knife's sheath and Beryl had the advantage. She pronged his eyes with her index and middle fingers and he stumbled, screaming into the jungle. The third warrior had pulled off his net and was swinging it around in the air like pizza dough.

Sensei still had the blowgun in his hands and could wield it as a weapon. It was longer than the kettukari with which he had the most experience, but the principles were the same. He stepped back, adjusted to the new length and, as the warrior hurled the net towards Beryl, he hooked the net, scooping it out of the air.

The man drew his knife and ran towards Beryl with his right arm raised intending to stab her. She reached up and blocked his arm with her left forearm and then jammed her left elbow into his armpit. She struck his chin with the heel of her right hand and grabbed his right wrist, pulling it forward and twisting it until he dropped the knife and stumbled onto the ground. He pulled his wrist free and stretched out to put his hand on the knife he had dropped. With his weight on his right hand, he began to push himself up, and Beryl was able to grab his left wrist and using both hands, twisted it until he was forced flat on the ground. She kicked his head, hoping that she would knock him unconscious; but his head snapped back and he was still holding the knife. He screamed at her as he adroitly jumped into a squatting position and then lunged up at her, trying to tackle her to the ground. She sidestepped his thrust and with a flat hand "knife" strike, she sliced at his neck. He fell and she conformed her hand into a mid-knuckle hammer and punched him hard at the base of his head. He gurgled in a strange way, until she pulled the knife from his hand and buried it into the back of his neck. She stood up and looked around for another assailant.

The first warrior, blood streaming from his mouth, had gotten to his feet and began to scream a war cry at Sensei as he drew his knife and ran towards him. Sensei, using the blowgun as a pike, pointed it into the man's chest. The man made a great "Uuf" sound as the wind was knocked out of him. Yet, he still grappled for the blowgun. Sensei hopped backwards pulling the man off balance. As he stumbled forwards, his chest met the punch of Sensei's knee which knocked the wind out of him again. He bent forward, dropped the knife, and began whooping for breath. Sensei conformed his hand into a blade with which he struck his neck, dropping him to the ground. With the heel of his hand he punched him between his shoulder blades and then grabbed his head and twisted it, breaking his neck as a *coup de grace.*

He looked around to see if anyone else was in the raiding party.

"We've got to make a stretcher for Jan," Beryl yelled.

They placed two nets, one on top of the other on the ground, and lay two blowguns lengthwise three feet apart. They folded the nets over the poles, creating a stretcher, and lay Jan on top of it. Beryl put her *Swamptec* hat over his eyes, and then she stooped so that Sensei could put the poles on her shoulders. He picked up the poles at other end and they both slowly stood.

Carrying Jan as evenly as possible, they did a double time step, carrying him back to the river. The boatman was gone.

Beryl carefully began to cross the rope and plank bridge. The hemp rope had stretched and the bridge swayed as she took each step. Half way across, a plank that Sensei stepped on tore loose and the rope bridge swung wildly to the side, sending him, Beryl and Jan plummeting into the swift current. Jan tumbled helplessly into the water and the stretcher fell apart. Beryl dove down to grab Jan's head and pull it up so that she could hold his face above water as Sensei tried to retrieve the poles and nets.

The sharp rocks that had prevented the boatman from going farther upstream now prevented them from being carried downstream, but as the current pushed Sensei against a rock, one of the nets unfurled and snared his feet as it became caught in the base of the rock. The current quickly washed the net over him and the rock, and he was trapped between the net and the rock he was clinging to.

Beryl braced herself against the rocks and one-by-one, pulled and pushed Jan to the South side of the stream, but she could not drag his body up the slippery bank.

Sensei struggled to free himself but the net was impaled by a spur in the rock and was held too tautly for him to dislodge. One of the blowguns had caught the top of the net and its weight helped to pull the net tighter over Sensei's body. He tried to slither down to grab the edge of the net and pull it free, but he had no leverage and no space to maneuver in. He was snared by the net and without a knife to cut it away he could not be freed. Beryl grabbed the back of Jan's collar and pulled him into the group of boulders. She was able to wedge his body between two rocks and hold him there with her foot while she grabbed the second blowgun that lay horizontally across the rocks. "Can you breathe through this if you go underwater?" she yelled to Sensei.

"No, but maybe you can use it as a lever to free the rock the net's caught on."

"I can't let go of Jan," she yelled. "Maybe I can hook the other blowgun with it and bring back the net. After repeated attempts she snagged the end of the net and pulled it towards herself, bringing the other blowgun with it until she was able to reach it. But still she could not let go of Jan. "How long has it been since Jan was hit?" she cried.

"At least half an hour," Sensei answered.

"Then let's wait until he regains some use of his muscles and can keep himself on this rock while I get you."

"A Dharani and two Hearts ought to do it," Sensei called back. It was a perfect way to stay alert but relaxed. Immediately the two of them began to chant, "Namu kara tan no tora ya ya..." After they finished the Dharani to Guan Yin they began the Heart Sutra, "Kan ji zai bo satsu gyo jin han nya ha ra mit ta..."

During the second recitation, Jan stirred. "You'll have to teach me that," he managed to say. Enough strength had returned to his arms for him to be able to hug the rock.

Holding the pole that snared the end of the net, Beryl moved towards Sensei and lifted the net up out of the water and brought it over and down the rock as if she were peeling an orange. Sensei was free. He quickly gathered the nets and poles, tossed them onto the bank, and went to help Beryl pull Jan out of the water.

Jan could not walk. "There was something else in the dart besides curare," he said. "I'm dizzy."

They rebuilt the stretcher and put Jan on it. Just as she was getting ready to stoop down to have the poles loaded onto her shoulders, she noticed her hat in the water, caught at the far side of the rocks. "Wait!" she shouted and jumped into the water, making her way through the rocks until she was able to retrieve it.

She put the hat over Jan's eyes and stooped to let Sensei hoist the two poles onto her shoulders.

Again, taking small double-steps they began to jog downhill to Granger's office. When they had gone half a mile, Jan insisted that they let him try to walk again. Since Beryl's shoulders were becoming seriously bruised by the poles and netting, Sensei agreed to set him down and to help him walk the rest of the way to Granger's. As they approached the house, Sensei shouted for Leighton who came running to help Jan walk to the house.

Beryl and Sensei wilted with relief and collapsed onto chairs, exhausted.

"My shoulders are rubbed raw," she said, without bothering to look at them. "And I ache all over. I can't move my hands. They hurt. My muscles are in spasm."

Leighton helped Jan to stretch out on a couch and then made coffee for everyone. "What the hell is going on?" he asked. "For months everything was so quiet around here; and in these last few weeks it's been crazy." He noticed that both sides of Beryl's neck were red and scraped. "Was that from the poles?" he asked.

"No... it was the coarse hemp net around the poles."

Sensei explained. "I'm taller than she is, so the weight sloped down onto her shoulders. There wasn't anything I could do about it. Because of the stumbling, the harder end to carry downhill is the rear end."

Jan was able to sit up and speak. "How the hell did you two manage to carry me all that distance? Are you all right?" he asked Beryl. "How do you feel?"

"Like I fired an elephant gun," she answered, rubbing her shoulders, "at myself."

"I feel as if I've been hit by a train," Jan said. He looked at Beryl. "Did you give me CPR?"

Sensei laughed. "Yes she did. I saw it for myself," he teased. "Personally, I thought she gave you much more CPR than was necessary."

Everyone grinned as Jan rubbed his eyes. "I thought I was dreaming... that this gorgeous plump angel was kissing me." Then he suddenly remembered that she had been darted first. "I saw you get hit," he said. "Why didn't you go down?"

"You know... waterproof... bulletproof... snakeproof... dartproof. You get what you pay for."

"It's those goddamn fat pants you're wearing. What are they made of? Steel?"

Beryl at first thought that the teasing proved that the crisis was over. "I'm going to take them off now before they rust." She tried to get up but she was too unsteady on her feet. Sensei helped her into the bathroom but, again, her arm and leg muscles were in spasm and her hands and fingers were swollen from the fighting. She could not unclasp the jeans or wading boots. Sensei came in and loosened her clothing. He turned the *Swamptec* wading boots inside out so that they would dry. Leighton handed in a pair of pajamas and slippers and she finally was able to rejoin the others in the living room.

"It's time to eat," Leighton announced. "I've got a lot of eggs and bread. I'm out of beer, but I can make warm iced tea. How does scrambled eggs and bread sound? He turned on his butane stove, put butter in a frying pan, and scrambled a dozen eggs.

"They look and smell wonderful," Beryl said. "But I really can't move my arms. You'll have to feed me," she whined. "And in case you think I'm joking... I'm not." Leighton sat beside her and eating from one plate, he took turns feeding her and himself.

Jan tried to stand up. He staggered and reached for Sensei who supported him and helped him to sit down again. "I can tell," Jan said, "I'm dizzy... they had something else on the dart. But what, I don't know. It could be one of a half dozen things they use. What doesn't kill you, usually wears off in a matter of hours."

While the men talked about the afternoon's adventure, Beryl went out and sat on the veranda steps. It felt good to be out of her armor and in nothing but the soft cotton of Leighton's pajamas. She was tired but still too filled with adrenalin to sleep. She sat alone, ignoring the insects as she studied the equatorial sky. Finally Leighton announced that it was time to get some sleep and directed his guests to their rooms.

Jan called, "Take your clothes off, completely. I mean get naked! Fleas get into the seams of your garments and when you get into bed and lie quietly, they come out and crawl and bite you. You will not be able to sleep." Beryl obeyed the order, stripped off her clothes, and slipped between the muslin sheets. It was her first night in the rainforest and with her attention free to fix upon sounds other than human, she was astonished to hear the riot of sounds that came from the trees all around them: the booming howler monkeys, croaking frogs, growling cats, shrieking nocturnal birds, and the peculiar echo-location clicks of the bats. It was, she thought, like a Charles Ives' symphony. Yet, despite the dissonance, it calmed her.

A damp breeze blew down from the hilltop, fanning everyone into a deep sleep.

SATURDAY, APRIL 2, 2011

While Leighton snored in his bed, Sensei, Jan, and Beryl awakened early and left money on the kitchen table to compensate for the hospitality. Beryl's shoulders and Sensei's, too, were badly bruised, and Jan still felt the after effects of the dart. Since their own cellphones were useless, they tried to use Leighton's to call for a motor canoe to come for them, but they could not get a signal.

They slowly began to walk back to the Vandermeer, feeling the increasing heat and humidity as the sun rose to its zenith. It had rained during the night, and rainwater had cascaded down from the hills, swelling the creek until the footpath that ran beside it seemed like its muddy bank. Each footstep pushed down several inches into the muck, causing an imbalance that had to be corrected before the foot could be pulled up and freed from the sucking mud. The mile trip began to feel like a marathon.

Jan had to stop and rest repeatedly. "I'm having trouble breathing," he said. "I felt it last night, too."

Breakfast was still being served when they reached the Vandermeer. Beryl said, "Let's eat and then either get Jan to the clinic or get a little sleep." They flopped into chairs on the veranda. Jan preferred to eat. He followed Sensei's advice to interlock his fingers behind his neck so that he could elevate his chest. Within minutes he felt some relief.

As the waiter placed their food on the table, Jan asked, "Do you know where Jackel Mazumi lives?"

"Sure. There's a landing at the fish taco place - where the trail to Jackel's house begins. So you can't miss the turn-off. You have to walk back a mile. If you think you're lost, just ask anyone you see. Everybody knows the place."

They finished eating, went back to their double room, and allowing Beryl to use the shower first, Jan and Sensei, fully clothed, collapsed on one of the large beds. Beryl gave twenty dollars and her "jungle togs" to one of the chambermaids to launder in such a way that they'd be dry by the afternoon. She turned her wading pants inside out. "Just launder this side," she said. Then she took a shower, put on an oversized t-shirt, and crawled into her bed.

Hendrik Holman had returned to Paramaribo to keep appointments he had made with important clients. His mind, however, was tormented by the doubts that were filling the spaces left empty by unfulfilled promises of "keeping him informed."

Of all the people involved in scamming Olivia, Hendrik believed that he had the most invested. In his mind, he was the operation's director. He had planned it. The strategy and the tactics were his. He had emphasized that the plan required a precise execution in all its segments, yet, already there was trouble. He had not heard from deJong. Moyer had not only married the mark, but had not deigned to call. And did anyone think that he was stupid enough to believe the story about Moyer being held captive in a doghouse? No... that story had to be part of a scheme cooked up between Moyer and Reinhardt Springer. Moyer couldn't be trusted, and neither could deJong. And what did the 'churchman' have to do with anything? Hendrik liked challenges. He did not like chaos.

Any day now the checks would arrive at the bank in Georgetown. And how were they going to pull off the transfer? The other three didn't need him. They could take a commercial flight to Georgetown. Springer could handle that. And what could he do about it? He decided to return to Cajana, and, this time, he would take a serious look around.

Wearing cowboy boots and trying to look casual, he landed at the Cajana Airfield, checked into the Vandermeer Lodge, and walked down to the dock to take the *Pink Dolphin's* motor-canoe shuttle.

He sat at the bar and, in casual conversation with a few customers, learned that Tony deJong and Rubem were very sick. "What's wrong with them?" he asked.

Someone answered, "Doc Von Bommel says they've got cholera. They've been quarantined!"

Everyone laughed heartily. "Let's hope nobody ever really does get cholera," Hendrik said.

The news encouraged him. Maybe Tony was 'layin' low' as he had been ordered. There was no better way to stay out of sight than to claim the contagion of disease. He wondered what news was to be had at *Springer's*.

He returned to the Cajana dock and transferred to *Springer's Roadhouse*'s shuttle.

As soon as the dinner crowd cleared out of *Jack's*, Gus, the bartender, and another worker rented an unmarked motor canoe from a boatman. They went down to the Gran Rio, turned left and continued downstream past the Cajana dock to *Springer's Roadhouse* turnoff.

Carrying a bolt cutter and some bottled water, they skirted the periphery of the roadhouse complex until they were able to approach the dog shed from the far side. No workers were in sight. Gus put his mouth up to a knothole and whispered, "Jackel! You there?"

"Yes, I'm here."

"DeJong sent us to rescue you. How are you two doing?"

"I'm better than Moyer. I go barefoot every day. His feet soft and easy cut."

Moyer groaned. "How is my wife?"

The workman cut the padlock and opened the shed's door. He handed Moyer a bottle of water. "Here, drink this. We don't know anything about your wife. Drink some more while we look around and see if we can get you out." He pulled Jackel from the shed.

"I ain't eaten since yesterday," Moyer said. "Find out where my wife is. Save her. Tell her my feet are throbbing. Flies been laying eggs in 'em. They're getting infected. She'll know what to do."

The workman looked at Gus and whispered, "He sounds half nuts." He tossed him a candy bar and closed the door to the shed.

"Aren't you gonna get him?" Jackel asked.

"We'll be back for him. We got no room in the boat. Springer's after your family, too. We gotta get them to safety."

They returned to the boat, started the motor, and pulled away from *Springer's* and headed to the river and the *Pink Dolphin*.

Faber and Donovan were waiting at *Jack's* landing. They lifted Jackel out of the boat and carried him to a bed in Jack's private wing of the roadhouse. There was so much mud and caked blood on Jackel's feet that they could not see the extent of his injuries. He was hungry and thirsty, and after he had eaten and drank his full, he fell into a deep sleep.

Reinhardt Springer had learned that an NBI officer and two civilians were reconnoitering the area. He had approved of keeping Moyer and Jackel Mazumi - two men who were vital to the scheme - out in the dog shed. Meanwhile, he had to determine if deJong and Henny Holman were signatories. Chico had brought him the news that two of his Yanos were killed and another was critically wounded. That, he decided, had to be the work of the National Bureau of Investigation.

Springer found it irritating to have to deal with so many disruptions in the smooth execution of his affairs. He decided that he might as well eat his dinner and then prepare himself properly to receive intruders.

Kaza Ross knew that he risked provoking his boss into a tantrum if he knocked on his door when, as he secretly put it, "Springer was feeding," but it was an important message. He knocked.

"As long as you've already destroyed my pleasure," Springer shouted, "tell me what you want."

Kaza opened the door and let himself in. "I thought you ought to know two things: the NBI guy, the man and a woman had been out to Granger's yesterday. They got back an hour or so ago and seem to be worn out from something."

"I already know that. What is the other thing?"

"Jackel has been taken out of the shed."

"Taken? By whom? When?"

"I don't know when someone took him out. Moyer is still in there. Half dead."

"Revive him and get him out of there. Be careful. He may be all we have left of this wretched business."

Kaza asked, "Where do you want me to take him? He can't walk."

"Bring him up the back stairs. Put him in the interrogation room. Bathe him and find some clean clothes for him, and don't forget socks. See to it that he's given water and food." He stood up. "Give him this," he indicated his dinner, "inasmuch as I no longer have an appetite. And don't let anyone see him. Put a blanket over him. Slip him something that will knock him out and keep him quiet. We don't know how he got there. Do you understand?"

Kaza nodded.

Reinhardt Springer took a deep breath. "Since there's still a possibility that our NBI friends will visit my establishment, I'll properly attire myself." He withdrew into his dressing room as Kaza got a blanket from the linen closet and hurried downstairs to find Chico.

Moyer was barely conscious when they pulled him from the shed and put a blanket over him. Ross lifted him onto his shoulder and casually walked back into the stone wing. Chico got a worker's uniform and white socks from the kitchen. They took Moyer into the guest bathroom and sat him on the toilet as they gave him drugged lemonade and the leftover food from Springer's tray. They filled the bathtub, adding fragrant bath crystals.

"How are your feet?" Kaza asked.

"They hurt like hell. They're throbbing."

"I'm sorry about that. I didn't know anything about it. Neither did the boss - or that you were out in the shed. He told us to take care of you the moment he heard. Who the hell beat you up and put you in the shed?"

"I don't know. Indians got Jackel and me and my wife."

"Jackel? And your wife? When did you get married?"

"A week ago. Where's my wife?"

"Can't help you. We don't know anything about it. Neither does Mr. Springer. He's full of questions." He dipped into the bath water and pulled up one of Moyer's feet.

Moyer was carried into the interrogation room. "Where is my wife?" he asked again. "Where is Olivia?" And then he was overcome with fatigue, the loss of blood, and the effects of the drugged lemonade.

Chico placed him on a cot. "Let him lay here and sleep it off," he said.

It was close to four o'clock when music from the bar awakened Jan, Beryl, and Sensei from their afternoon nap. Several groups of tourists had come to Cajana. There was a small dance floor in the bar, and all of the tourists, it seemed, were dancing at once.

Sensei and Jan both had blisters on their feet, but Sensei had not realized how serious his were until he went into the shower. He came back into the bedroom with bloody feet. "I'm gonna need bandages... more than *Band-aids*. Jan looked at his own feet. I can use the strips. I didn't walk as much as you." They exchanged a smile that said that they were lucky to have gotten away with only blistered feet.

Jan's first-aid kit was still in the room, and Beryl opened it and began to bandage Sensei's feet. "Are your feet ok to go to Jackel's house?" she asked.

They weren't, but Sensei said, "Sure."

She distributed the food and water and led the men out to the dock where the motor-canoes waited to be rented. None was there. "Where are the boatmen?" Jan asked a boy.

"Tourists take 'em down to Awarradam."

"All of them?"

"Yeah. Pay 'em good too. They's bringing 'em back late."

"I need a ride to Jackel's house."

"You a cop. You can make *Jack's* or *Springer's* shuttle take you."

"That's right," Beryl said. "Commandeer a boat."

It was true that Jan could have forced someone to take them, but between the grogginess he felt from whatever else was on the dart and the blisters on Sensei's feet, he thought that it wasn't in anyone's interest to take a boat ride at that time. "I know you want to get moving on this," he said gently to Beryl, "but rather than disturb everyone and create publicity that we may not want, I think we should go back."

Beryl looked closely at his eyes. "You're far from being over that dart. Let's go back and try again in the morning. If we ever fell overboard with Sensei's bloody feet in the water..."

"Yes," Jan sighed. "I've already put your lives in jeopardy. There I was, worried about you guys, and here I am, the weak sister in the outfit." He staggered and had to grab Beryl's shoulder for support. She winced in pain, and he tried to apologize. They looked at each other and began to laugh. "I think we have grown old together," he said. "Let's sit here on the dock without benefit of rocking chairs."

Cajana was quiet with the tourists and the boatmen gone. They leaned back against a few boxes and relaxed. As darkness fell, mosquitos came in swarms. Sensei removed a can of insect repellent from his backpack and sprayed his face and arms. He gave the repellent to Jan who did the same. Beryl let her hat's net veil down and threaded the chain through the hem. The boatman from Springer's lit several pots of palm nuts and all around, in places they could not see, people began to burn the oily nuts to ward off the mosquito attacks. The three exhausted investigators sat propped up against the boxes and studied the darkness.

The smoke from so many smoldering fires gave the night air a peculiar silky feeling and a slightly acrid smell. It created an aura around any illuminating thing... electric light, lamp or candle, and even the moon.

On either side of the river, trees stretched out from the black jungle and tried to reach each other. Where the river was wide, the trees could not touch, and a silver streak of moonlight ran along its center like a seam.

They returned to the Vandermeer, ate a light meal, drank a gin and tonic, and then limped back to their room and collapsed.

Reinhardt Springer was much annoyed. He had descended into the roadhouse wearing a dinner jacket and starched shirt with his favorite cufflinks. That he was the only person who appeared to have dressed appropriately reinforced his opinion that he was the only civilized person in the District. He looked over his clientele. Only the usual customers were there.

As he walked into the bar, he saw Hendrik Holman lift a bottle of beer to his lips and take a long drink. Hendrik looked at him and put the bottle on the bar. "You're lookin' like you've just stepped out of a gentlemen's magazine. What brings you down here?" Hendrik asked.

"I'm just looking around seeing if there's anyone worth recognizing."

"Will I do?"

"'Now is the winter of my discontent made glorious summer,'" Springer recited sarcastically.

Hendrik's heart thumped. He knew this quote! "Reinhardt the Third!" he shouted.

Reinhardt Springer was delighted. He laughed and slapped the bar. "Give him and me a Heineken!" he called. He pulled a bar stool closer to Hendrik's and sat down. "Culture in this wasteland? I am impressed. So, tell me, Hendrik the Fifth. What brings you to our band of brothers?"

Hendrik Holman had already exhausted his Shakespearean repertoire. "I'm looking for two friends."

"Anyone I know?"

"I don't know who you know. But in case you happen to know Tony deJong and Ananda Moyer, that's who I'm looking for."

"I think I can help you... but not by much. I was told that someone locked Jackel Mazumi and Moyer in my dog shed out back. I didn't know about it until someone told me Jackel had fled but Moyer was still in there. So I sent my men to bring him up here to my quarters. He was half dead. I told them to give him plenty of water and to feed him, bathe him, and give him a clean shirt, pants, and socks. He revived."

"Where is he now?"

"He fell asleep on a cot upstairs; but when I went in to check on him, he was gone. So I don't know where he is. He told my men that he had gotten married. Maybe he went to find his wife."

"Yes, I heard that he got hitched," Hendrik said.

"I haven't heard anything more about deJong except that he and Rubem have cholera."

"Jesus! Cholera?" Hendrik pretended that this was news to him.

"Don't get excited. That was Doc Von Bommel's diagnosis. Warts are symptoms of cholera to that incompetent fool."

"Where was it that he made his diagnosis?"

"At *Jack's Pink D.*"

"You know, I brought Tony down here when somebody from Jack's called to tell him that Rubem was very ill and was calling for him. Tony looked a little sick himself. I thought it was just a hangover. Are they still at *Jack's*?"

"I have no idea. I don't keep track of *Jack's* clientele."

Springer had gained important information. Holman clearly did not have access to the account in Georgetown. If he had, he would not be looking for the others. He pointed at the money Hendrik had put on the bar. "Put your money away," he said. "Come on, let's see what Lady Luck has in store for you and Reinhardt the Third." He lowered his voice. "Your money will be good at the craps table."

SUNDAY, APRIL 3, 2011

Overnight, the mud had dried on Jackel's feet and had fallen off, revealing the extent of his lacerations. It was evident to Faber and Donovan that much improvisation was needed.

The problems were daunting. In addition to the lacerations, Jackel's feet were badly swollen. He could not walk. He was wearing native clothing when Springer's men captured him and there were no men's garments that would fit him - at least in the style that a businessman would wear.

Donovan and Faber carried him from his bed in Rubem's old room to a bathtub filled with hot soapy water. As they finished scrubbing him, Donovan whined, "The only pants we've got are too large!"

"What about the girls?" Faber asked. "One of them has to have blue jeans that will fit him. Take off your belt and measure his waist."

As Faber supported Jackel, Donovan took off his belt, wrapped it around Jackel"s waist, measured and marked it, and ran downstairs to the girls' dressing room. One of the girls had the exact waist measurement. "I'll get these back to you as soon as possible," Donovan said to her. Then he ran upstairs. "Try these!" he said to Faber.

He found an old pair of briefs that were too small for him and put them on Jackel. Faber, being slim, had a shirt that came close to fitting. "Let's take everything off so that he doesn't soil them and give us more trouble," Faber said. "Do you have a wheelchair anywhere around?"

"Yeah. We keep a fold-up wheelchair in the lobby."

"Shouldn't we be sending the men to pick up the mill house guests and the papers?" Faber asked.

"Yes... we should. One of the men will have to stay with them at the mill house until you can get there. We have a lot of work to do here on

Jackel's feet." He turned to Jackel, "You know that you really screwed-up when you got involved in that scheme to get Olivia Moyer's money. Mr. Edwards, here, is kind enough to help you undo the wrong you've done. Until you set everything right, you and your family are in danger. So, tell Mr. Edwards where you've got the bank papers. He'll need them to straighten out the mess."

"All those papers are in that black attaché case. It's under my bed."

"We've got to protect your kids too. Springer is determined to force you to do what he wants and he'll hurt your family. We'll see what Lola says." Donovan handed him a bathrobe. "We can have food sent up here. How's that?"

"Sounds good to me," Jackel said. "I'm hungry."

"Eat up!" Donovan said. "Tomorrow we go to Georgetown and get things back to normal."

Beryl, Sensei, and Jan renewed their plan to rescue Olivia. They would rent a motor canoe to take them to the fish taco shack where the trail to Jackel's house began.

Sensei announced that he would be carrying his knife. "Will you be taking yours?" he asked Beryl.

"I'm not carrying a knife," she teased. "I don't want to dull the blade by letting it rub against my pants."

They laughed and loaded their backpacks again with water, protein bars, anti-venom and first aid supplies. Jan's satellite phone was still in his backpack. They had no other usable phones.

In the canoe, Beryl took her hat and threaded the chain through the netting's hem. Swarms of mosquitos and gnats were beginning to attack. The men sprayed repellent but still had to swat mosquitos. They looked at Beryl and feigned resentment.

"I'm gonna burn that goddamned suit of hers first chance I get," Jan teased.

"Jan, my brother," Sensei said, "what makes you think it's not fireproof?"

When they reached the fish taco landing, they checked to see that no one was waiting in the shadows and then walked on to Jackel's house.

Lola Mazumi hid her children until she saw that it was an NBI officer approaching. "Who you lookin' for?" she asked Jan.

"Do you know where Springer's Annex is?"

"It's about time you NBI guys got on Springer's trail. You here because he's got one of yours in the Annex?"

Jan was embarrassed. "I'm not going to be interrogated by you. Can you lead us there or not?"

"I lead you. What three people gonna do against Springer's Annex? I lead you but I can't stay to watch. I got to get back to my kids. Jackel be back soon I hope."

It began to rain. Water, in large drops that fell from the tree canopy, created a quarter-inch depth of slime that rushed over the ground, making a slippery surface that licked at their feet as the monkeys overhead chattered. The path quickly became impossible to walk on. Jackel's wife motioned for them to follow her onto semi-savannah type land. Soon, what had been clumps of wild grass, became sponges that were alive with insects. Everyone's shoes, except Beryl's, were soggy with slime water. She trekked on fearlessly. Lola Mazumi began to walk beside Sensei as Jan began to jog to get to higher ground where he could walk beside Beryl. Finally he reached her. "Don't leave me, Master," he pleaded. "I don't want to be alone."

"We'll see how you behave yourself," she said, as they approached a tree that lay across their path. Jan, in an exaggerated gesture, took Beryl's hand and put his left foot over the tree, alerting a nearby snake. As he put his right foot over it, Beryl simultaneously put her left foot over it and the snake uncoiled and struck the inside of her left leg at the knee.

Jan shouted and grabbed the snake and flung it into the bushes. "You're hit! You're hit! Sensei! She's been bitten! A bushmaster! Christ! I've got anti-venom in my bag. I can start the shots, but we have to get her to a hospital."

"A tailor would be better," Beryl said. "That thing ripped my pants! Look at this! And I don't have a sewing kit. Do you know how much these pants cost? The snake didn't bite me but it sure did a number on my new pants."

Jan was incredulous. "Are you trying to tell me that that bushmaster didn't bite you? What the hell are you wearing? Jesus! Is that stuff chain-mail?"

"They're magic pants," Lola said.

"And I thought the dart had probably hit you tangentially. I never really believed that it simply couldn't penetrate." He examined her pants at the knee where the flexibility folds were. The snake had struck where the 'bulletproof' wading pants had been doubled in a pleat. The fangs tore the denim pants but had not penetrated the wading pants. "I don't believe it." Still breathing heavily from fear, he sat down on the log. "Let me get my breath," he said. "If I didn't see this for myself, I never would have believed it."

"The joke," said Sensei, "is on us. I am pregnant with shame." He and Jan laughed momentarily; and then continued to swat mosquitos and gnats and to curse their soggy shoes.

Lola Mazumi had also observed the entire incident and could barely believe what she had seen. "That snake gonna need new teeth." Her father had been killed by a bushmaster. "Yes, they're magic pants."

Beryl lowered the gloves from her cuffs. Her left knee felt as though it had been struck with a puck from a well-aimed slap shot. She said nothing about the pain. "Ah, my *Swamptec* togs," she taunted her companions. "Cheap at twice the price."

As they approached the Annex, they could hear a car approach. They hid behind trees and watched as a Range Rover stopped at the paved stone entrance path to the Annex. The rain had become torrential and the four heavily armed men who were in the Rover got out and quickly entered the Annex.

"Springer's car," Lola whispered to Sensei. "They collect money."

Jan turned to ask, "How long will they stay?"

"Not long. They watch money being counted and check around to see that everything is ok. They don't mess with these sick girls. And they know Springer likes that car. They won't drive in muddy road. They know he worries if they stay out too long."

"Why are they so heavily armed?" Beryl asked.

"They afraid the women gang up on them or have made lovers from customers. That happen once. Two Reinhardt's men killed with guns when lovers try to free women."

"Well, Jan Kalashnikov," Beryl said, "your side-arm and Sensei's knife are no match for four AK47's plus whatever it was they have on their gunbelts. We're gonna have a fight on our hands."

"Let's wait," Jan said.

"Please," Lola countered. "You don't need me. My kids need me. I'll go back my house. The rain will be over soon. If my Jackel is home then he watch the kids. But now, my family need me."

"I don't feel right about letting you go back alone. But I need to say here," Beryl said. "My leg is stressed enough. I don't want to slip in the mud and make it worse."

Jan said, "I'll walk back with her. You stay here."

Lola laughed. "You NBI guys like to joke. I can walk back blindfolded." She turned to Sensei. "You keep these two out of trouble. Him specially."

Alone, she headed back to her house.

Lola quickly answered the tapping at her door. "We rescued your husband," Gus said. "He was badly beaten by Springer."

"Yes," she said anxiously, "I know. My boy told me."

"Jackel wants you and Dani to be safe. Springer knows Dani helped him when he was in the dog shack. He's lookin' for you both. So, we're gonna take you both to the mill house at the *Pink D*. As soon as we get Jackel fixed up we'll bring him there." All the kids were up and standing behind their mother. "Will the kids be ok without you and Dani?" Gus asked.

"Yes. They can go to my sister. She lives near us." Lola packed a few articles and put them in a bag.

"One more thing," Gus said. "We're supposed to get the black attaché case Jackel keeps under his bed." Dani looked under his father's bed and pulled out the black case. "Good!" said Gus, taking the case; and the four of them hurried back to the fish taco shack's landing on the Gran Rio.

Jackel Mazumi was confused. "Jack, what is goin' on? Why Springer hurt Moyer and me? Why he put us in shed?"

"He's trying to get Olivia's money that you put in the bank in Georgetown," Jack said. "Springer is a violent man. He'll stop once we get the money back for Olivia."

"Thanks, Jack. I let Henny and Tony talk me into that scam. I'm stupid. Lola gonna kill me when she find out. All that money. Big mistake for me."

While Faber went down to the kitchen to order lunch for the three of them, Donovan sat on the bed and practiced signing deJong's signature. He stopped for a moment to consider the future of Samuel Faber. He still had not made up his mind about what he'd do with him. He definitely did not want to have a witness around to the murder of Tony and Rubem, but he liked having a friend he could trust. He brooded about it. Faber had proven to be useful. But even useful things wear out. "Yes," he told himself, "things that aren't useful don't wear out... they go out of fashion... they are discarded or destroyed... or they just take up space while you wait to see if there comes a time that they'll be of use. But useful things? They usually have a short lifespan. Useful things do not last." These observations were worthy of notation although, at the moment, he was not entirely sure of the point they made. He did not resume his forgery practice until he had memorialized his thoughts in his wisdom book.

He knew that he had a few more days to make a decision about Faber. The operation had gone smoothly due to Faber's help. In a day or two the transferred money would be safe in his account. He would use the time to figure out how to get Faber's half. Make him a partner in the *Pink D.* as a Joint Tenant with rights of survival and then quietly let him disappear? Not right away, maybe. But why not?

Samuel Faber knew that he did not want to go back to Pennsylvania. It was true that a few days earlier he had considered buying the "enchanted" mill house; but after he spent a few hours working there with Jack, he had changed his mind. Tiny black gnats and mosquitos and cockroaches as big as mice did not constitute a fairyland environment. He rather liked living inside the *Pink Dolphin*. He was born for beauty, leisure, and sin; and if he went back to the states, all he'd be going back to was ugliness, work, and that goddamned righteousness he always had to project.

Olivia had begun to feel feverish but she knew better than to complain. She could no longer keep count of the number of men she had serviced. Thursday night, Friday night, and all day Saturday. By noon on Saturday, she knew she was becoming feverish. She felt thirsty. "*Vasser*" she cried to the madam. "*Bitte*." She wasn't sure which language it was she was speaking but she received water and finally, towards evening, one of the men reported that she felt warm and seemed half dead. After her condition was checked, she was taken to the building at the rear of the complex, the place they called, "the Sick Shed."

As she lay alone in the shed, she began to pray aloud again... a long prayer that guided her into feverish sleep.

For an hour Jan, Sensei, and Beryl studied the Annex. The rain had stopped and they were able to see the entire complex more clearly.

"It's been camouflaged to look like some kind of mining operation. Look at that fake mine entrance. They painted a big rock black and put a wooden frame around it. Jesus! From the air, you'd never suspect that it was fake."

On the left side of the Annex courtyard, a chain-link fence enclosed a large area on two sides. The rear property-line, which they could barely see, was a river that would have been sluggish in the dry months and torrential in the wet. A drop in the terrain let the water fall several meters into a shallow pool. There were fences on both sides of the river. The fence on the far side, they supposed, prevented caiman from sliding down into the pool. The fence on courtyard side had a gate that one of the administrative women opened to check the pool beneath the waterfall.

As Sensei, Beryl, and Jan watched, a worker entered the yard and, using a hose, filled a row of wash tubs and put scrubbing boards and bars of naptha soap in them. At noon, three women came out, carrying dirty laundry. They knelt at the tubs, picked up a bar of soap, and began to rub the sheets against the corrugated washboard. Two other women followed them out and knelt at the tubs to launder their dirty sheets and dresses. Olivia was not among them.

Soon the women had reached the lunch phase of the break. They sat in the shade and ate pastries and drank coffee, talking and laughing amongst themselves. Jan watched and shook his head. "They just don't look like they're being held against their will... not that I'm speaking from personal experience as a brothel patron."

At the rear of the courtyard was a row of rooms. A young man who wore only a sarong came out to sit in the sun and brush his long red hair.

A blonde woman who wore a gun belt and who obviously was in a superior position to that of the house madam, walked around the yard in her riding boots, breeches, long sleeved shirt, and heavy-duty latex gloves. With each step she took, she slapped the palm of her glove with a riding crop.

"But where is Olivia? I don't see her," Beryl said.

"We don't even know whether or not she's inside," Jan said. "She might have been moved. I see no advantage in waiting." He had noticed that Beryl seemed to be increasingly distressed by her knee. "Let's get you back to the Vandermeer and let you stretch that leg out. It's not helping to keep it in a crouched position."

"Let's give the guys with the weapons five more minutes to get out," Sensei said. "We're no match for assault rifles but if that's the only protection they have and those guys leave, we can take them."

Before the final five minutes were up they could hear the sound of motorcycles advancing towards the Annex. A heavily armed man arrived first. He parked his cycle and looked around as if he were making a security assessment. He took out what appeared to be a "walkie-talkie" two-way radio and made a call. Immediately, in the distance, several other motorcycles started their engines.

Soon, as the first man stood guard with his semi-automatic rifle, a cycle with a sidecar drove up and parked. A well-groomed man got out of the sidecar. Jan gasped. "Good Christ! I know that guy. He's a

Swiss national. Rich. Very, very rich. What the hell is he doing in a place like this?"

Beryl looked at Jan. "What they're all doing. The guy probably has an incurable disease and rather than risk a law suit or bad publicity he's indulging himself - or, maybe he just likes redheads." He walked up the paved entryway and the door opened. A bodyguard followed him in. Two other motorcycles drove into the clearing in front of the Annex and parked. The drivers picked up assault rifles and assumed sentinel postures, walking the fenced periphery of the complex.

In a few minutes, the man and his bodyguard emerged from the rear of the woman's building and walked to the men's building. The red haired young man immediately fell to his knees and crawled to the Swiss who stood there in a Mussolini "hands on hips - chest out" pose, waiting for him to kiss his boots.

"I'm gonna puke," Jan said.

"There's no telling how long this is going to take," Sensei said. "Let's head back. We can return tomorrow morning. I expect that there will be fewer customers on a Monday."

"You can go back," Beryl said. "I'm staying. Not all of the women have come out yet."

"There's too many armed guards," Sensei said. "You can't prevail against all of them, and if they get you, they'll put you in the whore's line-up. We can stay awhile longer and wait with you. But you're not staying here alone."

"If you need help subduing her," Jan said, "I'll happily put cuffs on her."

More dirt bikes delivered customers. The number of armed men who stood outside the Annex had increased to seven, and three more were inside, guarding their employers in the rear of the facility. Someone shouted, "Fan out and check the perimeter," and as several armed men started to walk in the investigators' direction, Beryl reluctantly agreed to turn back. Monday was bound to be a less busy day.

Helped by Jan, she limped back to the Vandermeer and dropped onto the bed as Sensei and Jan went into the bar to get a few drinks. Jan asked the barman to have one of the chambermaids stop at their room to see if Beryl needed any help with her garments.

Beryl stripped off her clothing, took a shower and shampooed her hair, finishing just before the maid arrived. The chambermaid agreed to launder the *Swamptec* clothing again and to repair the torn denim pants. Seeing the large purple bruise on Beryl's leg, she gasped. "What happened to you?"

"A bushmaster tried to bite me."

"Try? They don't *try*." She examined the bruise more closely as Beryl sat on the bed. "The skin of your leg is not broken!"

"It did bite my pants," Beryl said, indicating the garments that now lay in a pile on the floor.

The maid picked up the jeans. "Look at these big fang marks! That snake... he took a big bite." Then she looked at the wading boots. "But he didn't get in here. What kind of pants are these?"

"My friend calls them 'Magic Pants.' She says the snake must have broken its teeth and now needs to buy new ones. I guess the snake needs dentures... you know... false teeth."

The maid sat on the bed beside Beryl and laughed. "Out there is a bushmaster with store-bought teeth. Oh, that is funny. I'd like to meet that snake!" Then her attention returned to the bruise. "But that snake hurt you bad. You have something for pain?"

"No, not yet."

"You wait here. I have Percocet. Do you know Percocet?"

"Yes. It will do the job."

The maid got up and left the room. Beryl closed her eyes and tried to use a deep relaxation exercise to lessen the throbbing in her leg. In a few minutes the maid returned with a bottle of water and a plastic envelope that contained half a dozen large tablets. "You take one now?" she asked.

"No. I can't. I have to go now to have dinner and then I'll take one. Please let me pay you."

"No. No. Everybody in the bar is talking about that snake. Your pants are famous now. Just now my boss ask me, 'What happened to that snake?' And I tell him, 'He went to dentist to get some false teeth."

Beryl put the plastic bag of Percocet tablets into her shoulder bag. Then, trying not to limp, she dressed and rejoined Sensei and Jan who waited in the veranda's dining area.

A waiter brought menus to the table. The three of them watched him as though they were watching him on television. Then they closed their eyes and just sat there. Nearly five minutes passed before anyone picked up a menu and summoned the waiter to order food.

MONDAY, APRIL 4, 2011

Donovan and Faber got up early to prepare Jackel for the trip. Donovan began by putting the woman's jeans on him. Then he bandaged his feet while Faber pomaded and sprayed his hair and put one of his western shirts on him.

One of the two workmen who had stayed with Lola and Dani overnight came to the bedroom door to tell them that all had gone well at the mill house overnight. "Good," Faber said, "I'll be along shortly, and I'll be sure to bring something tasty with me for breakfast."

"Good idea," Donovan said as the workman left. "We can put a sedative of some kind in the juice. Keep 'em calm. If we're convincing about Jackel's whereabouts, they'll be cooperative. Never underestimate the power of a well-told lie." He made a note to include this caveat among his sutras.

"I've made special travel arrangements," Jack said. "Let's have breakfast and then I'll change into deJong's clothing and sunglasses, the whore's wig and corset, and your hat. I'll look the part."

Faber could not remember ever being so excited as he was at that moment. He had a friend who was important. The staff treated him with deference and friendliness. Money was in his future. And so was... he savored the delicious thought... a battered and destitute Ananda Moyer.

Donovan made a call to a friend in Awarradam, and then, with the help of two of his workers, he was laced into the corset, and breathlessly squeezed into deJong's pants. Speaking in a slightly higher pitch, he stood on the *Pink Dolphin's* lawn beside Jackel in his wheelchair. In a few minutes a helicopter's rotor was heard and then the aircraft landed nearby and Donovan, Jackel, and the folded chair were put aboard. The helicopter would return to Awarradam and then they would transfer to an aircraft that would take them to Georgetown. Guyana's time zone was an hour behind; but even with a refueling stop, they would arrive before Jackel's bank clerk went to lunch.

Faber went to the mill house to greet Lola Mazumi and her son Dani as they awakened. He carried with him a picnic basket filled with fruit, yogurt, coffee, and juice. There was no need for force of any kind. Faber had explained again that they were in danger and Jackel wanted them to wait there until he returned later in the day.

The mill house had been cleaned and furnished with a bed, sleeping mats, a table and chairs, dishes, lamps and oil and several cases of bottled water. The insects that plagued the building through the night were gone, and Faber looked around and lamented that there were simply too many little black gnats to overcome. The place could never function as a rustic kind of bachelor's pad.

To pass the time he played chequers with the worker, but soon boredom seized him and to free himself from it he began to explore some of the mysterious elements in the building's construction.

He and the worker poked around the water wheel's controls that were still in place inside the mill house. Intrigued by two long levers that extended from a housing in the corner of the room, Faber and the worker discussed the levers' possible function. "Look," the worker noticed, "there's a pulley system with cables that go up through a kind of chimney to the roof. What could the levers activate?"

"Pull one and find out," Faber suggested. The worker pulled one and discovered that it flopped around and accomplished nothing. "The cable it connects to has obviously been broken," Faber said. "Try the other one." The worker pulled on the lever and felt its strong connection to something outside the mill house. "Help me," the worker said, and Faber and the worker together pulled and could tell immediately that they had moved something.

Suddenly they heard the sound of rushing water and went outside to investigate. Faber and the worker inched their way along a narrow wooden ledge that was built just above ground level on the outside of the building. The mill house had been constructed on an elevated stone and concrete foundation which, except for the front entrance wall, had allowed the building to be nearly surrounded by water when torrential rains overwhelmed the sides of the coffin dam. Formerly, a worker, stepping sideways, could have gone completely around the three "water" sides of the house. But now, an accumulation of debris blocked passage at the farthest corner. Faber could see that the lever they had pulled had raised a top 'headrace' gate that allowed water to flow into a sluice that was supposed to channel the water to the wheel; but the sluice was broken and lay in pieces on the bottom of the coffin dam. The other lever had been intended to open the exit gate, the bottom tailrace, for the water to flow out of the coffin dam after it had turned the wheel. But this gate had been left in a closed position, and with its cables broken, they had no way to open it.

With the headrace gate open, the coffin dam was rapidly filling. Faber and the workman feared that the floor of the house would be inundated. So many vines covered the dam's wall panels that they could not see that even if the dam's enclosure was filled, the water, except in flood conditions, would not have reached the ground floor of the mill house which was several inches higher than the top of the panels. The water would have simply sloshed over the panel tops.

Faber and the workman understood that what they had done was to pull up a gate that let river water into the enclosure. They came running into the mill house and tried to push the lever back to close the gate and stop the water. Opening it had been difficult. Closing it proved to be impossible. They supposed that one purpose of the ledge must surely have been to enable a man to maintain the integrity of the sluice and a secondary purpose must have been to assist in closing the headrace gate. They watched helplessly as the enclosure filled. But then, miraculously, the water began to slosh over the vine-covered tops of the panels. They whooped and laughed, joyful to think how worried they had been about having caused a disaster.

Lola Mazumi had observed them as they pulled on the lever and she had heard the rushing water. She had also followed the men outside to see what they were looking at. She listened and watched, and, being familiar with "fish trap" fishing techniques, she understood what they had failed to grasp: they had created a weir, a trap. Piranha could enter but they could not get out. In their normal environment, piranha, although not what anyone would consider docile or sluggish, were not particularly dangerous. But when their environment was not normal and they were deprived of food, they became crazed with hunger and would devour anything that was edible. Unfortunately, they had the teeth that could realize their desire. The hint of food, such as a single drop of blood might offer, would send them into a macabre frenzy.

Faber and the worker continued to compliment themselves and the ledge that had held their weight and allowed them to get to the back of the building and see the problem for themselves. "We're lucky that wooden ledge held our weight," Faber wheezed.

"This building solid," Lola said. "It made of Zapote wood... Ironwood they call it. Last forever."

"Why do they have the area enclosed at all?" Faber asked.

"Caiman jammed up water works," she answered.

"Oh, alligators," Faber said. "Now I understand." He and the worker opened the picnic basket and a few bottles of beer. Relaxed, finally, they began discussions about Suriname, religion, and life's vicissitudes.

In Georgetown, Jackel Mazumi and Jack Donovan waited in a small open-air fruit market across the street from the bank. At noon, the tellers and clerks who took their lunch break at that hour began to exit the bank. Jackel studied a group of well-dressed men who came out together. "That's him," he said. "That one with yellow stripe in his tie help me and deJong."

Donovan marveled at Jackel's ability to see the tie's detail. Although he could not distinguish a yellow stripe, he took Jackel's word that it existed. He pushed four cotton balls into Jackel's mouth to puff out his cheeks and pushed the wheelchair across the street.

Donovan approached the desk that Jackel indicated that he had previously used and presented the documents to the clerk. "As you can see, Mr. Mazumi has been seriously injured."

The clerk accepted the papers and began to read them. "What happened to Mr. Mazumi?"

"Mining, Ma'am," Donovan explained, "uses dangerous materials. People think of explosives. They don't think of the chemicals that bathe the ore. Mr. Mazumi stepped into a pool of sodium hydroxide... that's lye. It wasn't deep but it sure did the trick. His feet were burned. He's lucky he didn't lose his balance and fall and burn his hands as well."

"What happened?" she asked.

Donovan gave the missing detail. "A large rock broke loose and rolled down right into his path and he had to side-step it. He had no choice."

"How terrible!" She looked at Donovan. "What can we do for you?"

As Donovan handed her deJong's passport and driver's license along with Jackel's passport, he said, "We'd like a couple of counter checks... unless, of course, our Wollenback printed checks have come in."

She checked. "No, not yet. Maybe in another couple of days." She handed Donovan two counter checks and returned his identification.

As he took the checks, he asked, "Where is the office for making international money transfers?"

She pointed to a side doorway that led into a corridor. "Out those doors and to your left. Winton International."

Jackel Mazumi tugged at Donovan's sleeve. Donovan tried to lean over to hear him, but the corset prohibited him from bending. He listened to Mazumi's string of incomprehensible syllables. "Ah," Donovan said to the inquisitive clerk, "Mr. Mazumi says he's glad you're so efficient because he's not feeling well." Then he tried to lower his voice. "I think his medication is making him a little nauseous."

"Then by all means let me hurry you through," the clerk replied. "There have been a few charges to your account. Eight hundred thousand, one hundred dollars American were deposited. You have eight hundred thousand three dollars remaining. Did you intend to close out the account?" She seemed alarmed.

"No. No... not at all," Donovan reassured her.

"Good. We don't want to lose a good customer. Now, if you are going immediately to the transfer agency, I'll keep your records right here and there won't be any delay when they contact me for verification. I'll fax everything right over."

Donovan pushed Jackel out the doors, into the corridor and into the offices of Winton International. He wrote the two counter checks for $389,000. to Jack Donovan's account in Suriname; and $389,000. to Samuel Faber's account also in Suriname. Phone calls were made, receipts were given, documents were laboriously signed, and in forty-five minutes everything was concluded.

They left the way they had entered. Mazumi weakly waved to the clerk and Donovan touched the brim of his hat and nodded to her.

They crossed the street and took a taxi to the airport where they boarded the waiting plane.

When they were airborne, Jack Donovan ripped off his shirt and unzipped the fly of deJong's pants. As Mazumi unlaced him, he asked, "Jack, where is the money going?" Donovan panted with relief as his abdomen bulged free of its restraints.

When he was able to speak naturally, he answered, "To Mr. Edwards and me. We had to split it into two payments since one large payment would have been suspicious. The money that is left in the account is yours. That's around twenty thousand dollars. Nandy Moyer's wife will get nearly all of her money back."

"You get nothing?"

"Ah... she'll give me a reward. She's not the type to cheat a person."

They did not speak again until they returned to Cajana.

This time, with Sensei carrying the shorter 'wakizashi' knife of the traditional sword and knife pair of samurai weapons, and Jan carrying his Colt .45 semi-automatic sidearm, they walked without a guide directly to the Annex. There were no guards anywhere in sight.

Crouching in the bush, Beryl, Jan, and Sensei searched for Olivia as they watched the women begin the lunch and laundry session. First, two collared women that they had not seen before - one with engorged breasts that were obviously filled with milk and the other, a pre-pubescent girl, came out and went to the washtubs and pushed their laundry down into the water and began to scrub the sheets.

"Jesus!" Jan whispered. "How old would you say that girl is?"

"Her breasts are barely starting to develop," Beryl replied. "She can't be more than ten or eleven."

"This is unbelievable," he exclaimed. "Why hasn't anyone done anything about this?"

"Probably because a whorehouse for people with incurable sexually transmitted diseases is a good way to curtail the spread of the disease. Who would have thought it also applied to pedophiles."

Sensei grunted. "I'd like to meet the S.O.B. who gave that kid a disease - the first time."

In a few minutes other women came out and also knelt at the tubs. When the first two were finished, they carried their laundry to the detergent and bleach vat and then went to the bathing station.

"Where can Olivia be?" Beryl asked. "I need to get into that compound."

Jan studied the complex through his binoculars. "The only way into that yard," Jan said, "without going through the front door, is to go to the far side of the creek and walk past the waterfall and then climb the fence to get into the pool." He handed the binoculars to Sensei.

"Yes," Sensei agreed. "The fence on this side has a gate. Neither fence seems to be very high."

"Well," said Beryl, "that's the way I'm going. The guards are probably inside the brothel."

"You don't want to meet the creatures that are on the other side of that fence," Jan said. "Wait here until we can form a plan."

"I have to trust my pants," she said seriously. "And yes... I know that I could step on an electric eel or tangle with a caiman and the pants won't help me. Do you have a better suggestion? Yesterday, after they ate, they rinsed their laundry in the waterfall. As soon as they start the rinsing, I'll go around. One of the women in the rinse cycle may know where Olivia is. For all we know she's dead or she's been taken away someplace. We may not have to enter the compound at all." They waited for the laundry tasks to continue.

The woman with the large breasts had finished eating and now went to the tub and, using a stick, extracted her laundry items which she identified by number. She placed the laundry in a net bag, walked to the river, and opened the gate. The girl got her own laundry and followed her.

Jan held Beryl's arm. "Listen to me!" he insisted. "There will be caiman on the other side. At least take my gun."

"No," Beryl said emphatically. "It's too noisy. But, ok, I'll take Sensei's knife. While they're rinsing the clothes, they'll be close enough for me to talk to. This is my chance." She extended her hand and Sensei unbuckled his scabbard's belt.

Jan did not want her to go. "Wait a minute," he said. "Suppose they don't speak English. Let me give you a few Dutch questions." He removed a small damp notebook from his breast pocket.

"Listen to me!" Jan was frustrated. "OK... here's what you should ask. Listen to my pronunciation. I'll write clearly and if necessary, show the paper."

As he spoke each word, Jan wrote, "*Wij zullen u nu bevrijden.* We will free you now. *Waar is Olivia?* Where is Olivia? Are any men watching now? *Zijn er mannen op wacht nu?* Do you understand? *Begrip je.*"

Surprised that she was able to use her *Swamptec* gloved hands so adroitly, Beryl pulled up the Velcro closure on her pocket and inserted the note. "Thanks. And don't worry. I no longer feel like Wonder Woman. I'll be careful."

Slowly, crouching low, Beryl circled around to the rear of the compound and quietly waded across the river just above the waterfall. A large caiman lay on the bank as she climbed it. It raised its head and hissed. She tried to remember what all the TV alligator wrestlers did at such a time, but nothing helpful occurred to her. Without knowing the proper way to approach a hissing alligator, she drew her knife from its sheath and slowly began to walk past it. As she ducked beneath a low tree branch, suddenly, from under nearby shrubbery, a smaller caiman darted towards her. She grabbed the branch and flung her left, injured leg up onto the branch and brought her right leg up in time to reach down and slash the animal's snout, striking bone. The animal tossed its head from side to side and then scampered into the bush. She wanted to scream from the pain she had just caused her knee, but she grunted a few times and when she was certain that no other animal threatened her, she dropped down and continued to walk to the waterfall. She startled the women in the water.

"Shh!" Beryl said, putting her finger to her lips. "*Wij zullen u nu bevrijden*. We will free you now. *Begrip je?* Do you understand?"

The older woman, wearing a metal collar and chain, stared at her and then seemed to nod. Beryl managed, after a couple of attempts, to ask her where Olivia was. The woman pointed to the sick shed. "*Infirma*," she said. "*Olivia está por allí.*" Beryl said, "*Gracias*" and shook her head at the absurdity of trying to speak Dutch to a woman who apparently spoke Spanish.

The blonde "overseer", who had been slapping her palm with a riding crop, noticed that the woman in the water was doing more than rinsing soap from the laundry. Suspicious, she briskly walked to the waterfall, quickening the crop's beat. Beryl saw her coming towards the falls and lowered herself among some reed-like water plants. The overseer stood in the gate's opening and called to the woman in the water. Beryl didn't understand the words but the meaning was clear. She wanted to know what was going on. The collared woman, obviously new to the Annex, was confused. She did not want to call attention to Beryl and she did not understand the words the overseer was barking at her. The young girl also stood in the water, trembling and saying nothing.

The blonde boss stood on the bank and ordered the collared woman to get out of the water. Beryl did not move. Her wet hat had blended with the color and texture of the plants and rocks and, for as long as she did not move, she was not noticeable.

A white-dressed woman approached the overseer and shouted at the collared woman, "*Fuera del agua!*"

The woman climbed up the embankment, and as the blonde woman stepped backwards, crawled until she was at the boss's feet. The woman then hit her on the head with her riding crop and reached down and grabbed the collar's chain, jerking it up while she called the captive woman names that Beryl could not understand. The woman tried to stand but the blonde pushed her back until she stumbled and fell. Then the blonde kicked her in the head and stomach with her booted foot, knocking the wind out of her. As she bent forward on her hands and knees, whooping to get her breath, the blonde stamped on the back of her head, pushing her face into the muck. She kicked her a few times and with a great shove, pushed her down the embankment into the water. The chain trailed behind her. The blonde then picked up the chain and hurled it down onto the woman's head. She snarled and then walked away. Beryl waited for the woman to stand up but she remained under water. Not knowing whether it was because of the kicks, the blows to the head, the weight of the chain, or the rolling turbulence of the waterfall's splash back that prevented the woman from standing up, but knowing that if she didn't help her she'd surely drown, Beryl jumped up and dove into the water and pulled the woman up, tossing her forward onto the bank.

As the woman gasped violently for air, the blonde looked back, startled to see Beryl who was clambering up the embankment, rushing towards her. The cumbersome latex gloves made the woman fumble as she tried to unbutton the security strap of her holster. Frantically she looked down at her gun, giving Beryl the needed second to conform her right hand fingers into an extended-knuckle fist. Fast and hard, Beryl punched the bridge of the woman's nose. The woman's head snapped back and Beryl followed the nasal blow with a left hand "knife blade" strike to her trachea. As the woman stumbled backwards, Beryl jumped at her and grabbed her left arm, twisting it until the woman fell forward onto her knees and then face. Still holding her arm, Beryl stomp-kicked her upper back. The woman made no sound, not even of breathing. Beryl released her arm and then reached down, grabbed her hair, snapped her head back and twisted it to be certain she was dead before she rolled her body down the embankment into the water. She turned around to see whether she had been noticed.

A half dozen "sarong" women were shouting and running towards her. Then from the opposite end of the yard, Sensei and Jan gave banshee cries as they leapt down from the fence. All six women stopped to look back at the source of the cries. Three ran towards it. Three turned again and advanced towards Beryl, and two of them, Beryl noticed, were carrying bullwhips.

The brothel's rear door opened and two male guards, who had been sleeping, came running out naked, shoeless, but carrying gun belts and assault rifles. Jan drew his sidearm and fired at the men, dropping both men with one shot to each. A third fully dressed guard emerged from the brothel, carrying his AK-47 ready for action, but the three administrative women suddenly moved between him and Sensei and Jan. The guard hesitated to fire his rifle and instead reached for his side arm. Sensei whacked one of the woman, knocking her out of his way, and, as he ran to the guard, he leaped, kicking him hard in the chest. The gun fired wildly into the air as he stumbled back towards the brothel door. As he fell onto the threshold, he shouted something. Sensei grabbed his hand that still held the gun, and turned it so that he could jam the barrel down into his throat. Then he pressed his own finger over the man's trigger finger. The gun fired and Sensei stood up and turned to help Beryl who was tangling with the two women with whips. Jan, he had seen, had his hands full with the three sarong women who were not armed with anything more lethal than mops.

No one had counted on opposition from any of the inmates, but the two burly men came out of the men's quarters. Used to beating compliant men, they lumbered towards Sensei as if their size and confident approach would frighten him into submission. They cursed and threatened, but he did not understand what they were saying. He stood there waiting to see what they would possibly think they could do to attack anyone. One extended his arms as if he were going to pick Sensei up by his lapels. In five moves Sensei dislocated his arm and broke his neck.

The freed inmates rushed to attack the women with mops. Jan tossed them a few zip ties and told them to put the women against the brothel wall. He turned to see how he could help Sensei and Beryl.

The woman Beryl had rescued from the water got up and ran to help her. One of the women who had a bullwhip raised her arm and with a furious snap made the whip crack the air. The other bullwhip was being used to force back two of the freed women who were rushing to Beryl's aid. The first administrative woman raised her arm and again snapped the whip which immediately coiled around the collared woman's neck. Beryl drew the wakizashi and with what seemed to be a flick of her hand, sliced through the braided leather whip. The metal collar had saved the woman from what might have been a death coil and she was able to unwind the whip's end from her neck. Beryl now attacked the woman who carried the whip. The whip, shorter now, was still a formidable weapon. She lashed Beryl's legs and happened to strike the snake-bruise. The pain seemed to enrage Beryl into mindlessness. When the woman raised her arm to lash her again, Beryl grabbed the whip with her left hand, pulled it towards herself, and as the woman stepped off balance, Beryl, with a fierce forehand, let the wakizashi slash her throat, nearly decapitating her. Blood squirted and sprayed out of her neck. Immediately, several of the inmates picked up the dead woman and carried her to the stream and threw her into the current.

The other woman who wielded a whip raised her arm, preparing to strike Beryl. Jan fired a single shot into her chest and she dropped to the ground near an unarmed sarong woman who was being beaten by several of the inmates. An inmate who had been much abused by this woman picked up a rock and smashed it against her antagonist's forehead. She then picked her up, carried her to the water, and hurled her into the current.

The other burly man who wanted to attack Sensei had turned back, looking for something he could use as a weapon. He picked up a large bushel-sized ceramic flowerpot and lifted it over his head, intending to hurl it at Sensei. From across the yard, Jan fired one round. The bullet entered the man's chest. The man's knees buckled and he crumpled into a bleeding heap as the flowerpot hit the walkway and shattered, spilling dirt and gardenias onto the concrete.

Doña Elena suddenly emerged from the brothel carrying a heavy miner's pike. She pointed the pike at Beryl and began to run towards her.

Beryl sidestepped the pike as a matador sidesteps a charging bull; but as the woman passed, Beryl slashed the side of her neck with the wakizashi. Again blood squirted some two meters into the air. Jan called, "Beryl!" Beryl did not move for a moment. He called again. "Beryl! It's over!" She turned and looked back at Jan and took a deep breath. To their surprise, another sarong woman came running out of the brothel into the courtyard, trying to attack Beryl with a knife. As she moved within reach, Beryl blocked her raised arm and automatically flipped the wakizashi in her hand, using the handle's heel to punch the oncoming woman's chest. The blow was given with such force that the woman dropped to the ground. Beryl turned and looked around to see if anyone needed help. Jan cuffed the stunned woman and carried her out of the brothel and put her against the wall with the three other women.

Beryl went to the sick shed and opened the door. The light that suddenly entered the room blinded Olivia and she could not see who had opened the door. She did recognize the American voice. "Olivia?"

Weakly, Olivia cried, "Yes, I'm Olivia."

Beryl said, "You're safe now. I'll get one of the men to carry you out."

She returned to the yard and called Sensei. "Olivia's back there in the shed." She pointed to the little building. "You'll have to carry her out. Get a clean sheet to wrap around her."

Then, without another word, Beryl walked to the laundry area, turned on the hose and began to squirt herself until all the blood had been washed off. The woman from Guyana who spoke English asked if she could help. "Do you know where the keys to the collars are?"

"Yes," she said. "I know. I'll get them." She ran into the brothel.

The doors of the men's annex opened; and the two captive "slave" men, fearful of everything, ran into the brothel and exited the front door. Many women followed them despite Jan's protests in Dutch, English, Spanish, and Portuguese.

Jan had already called for medivac helicopters. Now he called again for military help to track down the people who had fled. "They don't stand a chance out there in the jungle," he said. "Tell the men to wear protective gloves," he ordered. "They need to be warned about what they're going to take into custody. The women are diseased; but they are victims, not fugitives."

The sun suddenly broke through the clouds.

Sensei wrapped Olivia in a bed sheet and carried her out the front door of the Annex. He called to Jan, "I have Olivia. She's really sick. How long before help gets here?"

The yard was empty except for a few women who believed that they had no place else to go.

Something on the other side of the waterfall caught Beryl's attention. Springer's youngest victim was sitting there waiting for Beryl. "The young girl!" Beryl said, pulling Jan's arm. They rushed towards the embankment when the girl suddenly stood up and screamed, pointing to a caiman coming upstream towards her. The usual amount of detergent and chlorine had not been there to deter the animals. Jan fired four shots into the animal's head as Beryl crossed to the collared girl and picked her up. The fragile girl wrapped her arms and legs around her, whimpering. Beryl carried her to the other bank where Jan was waiting to receive her. She wrapped her arms tightly around Jan's neck and did not move as Sensei brought the key and unlocked her collar. Jan did not try to dislodge her grip.

It was over. Not until Jan's satphone rang was Beryl able to take the girl from him.

Jan's superior was calling to get details of the incident. Jan was asked to give separate accounts of the victims and the perpetrators. He told his superior that all of the victims and perpetrators needed medical care and should be quarantined because of their sexually transmitted diseases. He hadn't yet taken a 'body count.'

Jan listened and looked heavenward as his superior said he'd wait for a count. Jan whispered, "How many prisoners do we have?"

"The mop ladies," Beryl said trying to be helpful. "The one I hit in the chest will probably die by tomorrow... maybe sooner." She looked at her more closely. "Maybe she's already dead. So three women prisoners, definitely."

Jan's superior asked him why, with only three women prisoners, he had called the raid, "a big operation."

"Well," Jan said, defensively, "many people didn't understand that we were trying to help them and they ran into the Jungle. How many dead?" He looked to Beryl and Sensei for an answer. "Well... nine? Maybe eleven. Twelve? And three prisoners."

When asked who "we" was, Jan said simply, "Two combat trained civilians who happened to be on the scene." His superior told him to be sure to secure the guns for ballistics so that they could officially know who shot whom.

"Only my sidearm was used. Oh! Wait! One of the guards was shot with his own gun. The civilians did not carry or use any firearms. We had to use standard knife and hand combat because firing my gun early on would have attracted more armed guards and we were already badly out-numbered... something like thirteen to three. *I need not tell you that in a hand-to-hand combat situation, unless you have subordinates who can guard the prisoners, you do not take prisoners.* We had one handgun and one knife. They had three assault rifles, four handguns, two bullwhips, and an assortment of... *bats*. I should like to point out that officially I am on vacation, and with your permission, I'd like to continue my recreation. I happen to be with a lady who is very special to me." The remark, made with so many bodies lying around, seemed absurd. Beryl and Jan looked sheepishly at each other.

He concluded by telling his superior that he should inform the U.S. vice-consul that the American lady named Olivia Mallard had been rescued.

He hung up and shrugged. "Well," he said, "self-defense is self-defense. I mean... it isn't as though all eleven of them didn't try to kill us. Right?"

"Right," echoed Sensei.

Deposited once again at *Jack's Pink Dolphin*, Jackel, under orders to keep out of sight, was loaded into a motor canoe, and two of the workmen took him downriver to the fish taco shack and then lifted him onto a stretcher and carried him back to his house. He sang a familiar song as he neared his house and his smaller children tried to climb onto the stretcher to be with him. Finally he was deposited in his own bed. The two workmen left. No one knew that Kaza and Chico had followed them.

At the mill house, Jack Donovan went himself to let Samuel Faber know how well everything had gone. Lola, Dani, and the worker who had guarded the "guests" with Faber were free to go.

"Where is my Jackel?" Lola asked.

"By now, he's at home waiting for you," Faber said. "Just walk back to the *Dolphin* and one of my men will take you to the fish taco shack. Good luck, Lola."

Jackel, helpless with his feet bandaged, waited for Lola. He heard someone approach the front of the house and he propped himself up on one arm, expecting to greet his wife as she came through the doorway. Instead Kaza and Chico burst into the room and picked him up from the bed and took turns carrying him to *Springer's*. As they left they shouted a threat to the children, "If you tell anyone, we'll come back for your mother."

In the distance, Lola and Dani heard the children screaming. They began to run. When they arrived at the house the kids were standing in the doorway crying. They told her that men from *Springer*'s had taken their father and said that if the children told anyone, they would come back for her. "We don't want you to be hurt," they cried.

"I'm fine. We fix this. Daddy's fine. Don't you worry. We fix this." Lola comforted her children. Under her breath she said, "God damned Springer," and tried to determine what she would do next.

Reinhardt Springer put cucumber paste on his face. It refreshed his complexion, he thought, as he sat in a hot tub of water until it cooled. Then he showered in cold water, dressed casually, and to prepare himself for work, put new batteries in his larynx voice-changing device. Then he sat on his reclining chair and listened to Jessye Norman sing the *Liebestod*. Nearly weeping, he played it several times, lamenting the difficulties of trying to remain civilized in an uncivilized world. Then the boots of his workmen thumped on the stairs that led to his apartment. He grunted and picked up his "cricket" and voice changer.

Jackel was dumped on the floor. "What happened to you?" Ananda whispered as a hooded man came and blindfolded him and then Jackel.

When the footsteps receded, Jackel whispered, "Donovan rescue me and my wife and boy. Then he took me to Georgetown. My feet hurt bad."

Moyer replied, "My feet are infected. They're swollen bad. Do you know where my wife is?"

"No. How you get here?" Jackel asked.

"Kaza Ross got me out of the shed. They gave me a bath and some food. I'm hungry again but I think they forgot about me. What about my wife?"

"They after money–" The door opened and someone came in and sat down behind the screen that sectioned off the back of the room.

The weird voice asked, "Mr. Mazumi, I heard that you went to Georgetown recently. Is that true?"

"Yes. True."

"Why did you betray your friends and go to Georgetown?"

"Donovan say you want hurt my family. My feet got hurt here. I got put in hot shed. No water."

"Are you saying that *I* wanted to hurt your family? Are you saying that *I* hurt your feet? Are you saying that *I* put you in the hot shed?" His mechanical voice grew angry. "Are you saying that *I* denied a thirsty man water?"

"This your place. You boss."

"This is Reinhardt Springer's place! He and he alone is the boss!" He clicked the cricket.

One of the men whipped the air with a long thin bamboo strip. He swung it sideways against Jackel's feet. The gauze dressing tore under the blow and the pain radiated throughout his feet.

"Who told you that Mr. Springer wanted to hurt your family?"

"Donovan."

"Didn't your wife deny it? Did she lie? Did she say that Mr. Springer tried to hurt her?"

"No. No. She didn't lie or tell him anything."

"How did he know? What did he do to her?"

"He protect her."

"How did he protect her? Where did he protect her?"

"I don't know. I went to Georgetown with Donovan."

"What happened to the money?"

"Donovan has some," he wheezed, "American guy got rest."

"The American guy... you mean the Churchman... Mr. deVries?"

"His name Edward."

"Edward what? What is his last name?"

"That is last name. First name Jeff, I think."

"Where did Jeff Edward put the money... and Donovan too? Where is the money?"

"I don't know."

"That is a lot of cash, Mr. Mazumi. Weren't you supposed to get some of it?"

"Yes, but now things go back to beginning. Money goes back to Moyer's wife."

"Don't be absurd, Mr. Mazumi. You don't really believe that, do you?"

"I don't know what is true. I don't understand money stuff."

"Where are Mr. Donovan and the churchman?"

"I didn't see churchman. Donovan is back at *Pink D*."

"I think you are lying to me. How is it that nobody knows you went to Georgetown? You cannot walk to Georgetown. You cannot swim to Georgetown. You did not take a plane to Georgetown. Yet you went to Georgetown with Jack Donovan? How did you manage that?"

"We fly to Georgetown to get money. First we take helicopter. Then we take plane."

"You will start telling me the truth or your friend here is going to be hurt. I will have his Achilles tendon cut. First one and then the other. Now tell me the truth! Where is the money that was put in the bank in Georgetown?"

Ananda pleaded, "Tell him, for God's sake... Tell him!"

Jackel Mazumi did not know what an Achilles tendon was. He didn't know where the money was. "I don't know," he said. "I tell truth. I don't know."

The clicker sounded and a rough hand grabbed Moyer's foot and raised his leg straight up. Then the blade of a machete sliced against his ankle. Ananda Moyer screamed and the sole of a boot pressed down on his cheek, silencing his cry.

The door opened and one of his security guards burst into the room. "The NBI raided the Annex! Most of our people are dead. A lot of the women escaped into the bush. The NBI's got Moyer's wife!"

Springer stood up and walked out of the room. The workers followed him, shutting the door.

"Tell me what you know!" Springer demanded.

The security guard repeated the news.

Inside the interrogation room, Ananda forgot his pain. "Thank God. Thank you, God. Olivia! I am so sorry! Oh, Thank you, God." Blood oozed from his leg and began to soak the mat under his feet. His sobs contained only one intelligible word, "Olivia."

Springer wanted details. The workman said that all he knew was that some American people, a man and a woman, were with the NBI captain. Moyer's wife was very sick. Lola Mazumi had been with an American guy at Donovan's mill house.

"That old waterwheel mill house?" Springer asked.

"Yes. It's some kind of hiding place now."

Springer considered that the money may be hidden there. "Smart move to hide it there. If Lola Mazumi was with him then she'll know where it's hidden. Go get her and bring her here."

"You won't have time, Mr. Springer. The NBI captain and the other two are probably going to come here right now!"

"Give our two guests a shot of morphine. Make sure none of Ananda's blood gets on the rug." Springer paused at the door to his private rooms. He turned and said, "Now go immediately and bring Mrs. Mazumi here... and do it very, very quietly."

Jan and Sensei had no alternative but to leave the guards and the women who ran the Annex lying where they had fallen so that photographs could be taken. The military helicopter landed near the medivac chopper. Jan spoke to the Lieutenant in charge. "Treat the women with caution and respect." He ordered that Olivia, the girl, and the third "collared" woman to be taken immediately in the medical helicopter. "One of them is a missing American. Notify the U.S. Consul." He patted the girl's head. "Notify Child Welfare about this young lady." He smiled at her and then continued to direct his men. "Find out where the Spanish speaking woman is from and notify the appropriate diplomatic corps about her. All of the women will need to be hospitalized. Many have no place else to go and will need further assistance."

The soldiers began to secure the site and search for the men and women who had fled into the surrounding jungle. Jan, Beryl and Sensei boarded the medivac helicopter that would drop them off at the Cajana airfield before it continued on to the hospital.

Springer's men were not gentle when they descended on Jackel's house the second time. They grabbed Lola, tied her securely, and put her in a net bag. The larger of the men slung the bag over his shoulder and walked rapidly to *Springer's Roadhouse*. They took her to the interrogation room and dropped her on the floor.

When Lola first saw her husband, she gasped, thinking that he was dead. Finally she was able to see that Jackel's chest was still moving. She took several deep breaths and sat up in the net bag with her eyes closed and her hands tied behind her.

Springer entered, staying behind the curtained screen. Attired again for a meeting with the NBI, he was dressed in a starched white shirt with ordinary cuffs, a paisley silk cravat and a collar fashionably left open at the neck. His dark blue jacket was linen. He had ordered his tailor "to make it fit as though an artist painted it on" and in this his tailor succeeded. There was not a country club in Christendom in which Reinhardt Springer would have looked out of place.

Again the weird larynx device concealed his real voice. "Tell me, Mrs. Mazumi, where is the money hidden... the money that your husband says he took from the bank in Georgetown?"

She did not answer.

"I will repeat the question once more--"

"Repeat question all you want. I don't tell you. I tell only Mr. Springer. You only full of shit. Hurt my husband. Mr. Springer a gentleman. He do what is right. I tell him if he want to know. You go to hell."

Springer was emotionally disarmed by her unexpected response. In his mechanical voice he said to the men, "This woman wants Mr. Springer. Is he in the building? If he is, go get him."

Springer walked to the door, and opened it. In his mechanical voice he said, "We will see if Mr. Springer wants to talk to you." He then slammed the door shut and waited a couple of minutes before he opened it again. In his own voice he said, "What the devil is going on here? Why is this lady trussed up like an animal? And in a bag! *Free her immediately*!"

He walked over to her and helped her to her feet. "Bring me a chair for her. No. Better yet, we'll go into my private sitting room." He turned to the men and angrily said, "Her husband... is he sleeping?" When they answered that he was, Springer shouted, "What kind of way is that to treat this man? Get a cot for him! Make him comfortable! And be quick about it!" Lola's hands were untied and she stood up. Reinhardt Springer gently took her arm. "Please come with me. You and I will talk and have some tea and cake and as soon as your husband starts to awaken, I will have my men take him to the clinic. Would you like that?"

Lola nodded. "Thank you," she said. "Those men no good. I don't talk... I don't walk... I don't do nothing with them."

"My dear, do not concern yourself." He called the kitchen and ordered that tea and cake be brought to his rooms without delay.

Reinhardt Springer sat at one end of the couch and Lola Mazumi sat at the other. A tray of tea and pastries was placed on the cushion between them. He poured her a cup of tea. "Milk or lemon or sugar?"

"What you take?" she asked.

"Since the tea is Earl Grey, I generally take milk and sugar with it. I'll fix yours and if you don't like it, we'll bring you another variety." He pushed the plate of pastries towards her. "Now, can you tell me what you refused to tell that other man?"

"He want to know where money is. I can't show you. You too pretty dressed. We have time, but not in pretty clothes. And don't say then I go with them. I don't go with them. You change your pretty clothes."

Springer laughed. "Would you like me to wear overalls?"

"No. Blue jean pants. Regular shirt. Regular shoes. Hat if you need it."

Springer placed his cup and saucer on the tray. "Consider it done." He went into his dressing room and humming to himself, he changed his clothes. When he re-entered his living room, he raised his arms and said, "Now will you walk beside me?"

She smiled and stuffed an eclair into her mouth. When she swallowed it she said, "What you looking for is hid at old mill house. Special place. You know old mill house?"

Springer said that he knew it by sight... from above. But he had never been inside it.

"Then I have to show you where money is. They use funny names for places."

"Then will you be my guide?"

"Yes, but we need to go quick in your boat. I want to be here when my Jackel wakes up."

Springer sat at the motor in the rear of the boat and allowed Lola to direct him upriver towards the *Pink Dolphin*.

As they passed the Vandermeer, Hendrik Holman was sitting on the veranda drinking a beer. He saw Springer's canoe pass. Lola was kneeling in the front and, of all people, Reinhardt Springer, himself, was back at the tiller. He picked up his binoculars and made doubly sure of what he was seeing. And they were passing Cajana and going upriver towards - what else? - the *Pink Dolphin*. He put his beer down and hurried down to see if a motor canoe was available for immediate hire.

Springer had allowed Lola to direct the boat past Cajana and then to turn west into the stream that ran past the *Pink Dolphin*. She continued for a quarter mile past the roadhouse, and then she told him to cut the motor and nose the canoe into the stream bank. She jumped out into the water and tied the boat to a nearby tree and waited for Springer to leave the boat without having to step into the water. Then they walked together on the path that led to the old mill house.

Hendrik Holman hurried down to the river's edge where the boatmen congregated. He got into a vacant canoe and instructed the driver to follow the boat that had just passed. At Donovan's dock, the boatman turned into the stream that ran back to the *Pink Dolphin*.

They passed the roadhouse. Hendrik had expected to find Springer's boat tied there, but he was wrong. The motor-canoe Lola and Springer were in was nowhere in sight.

They continued on and in a few minutes they saw its wake. "Slow down," Hendrik called. The pitch of his canoe's motor lowered. They proceeded through the ruffled surface of the narrowing stream. The mottled shadows cast by the afternoon sun that fell on the tree leaves made it difficult to distinguish the way ahead. But they went slowly and finally, in the distance, they could see that Springer's boat had been pulled up and tied to a tree at the stream's edge.

"Cut the motor," Hendrik said. I'll get out here and walk up. You wait here for me."

"I can't wait no more than ten minutes. After that, you call the dispatcher at the dock when you're ready to leave. It's busy today."

Hendrik got out of the canoe and began to push and pull his way through the dense foliage of the "light gap" secondary jungle growth. He walked parallel to the stream and soon, at its junction with a much larger stream, the mill house was in view. He stopped, remembering that his sun hat had a bright crimson band around the crown. In the dark green background, a moving, crimson band drew attention to itself. He pulled off his hat, removed the band, put it in his pocket, and continued walking.

Jack Donovan asked the chef to make something special... an *anaconda en daube bourguignon* for him and his friend Samuel Faber to dine upon in celebration of their victory over Springer and Moyer and all the double-crossing bastards of the world who lay defeated before them. A celebration was in order. While the chef labored over a fresh snake, Donovan bathed and dressed and Faber cleaned up the mess that had been made while preparing Jackel for the trip to Georgetown.

Donovan, carrying his book of wisdom, entered the guest room, and while Faber bathed and shaved, he jotted down a host of wise remarks that had come to him on the flight home from Georgetown. He had to record them quickly before they "flew the coop of memory."

Gus the bartender heard the astonishing news that Lola Mazumi and Reinhardt Springer had just passed the *Pink D.* on their way back to the mill house. He sent a kitchen boy to deliver the news. Donovan tipped the boy a dollar and went to the window to see if the passing boat could be seen from the upstairs window. He could see only rippled remnants of the wake, but it was still evidence of his victory over Reinhardt Springer. "The son of a bitch is desperate!" He murmured and returned to the couch to resume memorializing his wisdom.

Faber, who was getting "the hang" of using a blow-dryer, emerged from the bathroom looking younger and more vibrant than he had looked in years. "I'm ready to celebrate," he declared. Donovan closed his book.

As they went down to the dining room, another boy met them on the stairs to tell them that Hendrik Holman had just passed the *Pink D.* in a motor-canoe, heading towards the mill house. "Sam," Donovan exulted, "let's really celebrate. All the goddamned losers of this world are convening at the mill house."

They ate snake with potatoes, carrots, and onions, drank champagne, and discussed the future.

Despite the joy of knowing that the high and mighty Reinhardt Springer was now reduced to going on fool's errands with a native woman, Jack was anxious. He looked around the dining room and despaired that it was half empty. "Easter season," he lamented, "is so hard on business." He needed Faber's half of the money. While Faber was still so "flush," it was a good time to proposition him with going partners in the purchase of land on which they could build Faber's dream resort, "a place where gentlemen of distinction could experience pleasure and pain." Donovan had no intention of letting the enterprise get past the planning phase before Faber became "fish food." He regretted that this was necessary, but he could see no other way.

"Faber," he said with stern conviction, "you are executive material. Take that 'BDS&M resort for queers' idea of yours. You could make it work. Running one of those 'Whack-a-fag' places ain't easy, but you have the kind of mind that could do it. You're smarter than Reinhardt Springer. Right now he has the Sicko market pretty much to himself, but you could give him real competition." Donovan regarded this endorsement as a compliment. Faber was not entirely comfortable with it.

"I confess," Faber admitted, "that the camaraderie I've experienced here brings out the entrepreneur in me." He poked at a potato. "You mentioned the lack of business during Easter. Why don't you expand into the BDS&M market at least in season? I can see university types who like adventure just flocking down here for spring break... you know, the Easter holidays. The schools all close and, let's face it, in the States, while you can't book a flight over Thanksgiving and Christmas because everybody's on the move, you can get any reservation you want over Easter. Nobody has a reason to go anywhere. You, Jack, *you*... could give them a reason."

"Let me think a minute," Donovan said, picking his teeth, trying to be careful not to discourage Faber. "I don't think I could do it alone. But if I had a partner with brains? Now that might appeal to me." While he doubted that he could ever see himself as the proprietor of a BDS&M joint, at least Faber was coming up with solutions to the Easter dearth.

"Somebody's got to take Springer down, and I think you're the man destined to do that. Nobody likes Springer. Men are wary of putting their reputations and their money in his hands because, as everybody knows, he's just not trustworthy. Everybody likes you, Jack, because you are."

"Do you think we could lure Springer's clientele away?" Donovan asked. "I hate to admit it, but the guy always beats me. I try something new and he copies it, only better. Food, Entertainment, Whores."

"Don't try to win when you know he's got the advantage. You named three categories. Food, recreation, sex. Do you know a book called *The Art of War*? Here's something for you to think about. A prince decreed that once a month he and his warlord would have a horse race. They had three races for three categories of horses: The first class was the young spirited horses that the nobility and the generals rode. The second class was the trained horses of cavalry officers. The third class was the ordinary cavalrymen's horses. The prince had better horses and he always won all three races. So the warlord asks this Chinese philosopher for advice. The wise philosopher tells him, 'Groom all your animals well and when the prince races his first class horses, you race your third class against them. You will lose. But then when he runs his second class horses, you run your first class, and you will win. And when he runs third class animals, you run your second class, and you will win. Instead of losing all three races, you are guaranteed to win two of them.'"

"That's great!" Donovan exclaimed. "Jesus! So what horses do I run?"

"Springer challenges you in ordinary vice... alcohol, whores, cards and dice, French food. He caters to the local trade. He doesn't make money from them. Why not? Because he caters to common perverts. Go instead for high-class international perverts and get their trade. Everybody misses Rubem. People eat that stuff up. Reinhardt wants to offer beef and oysters to crude people. That may be great for locals, but tourists can get that at home. You've got a great chef. Offer his exotic dishes... piranha and anaconda. Throw in a few caiman. Keep a few tables for the gambling addicts. The others will have more excitement having sex with a movie star... you know... somebody who's an addict or deep in debt or over the hill.

"Put in a swimming pool. Swimming pools aren't for swimming. They're for showing off one's physique. If there are too many mosquitoes, build a glass house around it. Advertise in all the Gentlemen's magazines. Sell memberships. With our money right now, we could make improvements in this place. Put in a dance floor. Hire celebrities to be seen here."

Jack was truly inspired. "I saw how we worked together to get Jackel ready. We really are a team. I can see it now. Why should this warlord always lose? And why should he be content to win only two out of three times? This warlord is gonna win 'em all." He ordered another bottle of champagne.

Faber radiated confidence. "We could also re-name the place, 'The Pink Dauphin.'"

Jack sat back, openmouthed, unable to think of words that could adequately describe the idea. "Stupendous" was not big enough. He searched his vocabulary as the waiter prepared to serve the champagne.

Lola Mazumi was not sure of how she would trick Reinhardt Springer. The coffin dam was full of water and the water was full of hungry piranha. But how would she get him into the water?

Reinhardt Springer had tried the mill house door and found it securely locked. He walked to the side of the house and looked through the window. "Why you look inside?" Lola asked. "They put money outside. They know everybody look inside for money, so they fool people. Money is outside."

"Where outside?" Springer asked.

"I don't know what pulley house is... but they put it there. They take money and walk along ledge. They put money in pulley house. I heard them say so. They go back ledge."

"Pulley house? Let's see." Springer went to the side of the house. He did not understand the construction of the waterwheel any more than Faber did when he stood guard over Lola and her son. He also did not wonder why the mill house was surrounded on three sides by water. It seemed natural to him.

Lola pointed to the ledge. "They walk along ledge... go and turn corner."

Springer could readily see that the ledge enabled workers, regardless of the water's depth, to move along the outside of the building. He saw, but did not understand, the significance of the water that had accumulated in the coffin dam. He sidestepped along the ledge until he came to the corner. There he paused to see what dangers might await him. Reinhardt Springer was no fool; and as seemingly friendly as Lola as was, he would not trust her with a dollar, much less his life.

When he reached the corner he was confronted by a scene of extraordinary beauty. He looked back to see the broken waterwheel, askew in the water, its axle having rusted through, inviting flowering vines to loop themselves around it. A flash of color caught his eye and he turned to look in the other direction as an iridescent ibis flapped its wings awkwardly to land on one of the pilasters that held the panels. Vines of various sorts that grew along the panel tops sent their creepers and tendrils floating lazily on the water, in no apparent hurry to find something they could cling to. The water was clear and fresh and reflected a few clouds that traveled across a blue sky. He saw a metal housing of some sort attached to the side of the house. This was what interested him. He did see a few silver streaks of fish, but he would have been more surprised to learn that there were no fish in the pool than he was to see evidence of them.

He was not comfortable with the narrowness of the ledge but, since he estimated the water's depth to be a meter or two, he thought that swimming out would probably be easier than shimmying out with his hands full. He could stuff the money inside his shirt. Of course, it would be a nuisance to dry soggy currency. But falling into the water posed no personal threat to him at all. "I see what appears to be a pulley housing," he called.

"Yes! Yes!" Lola answered. "That is where they put money. Pulley Housing. Good. I wait here. Take your time! Be careful!" Needing a cutting tool, she picked up two stones, vertically struck one stone against the edge of the other and chipped off a sharp flake. She cut her arm and dripped blood on the flake which she then threw out into the coffin dam.

Springer had found nothing but cables inside the pulley housing. "It's empty!" he called.

"Don't blame me!" she shouted back. "That is where Jeff say money is. Maybe he trick me and it is inside." She made a pile of rocks suitable for throwing and picked up a long split piece of zapote wood.

Cursing, Springer made his way back to the corner and turned it to see Lola standing there at attention, holding the long narrow piece of wood upright, as a knight would hold a lance.

"Don't play games with me, Lola!" Springer threatened. "Where did they put the money?"

He turned sideways and with his back leaning against the house, began to side step his way towards her.

Lola began to throw rocks at him. He raised his arms to shield his face. Springer had not wanted to get his shoes and clothing wet, but he saw no other way out but to swim. He would need only a few strokes to reach the wheel and hoist himself out of the water. Cursing her, he jumped into the water, raised one arm to begin a swimming stroke, and that was all. His other hand was already being bitten by the hungry, blood-maddened fish.

Lola watched the frenzied splashing and heard the choking cries. When it was quiet and calm again, just a few minutes later, she called, "Goodbye, Mr. Springer. You remember my Jackel. I remember. You remember."

She began to walk back to the motor-canoe. Immediately she saw Hendrik approaching. He stopped and put his hands on his hips as if he intended to block her path. "Where's Springer?" he laughed. "You're quite a clever little lady," he said. "I'm sure Springer never saw it coming. How did you do it?"

"What you want, Henny?"

"I want what Springer wanted. The money. Where is it?"

"Listen, Henny. That money bring nothing but bad times. Forget money. You enjoy your life."

"I intend to enjoy my life but I worked very hard to get that money, and one fourth of it is mine."

"It's not your money. It belong to Olivia. Let her have it."

Hendrik decided to use a more tactful approach. "You understand business. We made investments and that money is the return on our investment. You're right. Part of it is Olivia's money. But part of it belongs to you and Jackel. He wanted it for your kids... to go to college." He waited for an answer.

"How come part belongs to Jackel and me?"

"Jackel worked for it. Maybe he didn't tell you why he got all dressed up and why he was in Guyana last week. But that's why. And after all he went through to get that money, are you going to let it rot there or be swallowed by an alligator? Come on, Lola. Use your head. You can take Ananda's share, too, and give it to Olivia. I trust you. All I want is the part of it that's mine." He could see that he was convincing her. "Your husband always trusted me. When did I ever let him down?"

"You swear you take only your part and give the rest to Tony and Nandy Moyer?"

"*And Jackel.* I just want my share. You have my word. You know you can trust me."

"All right, but no funny business, Henny."

Hendrik Holman put his arm around Lola's shoulder, turning her back to the mill house. He decided to be absolutely sure she was being truthful. "So how did Springer find out about the money?"

"Kaza Ross got Nandy Moyer and hurt him bad. He told him and Springer that I was waitin' for Jackel down here at mill house. Jeff Edwards wait with me and my boy Dani. They want to be sure Jackel come back with money. This all arranged before Tony got sick. Jackel got back and gave money to Jeff Edwards and that's who put it in pulley house. They say that money is hot and will cool down in maybe one month." She noticed the cowboy heels on Hendrik's boots. "Springer just a thief. I told him they lock house to fool people, but put the money outside. He went out and found it in what he call 'pulley housing.' I didn't have nothing to do with him falling into the water. I told him, 'Springer, take the money out in parts, make couple trips.' But he want it all at once. Fall and hit his head. Stupid man."

As they approached the house he heard his boatman start the motor. No matter, he thought. He would use Springer's canoe to return to Cajana, and he would return alone.

Hendrik went to the side ledge, put his back against the house, and began to side step towards the rear. Lola watched him and told him repeatedly to be careful.

As soon as Hendrik turned the corner, she began to gather stones. "I see the pulley housing," he called. He put his hand inside the housing and discovered nothing but a few wires. "It's empty!" he shouted. Angry, he began to sidestep too quickly along the ledge.

When he turned the corner he faced Lola who let him take a few steps forward before she began to pelt him.

Hendrik's cowboy boots became his downfall. The heels kept him off balance and the leather soles were slippery. As Lola threw the stones, he flailed his arms in a fatal dance as he tried to deflect them. It required only three stones to cause him to tumble into the water. He thrashed and screamed in the roiling water for a few seconds. And then he was quiet even as the water continued to bubble with activity.

She did not move until she was sure that Hendrik Holman existed only in her memory. "Henny," Lola said to the place in the water where he had recently been, "you the reason my Jackel get mixed up in this bad stuff. You greedy man. You thief. Say hello to Springer."

The waiter approached Jack's table deferentially. "Sir," he said, "Gus asked me to tell you that the NBI has raided Springer's Annex, Cajana is crawling with military personnel, Ananda Moyer is rumored to be dead, and Jackel Mazumi is in custody."

Faber and Donovan looked at each other. "What should we do?" Faber asked.

Donovan told the waiter to bring Gus to the table.

Gus was helpful. "In my opinion you ought to head for Brazil. It probably would be to your advantage to leave before any warrants are issued. That way you're not fugitives.

"Maybe you can get someone from Awarradam to fly you down to Manaus. You'll never get past the ticket counter up in the capital. Or you can always go on foot. There are good guides available. A guy just came in sayin' that bank accounts are gonna be frozen. They're lookin' for Mr. Edwards' real name - checkin' with the tourist authorities. Jackel had a shirt on that was bought in Lancaster County, Pennsylvania."

As Jan was finishing his paperwork, Beryl sat on the dock and called George. "We've rescued Olivia. She's very sick... just how sick, I can't say. The government's paramedics have flown her up to Paramaribo, but I don't know which hospital they've taken her to. Sensei went back to the capital with the vice-consul. I'm here with Jan Osterhaus, the NBI chief who helped us. We're trying to get Olivia's money back... but that's another story. Deacon Faber is wanted for questioning. I'm exhausted. I'll give you all the news later, but I just wanted to let you know."

George was relieved. "You sound tired. Get some rest. I'll let Tracy and Father Haas know."

Jan, Beryl, and Sensei showered and dressed and met at a table on the veranda. They ordered a late lunch.

Twenty minutes later a commotion down at the riverside caused Jan to signal that they stop eating so that he could hear what was being said. "Oh," he finally concluded, "it's just the remains... clothing mostly... of the Annex's *Schutzstaffel* maiden - *the one who slipped and fell into the creek.*"

"Oh," said Beryl, returning to her omelette. She was still so exhausted she could barely say, "There'll probably be two more." When they finished eating, it was necessary to return to the dock. Vice-Consul Bernard McCarthy had immediately flown his own plane the hundred forty miles to Cajana to get a first hand account of the rescue of Olivia Mallard Moyer. He invited Sensei to return to the capital with him and Sensei, knowing that Beryl and Jan wanted to spend some time "alone together," accepted the invitation.

By the time they deplaned in the capital, news reports were circulating: Sensei was some kind of International Grand Master at Karate. He groaned at hearing the news, and as he and McCarthy drove back into town, he confided all the nationalistic oddities that had created "the secret of my success."

McCarthy laughed. "It's too late now to find a diplomatic solution to your quandary. Next time, get yourself a good Ka-Bar knife! I'm gonna be asked to produce you for talk shows and such... and naturally I'll have to tell people how proud and pleased I am to know that a fellow American has been instrumental in bringing an unsavory foreign element to justice in Suriname."

"Ah, yes," Sensei grinned. "Things are the same all over. The crooks are always aliens."

As Lola approached the Cajana dock in Springer's boat, Kaza Ross flagged her down. He had just spoken to the boatman that Hendrik had used and knew that Springer's boat had been tied up near the mill house. "What's going on?" he called to Lola.

Jan saw her stop. He asked Beryl, "What is she doing in Springer's boat?" Beryl neither knew nor cared.

Lola stood in the boat and explained that Springer, Henny Holman, and another man who was coming down from Awarradam didn't need Springer's boat but did need their privacy, and Springer told her to take the boat to the dock. The explanation satisfied Kaza Ross.

Lola called to Jan and waved to him to come down to the dockside. "You know that man Moyer?" she asked.

"Yes... Ananda Moyer. Why do you ask?"

"Because he bleed to death in Springer's upstairs private place."

"He's dead?"

"He look dead to me."

"When did you see him?" Jan asked.

"Springer's men take my Jackel to Springer's private stone house. When I get back from Mill House, they come get me and take me there, too. Jackel sleeps - maybe he got some drugs. But that Moyer guy, he look dead."

Jan told her to wait. He told Beryl, "Moyer is either dead or dying in Springer's apartment. Jackel is there asleep or unconscious. Are you up for one more trip?"

"I'm too exhausted to object," Beryl groaned, getting into the boat.

Ananda Moyer was cold, his lips were blue, and the blood that had oozed out of him had already congealed into paste that glued his flesh to the mat. Jackel was awake and in pain. Jan tried to make him comfortable as Lola cradled his head in her arms.

Jan summoned men to take Jackel and anyone else who needed treatment to the clinic in Cajana or, if necessary, to Paramaribo. They were also to take Ananda's body to the morgue in the capital.

"And now, we're finished," he said. He picked Beryl up and carried her to the motor-canoe and guided it to the Cajana dock. He carried her to the clinic.

Beryl needed help to get out of her wading pants and when the bruise was revealed, even she was surprised at the size of the area to which it had spread.

"Good Christ!" Jan yelled. "Why didn't you say something?"

The doctor whistled incredulously. "Are you telling me that a bushmaster's fangs actually came down on this?"

"Yes," Jan said. "And I was present at the time. I saw it yesterday when she was bitten, but it didn't look like this. She was wearing specialized fang-proof pants... bullet-proof... curare dart-proof..."

"Unbelievable," said the doctor. "It takes a while for a bruise to form. And this mess! Well, what might have happened is that the pinpoint pressure damaged deep tissue. Keep her off her feet and keep the leg elevated... just put a pillow under it. I'll write you a prescription for the pain."

"I'm fine," she said. "I've got some Percocet."

"Percocet?" the doctor asked. "Where did you get Percocet?"

"The Percocet fairy left it," Jan said officially. "Should we give her one as requested?"

"Yes. She should be having a lot of pain so don't be stingy if she asks for one. If you need more, come by the clinic and I'll write you a script."

"Thanks Doc," Jan said. "What do we owe you?"

"No money, just information. Tell me where the hell she got those pants."

"I'll have her send you the catalog," Jan said. "I'm told they're expensive but, as she put it, 'cheap at twice the price.'"

As they left the clinic, Jan insisted that she let him take her to a resort - any resort - so that she could recuperate. "We can spend as much time doing nothing as you need. I already told my people that I'd be doing some R&R up at the Lake. I'm officially on vacation and you're officially injured. Sensei can sub for you and my people are paid to replace me. We're going to one of Berg En Dal's coziest cabins, one that offers the best Dutch cuisine around. You are going to get fat."

"And you're not?"

"I plan on getting more rigorous exercise. You can't what with that bad leg. The doctor said you have to lie flat on your back, and that suits me fine. All this Bible preaching talk has brought out the missionary in me." He tried to kiss her but they were both giggling too much.

Military engineers had verified Lola's story about the problems with the intake gate at the mill house; and after finding Hendrik's crimson headband caught in the floating vines, they succeeded in completely closing the headrace gate and opening the outtake. The water drained away to reveal the skeletons of Reinhardt Springer and Hendrik Holman.

Since it was known that Lola and her son had recently spent the night in the mill house and further, that the last time anyone had seen Reinhardt Springer he was with her, she was questioned at the clinic as she sat beside her husband's bed.

She said that she could not account for the presence of either man's skeleton in the coffin dam. She had gone there with Springer and Hendrik had followed and the two men acted like friends. They didn't want her to stay so she left. She did explain that there was a problem with the pulley system that opened and closed the gates. It was possible that they had tried to effect some repairs and were attacked by the voracious fish that had grown particularly hungry while being trapped in the enclosure. The NBI engineers doubted that a ninety-pound woman could have caused the deaths of two grown men, and Lola was thanked for her cooperation and excused.

In the small community center that served as police headquarters, Kaza Ross confirmed that Jeffrey Edwards' real name was Willem deVries, but Bernard McCarthy promptly disabused them of that notion. He had been speaking at length to Father Haas.

The immigration and tourist authorities in Paramaribo verified that Samuel Faber had entered Suriname during the previous week.

But where was he now and where also was the suddenly missing Jack Donovan? Jackel outlined the original scheme to swindle Olivia and the second scheme to swindle the swindlers. Donovan's bank account as well as Faber's were immediately frozen as was the Wollenback account in Georgetown, Guyana.

Everyone had questions for Jan Osterhaus and Beryl Tilson but they could not be reached.

THURSDAY, APRIL 7, 2011

With Jan's help, Beryl made the funeral arrangements. A mortician in Paramaribo agreed to pick up Olivia's mauve silk from the Seabreeze Motel. A seamstress would line his coffin with it and also make a pillowcase.

The funeral was scheduled for Friday morning in a small church in Cajana. A stonecutter agreed to carve a headstone immediately and have it delivered to the cemetery. Many floral arrangements were ordered. Ananda's mother and his brothers would be brought to the ceremony, and Jan ordered that the ceremony be recorded and streamed to an iPad he had ordered for Olivia. Beryl agreed to give a eulogy that Olivia had written.

There was considerable confusion about exactly what had happened. When Olivia was shown a police photograph of Samuel Faber and asked if she knew him, she said that she did and that his name was Father Willem deVries. He was stalking her husband and had apparently threatened to confront him in Suriname. She denied ever having heard the name Samuel Faber and she knew nothing about a mill house, or a man named Donovan, or the wife of Indian businessman Jackel Mazumi. Hendrik Holman, she insisted, had nothing to do with anything. He was simply the pilot who had on one occasion flown her husband and her to Cajana. He had not even gone back to the Granger-Wollenback House and had merely witnessed her signature while sitting in an airport cafeteria. Shown an old wild eyeglass-free police mug shot of Anton deJong, she denied ever having seen the man in her life.

By Thursday she had recovered her senses sufficiently to watch television. What she was able to learn from the televised accounts confused her even more. When Beryl came to her room Olivia burst out crying. "For the love of heaven," she begged, "will you please tell me what is going on?"

"First, do you know the details of your physical condition? Beryl asked.

"I've been told that the tests thus far indicated that I don't have AIDS but do have two contagious diseases that are responding well to the 'heavy-duty' antibiotics they're giving me. And I've one disease that is "manageable" by which I suppose they mean that they can't cure it but they can control it to some degree. My cuts and abrasions are scabbed up and itchy. I asked when I could go home and they said I could leave this weekend; but they didn't know whether the civil authorities had any conflicting plans.

"Now," Olivia asked, "what is going on? I know my husband is dead. Can you tell me again - and in detail that makes sense to me - how he died?"

For the next hour, Beryl told her all that she knew. Finally, everything made sense to Olivia. "I miss Ananda so much. We had only a few days together, but they were wonderful days. Sensei kindly brought me a set of our wedding pictures. We were happy together. I think the pictures prove that."

Beryl agreed. "Tracy is anxious for you to come to live with her in Philadelphia."

"I talked to my sister," Olivia said. "She said we owe a great deal to you, Jan, and the celebrated Mr. Wong. He's been on TV. I saw him in a few news clips."

"Yes, and he's getting more attention than he likes." Beryl checked her watch. "I have to go now. My partner George has set up a conference call. I'll check in on you later and let you know the latest news about our departure."

In Paramaribo, Jan, several NBI officers, Beryl, Sensei, and Vice-Consul Bernard McCarthy waited in the vice-consul's office; while in Pennsylvania, at the prison, Warden Conner, Fathers Haas, Willem deVries, Ananda's next-door cell mate, Mike Delaney, a gentleman from the State Department, and George were assembled.

Beryl was on screen in Suriname and Mike Delaney sat before the laptop in the warden's office. "I think we nobodies can get our issues resolved so that the important folks can talk 'legal shop' in private. You know how these lawyer types are."

"Tell me," Mike laughed.

"My concern is how my client got drawn into this scheme. She'll get her money back and she's agreed to place herself at the disposal of the Surinamese authorities when she's back in the States. At home she is not going to press charges against anybody for anything. What happens to Samuel Faber down here has nothing to do with us. But I think that all of us would like to understand how she came to be involved in this affair. So Mike," she began, "I'm going to limit my questions to you about the scam as far as you know it. What can you tell us about Moyer and Deacon Faber?"

"Faber loved Moyer and getting spanked. Moyer hated Faber. But everybody was afraid of Faber so Moyer knew better than to try to cross him."

"What can you tell us about the letter-writing scam?"

"Faber wrote rich women letters in Moyer's name. After he got them interested he'd ask for money to get a lawyer. I remember one day he took pictures of Moyer holding up a sign that said, "Hi, Judy" and then he flipped it over and it said, "Hi, Louise" and then he put another sign in his hand–" Mike Delaney began to laugh. "I can't remember all the names. It wasn't Moyer's type of con... but he was bitter about being accused of hurting that kid. He said he never touched the kid."

"If it means anything, from what little investigation I was able to do, I believe him. Did you know anything about Olivia Moyer?"

"I think that of all of them, she was the only one he really liked."

"Faber was associated with the prison for more than twenty years; Moyer only a few months. How long were you there?"

"I had just celebrated my fourteenth anniversary a couple of months before I finished my time. I think I was supposed to get ivory for an anniversary gift, but the trade in ivory is illegal. So I got stiffed." He laughed.

"Look on the bright side. It could have been your Golden anniversary."

"Brighter yet... paper."

Beryl laughed, too. "When did you first become aware that Faber was sexually involved with the inmates?"

"Faber had a history. I don't know how far back it went. But about eight years ago I had a cellie named Roy Remington and Faber fell in love with him. Roy was big and strong and good lookin' but he wasn't interested in Faber. Faber started to intercept Roy's mail and make threats. Roy didn't take him seriously until he was denied parole. Then he began to humor him. Roy had a wife and kids down in West Virginia. They were all he lived for. He blamed Faber for screwing up his parole. And now, because he was pretending to be an item with Faber, he couldn't let his wife visit or even write to him. Roy really hated Faber because of that."

"What happened between him and Faber?"

"When her letters stopped coming to Roy, Faber figured they were busted up. Roy was afraid of what Faber could do so he led him on. This went on for a year and then Roy was released. Faber wanted to be Mrs. Remington. He had big plans. Roy had a trade. He could lay ceramic tile floors. So Faber wanted to go into the flooring business with Roy and he found a small tile company for sale in Jersey. Faber said he'd handle the showroom and office and Roy would go lay the tile.

"It cost fifty thousand for the stock and fixtures, and Roy said it sounded great. Faber borrows money from a bunch of church people and deposits it in a bank in both their names. Faber also runs up his credit cards buying clothes for Roy and he borrows more money to buy Roy a car as a 'getting out of jail' present; and he buys insurance for the car. Roy gets released and is supposed to go drive down to check out the tile shop and make an appearance at the bank to sign signature cards. Roy waits a couple days and takes all the money out of the account and goes to West Virginia. He wasn't on parole. The car was in his name and there was no lien on it. The debt was all Faber's. Roy was home free. What could Faber do about it?

"How did Faber react?"

"He had a sort of nervous breakdown. He moped around like a zombie and then a few years ago Father Willem joined the staff. Faber came to life. He fell crazy in love again. The priest tried to be nice; but Faber wanted more than nice. Their church has a kind of sacred confession–"

"Wait!" Beryl interrupted him. "I don't want you to tell us anything about what Moyer said that Faber told him about the Confessional. We can imagine how Faber secured Father deVries' silence. So, go on..."

"Ok... I understand. But we knew that it was Faber who stole the money and blamed it on Father Willem because he bragged about it. Faber was still paying the credit cards and the big loans off. He also wanted to get even with Father Willem here for rejecting 'his advances,' as we say.

"And then last fall Ananda Moyer got the next cell to me. He was only supposed to be temporary. And Faber fell in love again. But now he was mean. Skyspirit Ministries gave him a real way out of his problems. He hadn't bothered much with it before but he figured that if he could get Moyer to con lonely women out of money, he'd get a cut of the proceeds."

"You said Faber bragged about stealing from the church. How did you hear about it?"

"I heard him. He threatened Moyer, telling him he took deVries down and he could take him down, too. I heard all the details about the embezzlement he pinned on the priest. Faber wanted to be Mrs. Moyer. He saw some big money coming down the pipeline. They were gonna build a resort that catered to perverts."

"Ok, that brings me up to date." Beryl turned to the others. "Any questions for Mike?" Nobody had any questions. Beryl thanked him and added, "You've got my partner there with you. If you think of a name or anything that might be helpful, let us know."

The laptop in the warden's office was turned slightly and George's face came on the screen. "How's your leg?" he asked.

Jan stared at the screen. He had considered only Sensei in terms of Beryl's professional life. Yes, her card read "Wagner & Tilson" - but he had never thought about Wagner. And here was this handsome man. "So this is George," he said softly.

Beryl grabbed his sleeve and pulled him down beside her. "George, this is Jan. Jan, say hello to George."

Jan sat down and put his arm around her shoulder. "Hello, Wagner. I'm taking the best care of her that I can."

"She's not easy to look after," George replied. "And you're the famous Jan I've been hearing about."

"I don't know whether to confirm or deny. It all depends on what she's been telling you."

The two men laughed as George said, "Father Willem wants to say something to Beryl."

Jan expected an ordinary priest to come on the screen. Instead, as George got up the handsome blonde priest came on the screen. Jan suddenly felt angry, although he could not identify the feeling he had as such. He felt an impulse to get up and walk out of the room.

Father deVries was laughing at something George said as he appeared on screen. He looked particularly handsome when he smiled. "I'm taking good care of your car. But please come home soon. It's giving me hives worrying about somebody stealing it or taking it to a chop shop." He spoke with complete seriousness. "I keep it parked in the back, wedged between a hearse that's up on cinderblocks and my office door."

Beryl fought to keep a serious expression, but Jan noticed that she gulped a bit when she spoke. "Won't you be going back to Harderwijk?" she asked.

"It's the damned decisions," deVries said. "I can't get away until I pick my replacement. And there are so many applicants clamoring for the position..." He was a better actor than she. He truly seemed sincere.

"What about Faber?" she asked. "We don't know how long they'll keep him down here. Maybe you could train him. He's probably used to a little gas." She burst out laughing and not even priestly discipline could prevent Willem deVries from giggling at what was obviously an "inside joke." Beryl managed to say, "I'll see you when I get home. Here... say hello to Jan in Dutch."

Willem deVries spoke a highly educated Dutch... refined and articulate. Jan tried to smooth his "colonial" accent as they exchanged formal greetings. Father Haas came on screen and soon everyone but George and Beryl were chatting in Dutch. The call ended with everyone exchanging private phone numbers.

Bernard McCarthy called Beryl aside to ask if she wanted a lift back to her hotel. She had expected to go back with Jan, but he had left with other members of the NBI. She said that she'd be grateful for the ride.

Jan needed to organize his thoughts. He sat at his desk and shuffled papers. His department chief passed his office, noticed him, stopped and backed up. "You look like you're ready for another vacation."

"I'm ready for something," Jan said. "I'm just not sure what it is." He did not look up.

"What happened to you back there? You looked like you got slapped with a dead fish."

"Ah... I don't really want to talk about it. I've got a few reports to write up." Jan stood up and reached into his inbox. "The work backs up."

"Come on, Jan. I've worked with you for twenty years. I've seen a lot of looks on your face; but this one today was a new one. What's bothering you?"

"It's something I have to work through myself–" His phone rang. He answered it, waving a short goodbye to the Chief. The secretary of the Japanese Ambassador was calling.

Near midnight, Jan softly knocked on the door of Room 822 of the Tropical Haven. Beryl and Sensei were watching a late movie.

"I have news," Jan said as he flopped onto Beryl's bed. "The Japanese ambassador is giving a party at their embassy tomorrow night. We three are invited. I said I would RSVP, ASAP. It's black tie."

"Not me," Sensei said. "I made it clear before we came that I didn't want any social froufrou."

"Sorry, Percy. I forgot to mention that you are the guest of honor. Master Nakayama will be there. The Ambassador wants to see the knives Nakayama gave to you as a gift."

““I thought you paid for them,” Beryl said.

“No,” Jan replied. “Master Nakayama never sent the credit card bill in. He called my secretary on Tuesday and told her the bill was merely written up so as not to embarrass Master Wong.”

Sensei sighed. “This is what happens when you're a man of Chinese ancestry and you prefer Japanese Karate.” He stood up. “I can't allow myself to become cynical. I have to believe that if we had fouled-up down there in Cajana they would still want to pay for the knives.”

“Of course they would, Master Wong.” Beryl imitated Master Nakayama. “You're so good at straw cutting... such form!” Sensei threw a pillow at her.

“Seriously,” he spoke to Jan, “I appreciate the honor but the truth is that while I'm a good martial artist, I know guys who could take me in a heartbeat. I feel like a fake.”

“Ah, we're all being praised way beyond the truth of things,” Beryl teased. “You're big box office stuff... enjoy it.”

“Don't we have something else to do tomorrow?” Sensei said hopefully.

“I don't know about Beryl, but you're supposed to address the Police Academy and I'm supposed to introduce you.”

Beryl sat up. “Tomorrow I'll be visiting with Olivia.”

Jan got up. “That's my news. Time to go. I'll see you, Sensei, in the morning, and then I think I supposed to pick you both up at 6 p.m. tomorrow night in the Ambassador's limo. And my final news is that Master Nakayama is sending you Buddhist robes of some kind so you'll look good when you're photographed holding your sword or whatever you call it.”

Sensei groaned. “It never ends.”

FRIDAY, APRIL 8, 2011

In the morning, Bernard McCarthy, paying his respects to the deceased husband of an "important American citizen," flew with Beryl down to Cajana for the little funeral service.

The "beauty consultant" put makeup on Ananda Moyer, giving color to his cheeks. She brushed Ananda's hair back so that it radiated from his head like an aura. The curls formed a kind of rippling fountain stream that cascaded over the mauve silk pillow. The lower half of the casket was closed. The banner on the floral spray that lay on it said simply, "Beloved Husband."

At eleven o'clock Olivia was able to watch the church fill with people and the camera slowly move up to show Ananda's handsome face and golden brown curls spread out - exactly as he would have wanted to arrange them.

Finally, Beryl read the eulogy Olivia had written. She ended with a few lines from a poem by John Keats.

Bright Star! would I were steadfast as thou art–
Still, still to hear her tender taken breath,
And so live ever, –or else swoon to death.

At Olivia's request, Beryl had the sewing machine and the rest of the mauve silk sent down to Lola. Olivia, now out of quarantine and looking human without any facial scabs at least, looked forward to getting home to Tracy who awaited her in Philadelphia. Beryl said she'd be by to pick Olivia up for the flight the next day and, at four o'clock in the afternoon, she returned to the Tropical Haven.

As Beryl opened the door to the hotel room, she found the black and silver beaded sari that Sensei had purchased for her from the silk shop. Sensei had stretched it out across her bed. "I didn't mention that I got it for you because you wanted to wear that other dress you really liked. But for now, I had it pressed since you're going to be seen beside me and my splendid raiment." He pointed to the closet. Silk robes, more in the style of samurai warrior than Buddhist priest, hung there.

"You bought this? When?"

"The day we went to the silk shop. You'd better hurry. Jan will be here in two hours."

The hotel beauty parlor regarded Beryl as a "celebrated person" and, as such, gave her immediate attention. When Jan called for them at six o'clock, he arranged for the limo to be waiting in the rear of the hotel, near the loading platform. He stared at Beryl as he called for her in Room 822. "You look beautiful," he said simply.

Sensei grunted. "I feel like the Pope of Zen."

The party was as they expected it to be, a celebration among strangers. As soon as the seemingly endless sequence of photographed introductions was over, more photographs of man and knife were taken, and the party wound down and stopped. Everyone thanked everyone profusely and then the lined-up limousines reclaimed the persons they had earlier deposited.

When they were close to the hotel, Jan asked the limo to stop. "Can we walk on the beach for a few blocks?" he asked Beryl. "I want to talk a little. Do you mind?" She said that she didn't. They got out of the car as Sensei continued on.

They walked along the shoreline. Beryl took off her shoes and lifted her sari so that it wouldn't get sand or water on it. The evening was clear and the ocean breeze refreshing after the smoke-filled reception room at the embassy.

Jan picked up a perfectly formed conch and a few smaller seashells as they walked. "Did you know," he asked, "that the English swapped New York City for Suriname? Yes... New York used to be New Amsterdam. Dutch Guyana used to be part of British Guyana."

Beryl grinned. "And then they lost that in the War for Independence. Poor Brits. No luck in real estate."

Jan smiled at her. "I guess you noticed that I've been sort of quiet since the videoconference."

"Yes. I noticed. What was wrong?"

"I was mad... really mad. I felt like kicking the cat or something. I tried to duck my boss's questions, but he wouldn't let me escape. He said he had worked with me for twenty years and had never seen me in such a mood. I said I didn't know what was wrong. He called me an idiot. 'You're in love,' he said. I countered, 'Love isn't supposed to make you mad.' And he said, 'but jealousy is. You're jealous of her partner and that Dutch priest." 'Yeah,' I said, 'and probably a dozen other guys! I feel like a goddamned groupie... one of those silly girls at a rock concert.'

"And that's why you were so quiet?"

"There's something about you that comforts me and excites me at the same time. I thought I loved my wife and that she understood me, and then one day, after I shot and killed a drug dealer who had shot and killed two kids, she says to me, 'How could you kill a man like that? Take another life? How will you live with yourself?' I thought my brain was going to ooze out of my ears. 'I'm a cop,' I said. She says, 'A cop is supposed to keep the peace, not murder people.' I divorced a stranger. And it made me so skittish about women. They fall in love with a uniform and then tell you they're conscientious objectors. But when I saw you in action, I wanted to stop everything to kiss you... just kiss you... and kiss you..."

"And look over your shoulder and shoot somebody and then kiss me again... and then look–"

"No! Kiss you with one eye open and one hand on my Colt. Simultaneous action. So I meet a woman who is perfect for me... and she's got all these men in her life. Yes. I guess that's what was bothering me. I got jealous."

"Jan, there's nothing romantic between George and me and Willem's a priest. What can I say?"

"You can think of something. I finally meet a woman who fits me like somebody made a mould of me and poured her into it... poured *you* into it... and now it's over and other guys are gonna go back and..."

"What? Play with a Jan doll?"

He laughed. "That's it. That's what I mean. You have to make me laugh. Smile through my pain. I'm going to miss you. Do you care that I'm gonna miss you? Forget the Jan mould. You're like parts of me that I never thought I'd find. I'm serious. I never thought I'd meet someone who'd be all my missing parts. I'm gonna look like a horror show when you get on that plane tomorrow... with all those parts in your luggage."

"Will I be embarrassed when I declare them in Customs?"

"Arrested, probably."

"Ah, Jan... you know that I'll miss you, too. I owe you so much. But it's not debt I feel. You're special to me, too. You're one of a kind... that rare breed that enters the bloodstream."

"What? I'm like malaria?"

Before she could protest, he kissed her for what he feared would be the last time.

SATURDAY, APRIL 9, 2011

Samuel Faber and Jack Donovan were picked up by the District police as they sat in an unnamed notch in the Gran Rio, waiting to rendezvous with the bush pilot who had actually turned them in. They had rehearsed in great detail their story about taking deJong and Rubem to the pontooned helicopter. They felt certain that they had covered all the minutia that invariably trip up liars.

They could not even imagine that the testimony of others would conflict with their version of events. Only Jackel spoke in their defense. He had described in as much detail as possible all that he knew about the swindle; but he was confused about the swindle of the swindle. Donovan and Jeff Edwards had been his allies.

Until a determination about the disappearance of Rubem and deJong could be made, bank fraud and a host of related crimes were sufficient to hold Faber and Donovan for trial. And then, they'd have to go to Guyana to answer charges.

Sensei, Olivia, and Beryl sat together on the plane. The flight landed at Philadelphia at two in the afternoon. George and Tracy were standing together, their cars parked outside the International Terminal building.

Nobody had much to say. Beryl had a new little collection of seashells that she intended to put in her lotus pool. George was tired... but not too tired to go out with Sensei for a few beers and some shuffleboard.

"Let's just drop *Our Lady of the Magic Pants* at the office," said Sensei. They did not tell her that Willem deVries would be calling on her.

Beryl got out on Germantown Avenue, said good night to them both, and unlocked the office door. She carried her luggage up the interior stairs that led to her second storey apartment, unlocked the door, and turned the lights on. Everything was just as it should be.

She went into the kitchen to make some tea and see what there was in the freezer. As she looked, someone knocked on the kitchen door. She turned and saw deVries outlined against the glass.

"You're just in time," she said, "I was just going to make tea."

"Here are your car keys. I did not have any accidents."

"I wasn't worried. What is that you're carrying?"

"From the good people of Harderwijk. Cookies. Bear claws made with butter. There are more in the Bronco. They are grateful to you and ashamed of having doubted me."

"To my knowledge nobody doubted you. Nobody believed that you ever stole anything except Violet Miniver's heart. Not the prisoners. Not the warden. Not the newspaper guy."

"Father Haas gave Van Kempen the story. It's all the rage up there, I'm told. But that's not why I'm here."

"And why are you here?"

"To give you these cookies!"

"You could have mailed them."

He sat down and pulled off his shoes and put the slippers on. He also took off his jacket and revealed that he was wearing ordinary street clothing."

"Where is your collar?"

"Back at Hospice."

"Are you going back to Harderwijk?"

"No. I'm staying in Jersey. A friend of George's named Alicia Eckersley has sent a crew to the hospice to renovate the place. I have no place to sleep. Does that sound like a hint to you? If you say 'No,' then George says I can stay with him."

He put cups and saucers on a tray and loaded a plate with pastries. The teakettle was boiling and he poured the water into a teapot and handed Beryl the Jasmine tea container. "You do the honors."

She put a few teaspoons full of tea leaves into the pot and said, "You know the drill."

As they passed her son's bedroom she said, "You can bunk here for as long as you want." She flipped on the light so that he could see the room. "But for now, let's listen to a little flute music..."

"*Om,*" he said. "*Mani padme hum.*"

They were still laughing as Beryl switched on the music and slid open the shoji screen.